SERIAL VENGEANCE

Melissa Wren

ISBN: 1481870300
ISBN 13: 9781481870306
Library of Congress Control Number: 2013900337
CreateSpace Independent Publishing Platform
North Charleston, South Carolina

Acknowledgements

Thank you Lord for blessing me with the passion and creativity to write from a very early age. I love you because you first loved me!

Special thanks to my agent at the time, Tony Outhwaite at JCA Literary Agency in New York, NY, for sticking with me for three years while I revised, and for his great wisdom and dedication.

A very huge thank you to my friend **Michael Proul,** who suffered through several versions and countless "writer's lunches" to brainstorm ideas. I'm lucky he still considers me a friend!

Thank you to Robert Diforio at D4EO Literary Agency who I had the pleasure of meeting at Thriller Fest in 2008. I appreciate his belief in my writing.

Much gratitude goes to author, Kathryn M. Johnson, for being a wonderful editor and mentor. She's written 40+ novels, works in the Washington, D.C. area, and provides writing services through WriteForYou.com.

Thank you to Carol Leonnig, a crime writer at the *Washington Post*, who graciously gave me a thorough and insightful tour of all the positions that make up the infamous "fifth floor." Her generosity added depth to my main character's career.

My appreciation goes out to others who read through drafts more than once and helped encourage and give me feedback: Lucy Gammons, Sheryl Davis, Jan Williams, Kendra Fox, Jim Greer, Jim Krol and others.

Thank you to the team at Create Space for doing an outstanding job, being wonderful to work with, and making one of my dreams come true.

"Eerily enough, there's a scene toward the end of the book that foreshadows something haunting that happened in my life seven years after I wrote it."
Melissa Wren

Prologue

Two Years Earlier

Olivia Penn surveyed the dimly lit room and avoided eye contact with the politically correct D.C. crowd at Off The Record. If only the red velvet walls would gush open and pour out the many enigmas from the elite power lunches and cocktail hours over the years, she thought. Her friend Stacy Greenburg frantically searched the depths of her knock-off Gucci handbag for one last cigarette.

"Remind me again why we're here," Olivia sighed and fingered the decorative charm on her silver necklace.

"I told you, it's the place to *be* but *not be seen*." Stacy smiled and yanked her vice out of her purse.

Olivia just looked at her friend. How could anyone *not* be seen here? They might as well have been standing on the White House lawn as close as they were to it. She could almost feel the keen eyes of the President's sharpshooters bearing down on them across Lafayette Square through the basement windows.

But Olivia knew Stacy's real reason for their meeting there. It was her favorite place because she actually believed sitting in a bar called Off The Record confirmed her status as a powerful and all-knowing reporter. She also thought that being seen in public made her less likely to be scrutinized by her press corp buddies. Her affair with a U.S. Senator wasn't exactly a secret, but it might not attract the vultures if she kept a low profile.

"You're not actually going to try and smoke that in here, are you?" Olivia stared at the cigarette in Stacy's left hand. Smoking hadn't been permitted inside public buildings in Washington for years.

"Of course I am. It's necessary."

Olivia held back her amusement. Stacy really was a piece of work, but Olivia had to admit that's what she liked about her. Stacy was fearless and didn't care what anyone thought about her. Olivia knew she had an equally strong backbone, but she liked to think she chose her battles more carefully. She hoped the risks Stacy continued to take wouldn't catch up to her.

"You're hoping Price will show up, aren't you?" Senator Sterling Price.

Olivia peered over her glass of Merlot and took a long sip.

Stacy rolled her cigarette back and forth between her fingertips, appearing deep in thought.

Up until this point, Olivia had done everything she could not to gawk at her friend's chest. Stacy's cleavage looked as if it was desperately trying to escape the Filene's Basement special that appeared to be one size too small. Her blouse had just enough fabric to get them through the Hay-Adam's Hotel lobby without being solicited for sex.

Stacy lit her cigarette, took a long drag, her eyes darting back and forth as smoke billowed around her. "You know what I like about you?" She paused. "I like that I can be myself around you." She took another puff. "I also like that you don't harass me when I need a cigarette, even if *it is* illegal. And, I like that I can tell you anything without feeling judged."

Olivia scanned the room as she listened. A sea of dark business suits and the backs of heads had slowly begun to turn around and stare at them. Smoking wasn't exactly the best way to "not be seen." She shifted in her seat. What was going to happen next? Her instincts told her she was on the verge of a breaking news story. A story she wasn't sure she wanted to witness, much less write about.

"I don't see him." Olivia pulled her blond hair down around her ears. "What time was he supposed to meet you?"

"Nine o'clock. He had to play the role of doting husband at some sort of dinner with his wife first."

Olivia looked at her watch. "It's ten. Are you sure you want to wait for him? Let's go some place and grab a late dinner. Forget about Price for the night."

Stacy flippantly twirled her right index finger at the bartender across the room to signal for another round. "I'm drinking my dinner tonight."

Olivia raised her eyebrows. "Okay then."

Instead of bringing more drinks, the waitress came over to their table with an ashtray in one hand and a folded piece of paper in the other.

"It's against the law to smoke in here." She placed the buzz-killer on the table while Stacy nodded and said a quick good-bye with one long last drag.

Olivia waved the smoke out of her face and watched the butt smolder.

"Thanks." The waitress rolled her eyes.

Stacy looked distractedly around the room, and Olivia could feel her desperation. As much as Olivia hated the idea of the affair, she only wanted to see her friend happy. And for some reason, Price made her happy.

The waitress continued to stand there. "Ms. Greenburg?"

Stacy looked up at her. Then at the piece of paper in her hand. "Yes. That's me. What is it?"

"There's a message for you." She shoved the paper in Stacy's hand, turned and walked away.

Stacy beamed. "It's got to be from him. He's probably on his way."

Olivia shook her head back and forth and frowned. "You know he's never going to leave his wife. Maybe not showing tonight is the coward's way of breaking it off with you."

Stacy unfolded the note. "He said he'd be here, and he will. He almost always keeps his word. Besides, that's a very hurtful thing to say."

Olivia could see tears well up in her friend's eyes as she read. Why didn't she have more respect for herself? Olivia couldn't help thinking how smart Stacy had always been, except when it came to her relationships with men.

"I guess I just don't understand. You've been with him for three years and he's been feeding you the same line about leaving his wife this whole time."

"We're in love," she mumbled, as if on autopilot.

"Stacy. He's a Senator." Olivia looked her in the eye.

A different waitress returned with their third round of drinks.

Stacy crumbled the note in her palm. "Actually, could you bring two shots of tequila? Pronto please."

"You know I don't drink tequila." Olivia sat back in her chair.

"They're both for me."

"Oh." Obviously it wasn't the news Stacy longed for. "So what does the note say? Is it from him?"

Stacy was too busy downing her rum and Coke. Finally she looked up and said, "I don't want to talk about it."

"Is he coming?"

Stacy cleared her throat and looked away. "No," she whispered.

Olivia had never seen her friend act like this. What was going on?

After Stacy's second tequila shot, her mood intensified and she got very quiet, until she finally mumbled what sounded like, "What goes around comes around. He'll get what he deserves."

That's when Olivia knew it was time to hail a cab and go home. She desperately wanted to know what was in the note that had upset Stacy so much. Odd that he sent a hand written note, she thought, but figured it was wise of him not to leave an electronic paper trail with an email or text.

The doorman motioned to one of the black sedans lined up in front of the hotel. An older gentleman rolled down his tinted window and

4

offered to take the two women home. Before Olivia knew it, they were at Stacy's apartment.

"I got this one." Olivia winked. "You can pay the fare the next time."

"Thanks." Stacy leaned over, gave her a hug, and said, "Goodbye Olivia," before she stumbled out of the car.

As the driver sped away, Olivia looked out the window and watched Stacy struggle up the steps and disappear inside her building. Maybe she should have walked her up to her apartment. But it was too late now. Anyway, she was sure Stacy wasn't so drunk that she couldn't make it upstairs safely.

She glanced down and noticed a wadded up piece of paper beside her on the leather seat. Stacy's note. Olivia opened it and smoothed out the wrinkles.

The note read: *Stacy, it's over. Are you ready for what's next?*

1

The sun was setting on a warm April evening in the nation's capital. He slipped through the large kitchen window of Olivia Penn's brownstone home, knowing that she and her husband had gone out for dinner, giving him plenty of time to complete his mission.

He couldn't wait to see the inside of Olivia's house. Catch a glimpse of her private life. How did she live when she wasn't in the spotlight? He wanted to know all her secrets.

His eyes adjusted to the darkness as he moved into the room. The kitchen was quaint and clean, with the exception of a broken wine glass sitting in the bottom of the sink. But the condition of the narrow living room a few feet away surprised him.

The place looked like organized chaos. A heap of newspapers sat stacked in piles next to a brown leather recliner that faced a fireplace. Unused green candles and hardback books littered the shelves and coffee table and looked new but dusty. The space gave the illusion of being comfortable and cozy, but it also felt empty. Something was missing.

A hand-made quilt had been thrown over the end of the couch. When he moved closer, he noticed a delicate black lacy bra peeking out carelessly beneath it.

His heart raced as he ran his fingers over the bra, fantasizing about snuggling up against her on the couch. He let the vision play out in his head. Some day. Soon. Then he turned and spotted a framed photograph across the room, standing guard on the end table. He walked over and scooped it up.

The picture of the "happy couple" interrupted his fantasy. Cameron. Olivia's husband had his arm wrapped around her waist and was looking deep into her eyes. The light in her eyes and smile on her face returned his affection. Her love remained frozen in time, looking as if Cameron was the only person who mattered in her world. It wasn't fair. That's how *he* felt about her.

It didn't help that Cameron had dark, handsome, rugged features, with only a few stubborn gray hairs and a subtle half-moon scar beside his left eye to mar his near impeccable looks. He suddenly wondered how else Cameron might be flawed. Did any of that matter? No. *He* was still far better looking than her husband. She belonged to *him*, not Cameron.

He gazed at the image of Olivia captured in her special moment, and a knot formed in his throat. He couldn't help wondering if the photo had been taken the day she'd won her Pulitzer. Then he remembered just how bittersweet that award must have been for her. Surely this photo had been taken on a happier day. Yes. In fact, given her slim figure, it had to have been taken very recently or before she'd gotten pregnant.

He stood, mesmerized for a moment by her sea-blue eyes, and thought about how it would feel to run his fingers through her bright, sandy blond hair. He noticed that she liked to wear her hair down, and it was cut stylishly to enhance her big natural curls, which stopped right above her shoulders. The times he'd watched her, he'd recognized her nervous habit of always making sure her ears were covered. He'd only gotten a glimpse of them once.

Curious, he thought, to be so sensitive about them. So what if they were a touch too big. He'd give anything to nibble on them. She was the most striking woman he'd ever met. Her effortless beauty captivated him. Her spirit infected him. But that wasn't why he loved her.

He loved her because she was the kind of person people were drawn to. Her energy, her passion, and her drive kept him up at night....thinking, and knowing that one day they would be together as one. The women he'd met his own age had none of those qualities. They didn't interest him at all. He knew with his devilishly good looks and charisma, he could have any woman he wanted. But he only wanted one. Olivia Penn.

He ran his index finger over the strong features of her face. Her stubbornness and strength were reflected through the contour of her cheekbones. He liked those qualities in her. What he would give to have her look at him the same way she was looking at Cameron in the photo, madly in love. Someday he vowed to have her all to himself.

He reflected on Olivia's articles in the *Washington Post* that had always moved him. That was how he'd come to know her. He wondered if she recalled when they'd first met. He'd never forgotten. She had been humble, complimentary of him, and even said they had something in common.

He was delighted that she saw it too. They were meant to be together. Soul mates. Some day he would have to remind her since she'd obviously forgotten and married someone else instead.

He turned to explore the rest of the house and took another sweeping glance over the living room, savoring all the details, especially the bra. Imagining how her breasts would feel in his hands made him long for her. He put it back where he found it and walked back toward the basement door and put his hand on the brass doorknob. The coldness of the metal shot a chill up his arm, and he backed away. He'd check it out later; it could be useful at some point.

He turned around and quickly made his way up the small wooden staircase instead. The floor moaned a little when he walked, and moments later he found exactly what he'd been looking for. Her office. Her sanctuary. Her world. He'd found the heart of Olivia Penn.

Her office looked nothing like the rest of the house. It appeared organized and clean, nothing out of place. He'd always had the impression that she was a neat freak. Apparently, her husband was the messy one. Looking around, he realized the living area hadn't given him an accurate sense of who she was at all.

The dark cherry wood bookshelves and fireplace made the space feel quaint. Strategically placed papers and journals sat stacked on a large oak desk in the middle of the room. He pictured her poring over them, hard at work.

An inviting leather recliner, like the one downstairs, sat in the corner. The scent of her perfume invaded his senses, and he could almost sense her presence. The aura of the room was like a magnet, and he knew he'd have to pry himself away. Finally he could understand why she spent so much time working. Her career was her life. Without it, she'd be lost.

His hungry eyes scanned the worn books that lined her bookshelves until he spotted another framed photo. He could feel Olivia's radiant smile from across the room, and when he walked closer, he saw the woman he'd been looking for all along. The picture showed her wearing a t-shirt and pair of blue jeans. Her hair had been longer then and pulled back in a ponytail. She looked like she'd just rolled out of bed.

A group of children surrounded a happy Olivia like a giant hug, and she was reaching her hand out to one of them. When he looked closer, he could see that her t-shirt read, United Way. His heart sank and suddenly ached for her. She really did love children, didn't she?

He moved away and sat down at her massive desk, making himself comfortable and shifting his focus from the distracting surroundings. Now all he needed was a pen and paper. He quickly found a box of stationery and a pen in a drawer, pulled out a couple of sheets and began to write. He had so many questions. He savored every word he scribbled, anxiously anticipating her reaction. Maybe he would even stick around and watch her find his letter.

Now she would begin to understand. See how real he truly was. See that he *was* somebody. More than anything, he wanted her to know that he was there. For now he had to be patient. But he knew it was only a matter of time. There was a time for everything. A time to live, and a time to die...if necessary.

2

The next morning Olivia couldn't force herself to read past the first few lines of the letter her stalker had left. "Dear Olivia, I've been watching you. How does it feel to know that I've been so close? I waited until you and Cameron left last night before I enjoyed a private tour of your world….a world we will soon share."

Her eyes quickly scanned the walls of her office, and she suddenly felt a heaviness in the room. Another presence. Was it him? He'd been in her home! Was he still here? Hiding…waiting…watching? She caught her breath as she looked at the closet door across the room.

Her heart raced and felt like it might explode. Was she having a heart attack? At 33? She needed to find her husband and get out of the house—now!

Instead, she sat frozen. *This isn't happening. This just can't be happening.*

Her head began to spin. Tears stung her eyes, but she willed them away. Maybe she should call the police first. No, she had to tell Cameron and make sure he was okay.

Olivia grabbed the letter, raced down the hallway and up the second flight of stairs, trying not to make too much noise. Cameron was in his office, intent on whatever he was working on. She stood in the doorway, gasping for breath. The only light in the room was a green glass-hooded desk lamp, which he sat hunched under. Olivia caught her breath and whispered, "Cam, come quick!"

He jumped and turned around to face her. "You scared me."

"Sorry, but Cam, we've got to get out of the house!"

"What's wrong?" He raised his eyebrows and jumped up from his seat.

"My stalker's been here and left me this." She handed him the letter. "I haven't read it all yet because I think he might still be here." She watched him scan the letter, his eyes growing big, his facial expression changing from shock to anger.

"Let's go," he said. "I'm going to grab my gun."

"No, we don't have time, it's in the basement," she said. "Come on, we need to get out of here." Olivia heard a noise below and jumped. "Like now! He *is* here." It sounded like their intruder was in the room neither of them dared to enter any more.

"He's in Patrick's room!" Cameron grabbed Olivia's arm, rage in his eyes. "Move as fast as you can down the stairs. If that's him, he's going to hear us, but I'll be right behind you. Do you have your cell phone?"

"It's in my purse downstairs."

"Grab it on the way out and go next door. Call 911." Cameron stuck the note in his pocket and led her to the door. "Go," he whispered. "I won't let him hurt you."

Olivia tried not to hyperventilate as she flew down the first flight of wooden steps. The floor was unforgiving and creaked loudly. A thud from the other room kept her moving. She could feel Cameron on her heels as they made their way down the lower flight of stairs.

"Hurry up," he said. "I see your purse."

She dashed across the floor, grabbed it and ran out the front door.

Olivia spotted their neighbors reading the paper on their tiny front porch and waved frantically. She squinted into the sunshine and felt dizzy. "Can we come in?" she cried, running toward their house. Olivia saw the confusion on Jack and Beverly's faces.

"There's someone in our house," Cameron said. "We should all get inside." He grabbed his wife's hand and pulled her along, and the four scrambled into the home. "Maybe if you called Rex, he could make it here even faster than the cops could."

"I'm dialing 911 first," Olivia said. Somehow she remained calm talking to the operator, explaining that she believed there was an intruder in her home but that she and her husband had made it out safely.

"The police are on their way," Olivia said. The next call she made was to Rex Conner, her friend and confidant at the D.C. Metropolitan Police Department. She knew this was his day off but prayed someone would pick up his phone. No answer. She left a message and knew he'd call her back as soon as he could.

"What's going on?" Jack asked. He was a bit of a firecracker and acted younger than he looked. He and Beverly were transplants from Oklahoma.

"We're not sure." Cameron pulled back the curtain of his neighbor's front window and looked at his home. "But someone's been stalking my wife and broke into our home last night. He's still in there."

Olivia looked at Beverly, who had settled into her old yellow recliner with her newspaper, oblivious to any danger next door.

"You're safe now," Beverly said. "Jack's got a gun, don't ya honey?"

"That's right, Bev. I'll be right back." He disappeared in the other room.

"By the way, Olivia," Beverly said, "nice story today. Another one above the fold I see. I just love living next door to a famous reporter. Never a dull moment." She smiled and went back to her reading.

Crazy old woman, Olivia thought.

Jack reappeared moments later with a rifle and a revolver. "Do you know if this clown is armed?"

Cameron turned around and stared at the guns. "I have no idea, but if he's bold enough to stay in the house with us there, then I'm betting he is."

"Here, take this." Jack handed him the revolver.

"Thanks." Cameron studied the piece, turning it back and forth in his hand.

"I don't believe this," Olivia exclaimed. "How did he get in? He's been there all night, and we had no idea." The hairs on the back of her neck stood at attention and she shuddered, picturing him standing over their bed, watching them sleep.

"Do you think it's someone we know?" Cameron asked. "Who all has access to our home?"

"A couple of contractors used to have a spare key."

"I'm changing the locks today," he mumbled.

Shaken to her core, Olivia covered her face with her hands and sat down on the couch.

Cameron walked up beside her. "Liv, I think you should read the rest of the letter. At least while we wait for the police. I'll keep an eye on the front door."

Wiping hot tears from her eyes, she took the letter from his outstretched hand. She didn't want to read the rest of it. It would probably be as disturbing as the ones the police had been reviewing over the last six months. They still had no leads.

But this time, her stalker had gone too far. The idea of a stranger in her home, going through her personal things unnerved her. What did he want from her? Olivia's chest tightened as her finger's gripped the paper. She picked up where she'd left off.

Dear Olivia,

...I know it wasn't right for me to come into your house, but you haven't invited me yet, and I couldn't help myself.

I have to admit when I saw your black lacy bra, it's exactly the type of underwear I've imagined you'd wear. After the last ten months you're feeling more confident as your body and your life find some element of normalcy again. I can't wait to find out what you'll wear for me.

I realize now that you work too hard, although that is one of the things I admire most about you. But there are still some things I'm dying to learn. For instance – does your career help take your mind off of losing Stacy? I read every article you wrote about her. She used to be a good writer too, just like you. Perhaps there is someone out there who knows where she is or what happened to her the night she disappeared. You just never know. It's a small world.

I also wonder how you dull the pain of losing your baby boy? But for now, I'm just glad I've gotten to know you a little better after seeing how you live. Don't worry, we'll have plenty of time to pick up where we left off when the time is right. I remain – your biggest fan.

3

He sat parked at the corner of 19th and T Street in the northwest section of Washington, D.C. He watched. And waited. Monica Habershamm, the world champion tennis player, was about to arrive back at her condo.

He knew her routine by heart, and today she'd even told him her exact plans, which simplified everything. The music inside his car moved him. He felt high and immersed in the melodic melancholy of Beethoven's *Moonlight Sonata*. Senses heightened, every chord of the music seemed to light his skin on fire, the notes tingling like a secret whispered in his ear. A cloud of smoke blew past his face and broke his trance. He'd forgotten he wasn't alone in the vehicle.

Sam Camp sat in the passenger side, puffing away on his cigarette. Most of the time Sam portrayed a strong, confident persona, when in reality he was just a scared little kid. Sam looked like a young Brad Pitt and never had a problem with the ladies. He also resembled an "old friend," one who he'd like to forget. One who'd stolen his beautiful wife and wrecked his marriage.

As hard as he tried, he'd never gotten past the image of walking in on his wife making love to another man. He'd tried everything he could to remove the memory from his head. She'd been the love of his life. But she'd walked out on him, just like that. He could have killed the guy… and her…if they'd stuck around. Both had vanished without a trace. He'd never had the opportunity to hurt them the way they'd hurt him.

But now he had his chance for vengeance. Monica's lover had it coming to her; she deserved to die.

"Why are you going to see Monica?" Sam asked.

"I have a gift for her." His eyes remained focused straight at the condo.

"What is it?" Sam's eyebrows shot up.

"A locket." He felt very pleased with his purchase. "I remember her saying she'd had one once, and that it meant the world to her. I wanted her to have another one. A nicer one."

"You think you might be setting yourself up for failure?" Sam smiled and took a drag.

"I don't fail." He pretended to conduct an orchestra to the beat of the chords with an invisible wand in his hand. "I'll get through to her this time."

"You're crazy, you know that?" Sam sighed and lit another cigarette.

"This time will be different. I know she has feelings for me."

Monica had a secret, and she'd confided in him. She said she'd be destroyed if anyone ever found out. She had pleaded with him to help her. And he had. Now it was her turn to give him what *he* needed. He could hardly wait any longer. But for now he sat patiently. Timing was everything.

4

Thirty minutes later, the killer left Sam in the car and walked into Monica's condo building. She'd given him a key once. He felt aroused as he pushed the elevator button for the fourth floor and the car quickly escalated. He walked down the long, dimly lit hallway, running his fingers over the gift-wrapped box in the left pocket of his windbreaker. The gun remained in his right pocket. He'd also brought a camera along. It always proved to be excellent leverage while providing souvenirs for later.

Standing on the other side of her door, he listened to the music inside his head and smiled, aching for his reunion with Monica. He was certain he'd timed his appearance just right. He heard her footsteps nearing the entryway and almost climaxed with anticipation.

Monica whipped the door open. Her red satin robe clung to her tall black muscular physique. He gave her the once over.

"What are you doing here?" Her words sounded slightly slurred. "I thought we were meeting tomorrow. I was expecting pizza."

"I'm sorry. Is this a bad time?" He looked past her and noticed the empty bottle of red wine and glasses in the living room. Both glasses displayed similar shades of red lipstick smeared around the rim.

"Um…" She pulled her robe around her, protectively.

"I wanted to give you something special I picked up for you today while I was shopping." He lied.

"Well…right now might not be the best time," she said.

"Oh, you're busy?" He bathed himself in the awkwardness of the moment.

Monica scratched her head and didn't say anything.

"I know I should have called, but I couldn't help thinking you'd appreciate this." He reached in his pocket and handed her the gift. "I can assure you, you won't be disappointed." The gift was significant.

His handsome, disarming smile carried him swiftly through the entryway. He walked past Monica and into the living area. Every inch of her condo was familiar to him. He had been there time and time again. The modern, art deco furnishings, the brilliant blazing red accents, the not-so-comfortable black leather couch, and the "this-is-the-type-of-expensive-condo-superstar-athletes-are-supposed-to-have" ambiance.

Monica walked next to him and called out into the back room. "It's okay...you can come out. A friend just stopped by, but he's leaving shortly."

He watched in amazement as a figure appeared in the doorway leading to the back bedroom. The woman's short brunette bob appeared messy as she zipped up the jacket to her matching tracksuit. She looked much more petite than she did on television. She gave him a surveillance glance.

"Well, aren't you going to open your gift?" He prompted.

"Sure." Monica ripped open the wrapping and box. "A necklace?"

His spirits sank after watching her reaction. "Actually, it's a locket... like the one you said you lost that meant so much to you." He'd looked so hard to find just the right one and had finally mustered up the nerve to give it to her.

Her expression said she didn't understand what it was.

"It meant so much to me, but that was in grade school." Monica turned to her friend and laughed. "Like twenty years ago."

Heat rushed over his face. "Just open it."

"Oh no," she mumbled. "You didn't..."

All he could hear was laughter and rejection. Betrayal. Who did these women think they were? He was trying to do something noble.

Suddenly, it felt just like the day his wife told him she'd fallen in love with someone else and was pregnant with his best friend's child. She'd simply gotten up and left the restaurant. Just like that. He'd never laid eyes on her again.

He could still see her face. He'd always taken such good care of her. Just like he had with Monica. The women's' laughter echoed in his ears. He pulled the revolver out of his pocket and fired.

5

He missed his target, but the shot had gotten their attention. Monica's lover also looked slightly inebriated, just enough to let her guard down for a moment. However, she still stood her ground. She was a very important person after all. He stood still, unable to speak for a moment, given the magnificence and finality of the situation.

He pointed his revolver at Sandra Schelbert's head. Her giddy schoolgirl smile, despite her age, turned taut.

"What is this?" she demanded. "Who are you and what do you want?"

Monica cried out, "What are you doing? What's gotten into you?"

He turned to Monica and pointed the gun at her, keeping a safe distance between the two women, as he guided them into Monica's bedroom. "You betrayed me. Now you and your girlfriend are going to pay. You deserve to die."

"You're sick." Sandra sounded very much in control of her voice, even though he hoped she was frightened. "You don't scare me. How much money do you want?"

That amused him. "You think this is about money?"

"What else could it be about? Everyone can be bought. Just name your price."

"Sandra!" Monica pleaded. "You don't understand."

"What don't I understand? That this lunatic can burst in here and think he can blackmail us because he found out about our affair?"

Sandra asked. "Trust me, I've dealt with it all. And much worse than *this*."

"Monica, lie on the bed," he instructed.

"What exactly do you think you're doing?" Sandra asked. "Do you know who I am?"

Of course he did. She was the Secretary of State. And he despised her for cheating on her husband and misleading the American people about her character. She was an adulterer who pretended to have a perfect family and perfect life, and she'd taken Monica away from him.

"Please don't do this." Monica pleaded. She was shaking from head to toe. "What do you want? Please!"

"Be quiet. And you, sleazy Sandra, not another word."

Monica begged for her life with her eyes. Tears raced down her cheeks. Her body was beautiful. She was tall, toned and fit. She matched him in height and probably in muscle.

"You can't be serious. What's wrong with you?" Monica couldn't stay silent. "I don't understand. I trusted you. I don't believe this is happening. Are you okay? Here...see I'm putting on the beautiful locket you gave me. That was very thoughtful...and the picture inside..."

"Sandra, lie down beside your lover."

"Don't you dare address me in such a way," Sandra said. "You're a pig, and you *will* be caught. I assure you. You will *not* succeed." Her voice remained adamant and unwavering.

"Sandra, please," Monica pleaded. She clutched the nearest pillow over her chest. "Come here. Just do as he says before he kills us."

Sandra looked shocked. "What? He's not going to be stupid enough to kill us. There are only about a dozen secret service men posted all around this place."

He positioned himself close to Sandra, anticipated the predictable knee to the scrotum trick and hit her hard across her left cheek with his revolver. She landed flat on her face on the floor beside the bed. From the strong force of the blow and the effects of the alcohol, he figured she'd be unconscious for a few minutes.

He turned to Monica with fire in his eyes. "You've betrayed me with this disgusting affair, and now you will be punished." He put a bullet in her head before she could respond, and watched her body slump sideways on the bed.

He watched blood gush out of the hole in her head. A slow motion replay of the blood stuck in his mind like a scratched record. What had he just done? He'd killed her. Was she really gone? He felt a wave of adrenaline shoot through him along with the most satisfying release of the sweetest pleasure he'd ever experienced. Nothing could even come close to this euphoria.

He propped Monica's body up on pillows so he could look at her, as if she were still alive and just resting. Ignoring the gaping wound in her head, he knew he'd never forget her last expression or the tearstains left on her face. Her eyes looked hollow, yet they seemed to be fixed on something further away than he could see. Her mouth hung open, as though she still wanted to say something. He cupped her chin with the palm of his hand and closed her open lips. She really *was* dead.

Moments later Sandra came to. He couldn't think about Monica any more. He bent down beside Sandra, close enough for her to feel and smell his breath on her neck.

"Up!" He kicked her in the side. She grunted and continued to lie with her face in the carpet on her stomach. "Oh, I can't wait to read the headline in tomorrow's *Post*. My bet is that your murder leads the front-page headlines for a long time. How about that for press? Bet you never counted on this type of attention. It's rather unflattering, but it will serve for good shock value. Especially after the American people find out about your nasty little affair."

"What've you done?" She winced and put a hand up to her head.

"You mean, what am I about to do?" He laughed hysterically. "This is only the beginning. Hop up. Monica needs you."

Sandra peeled herself off the carpet and looked at the bed. She gasped and turned to look him in the eye. He recognized Sandra's military training, her attempt to put herself in another state of mind, her ability to try and remain in control of her emotions. She was almost convincing. She'd been trained to remain composed, no matter what the situation.

"Let's talk about this," Sandra suggested. "Nobody else has to die. Just put the gun down, and let's work this out. I'm the one you really want to get to anyway, right?"

"I've never seen a dead woman talk so much." He smirked. "You don't get it, do you? You have to die for justice to be served. Any last words?"

A realization of pure terror swept over her face. She went pale. "You won't get away with this," she said. "You're nobody. You're pathetic."

"You're wrong. I'll never be caught. But you will. And after all of this, your life will have been nothing but a joke. Your family and fellow Americans will see you for what you really are. An adulterer, a liar and a fraud."

Before she could say another word, the compulsion to kill overcame him again, and he shot her square between the eyes. Sandra fell lifeless onto the floor. The same euphoric climax rushed through his loins, this time more intense. He never wanted to wake up from this dream, this sense of ultimate freedom and control. He wanted to do it again, and again, and again. And he would. He was certain of that. *This* was only the beginning.

Standing in the presence of two very attractive and powerful women, he relished in his power. What excited him the most was the satisfaction of knowing that he could do whatever he pleased with their bodies. And he did. Justice had been served. He fished for his camera in his jacket pocket. Sam would want pictures. After all, he'd just killed a legend. Make that *two* legends.

6

Olivia heard the howling of police sirens growing louder before two cars with flashing lights pulled up close to her home.

"Stay here." Cameron grabbed the letter out of her hands. "I'll be back."

Olivia didn't argue. From the window she watched him cross the street to greet the officers, as they jumped out of their vehicles, guns drawn. One of the cops looked short and pudgy, as if he'd just hit puberty. Was he experienced enough to be a good cop like Rex? Where was Rex when she needed him?

A second cop got out of the same car, his muscles bulged unnaturally out of his short-sleeved uniform. Olivia had more faith in the two African American cops who climbed out of the other car. They appeared confident, as if they'd answered dozens of calls like this before. They also towered above the other two.

Pedestrians stopped to stare. The youthful policeman and Cameron exchanged a few words before the four officers huddled for a moment, and then scattered. One went to the back of the house, one around the side, the other two prepared to go through the front door.

Olivia said goodbye to Beverly and Jack and joined her husband on the sidewalk once the officers were out of sight. She slipped her arm around Cameron's waist and looked up at him. His round, dark-framed, much-too-old-for-him reading glasses sat slightly crooked on his nose and reminded her of something George Burns might have worn. She couldn't help noticing that he looked sexy when he didn't shave and sported a t-shirt and a pair of jeans.

It seemed like hours before the officers emerged again. Completely empty-handed. "I'm sorry, but we didn't find anyone," the meaty cop reported. "Looks like he came and went through the kitchen window though. It was wide open." The other cops went back into the house with what appeared to be a camera and other equipment.

"So that's it?" Cameron said.

"You mentioned you heard something in one of the bedrooms. Must have been your cat."

Cameron shook his head. "We don't have a cat."

"Hmm…could be a stray that came in through the same window, hoping to find some food. Either way, we left the little fellow in the baby's room where we found him. Probably explains the noise. Noticed a few things were knocked off the shelf. Like a picture frame and a piggy bank."

Olivia rubbed her temples and hung her head.

"By the way, where *is* the baby?" The officer took his hat off and wiped sweat from his forehead with the back of his hand. "You don't look too concerned, so I'm assuming there hasn't been a kidnapping or anything."

"No," Cameron said, "our baby isn't here."

It was the truth, but Olivia frowned at her husband anyway. "What are we supposed to do now? I don't want to sleep here tonight, knowing he's been in our house. What if he comes back?"

"We're going to see if we can get any prints off of the window ledge, dust for them in your office and take a few photos." The cop scratched his head. "Then we'll be out of your way."

"If you guys hadn't taken so long to show up, maybe you could have caught him." Cameron thrust the letter toward the officer. "He's been stalking my wife for the last six months, and nobody seems to care to do anything about it."

"I'm familiar with the case." The cop cleared his throat as his eyes scanned the letter. "We've done the best we could with what we've had to go on. So he left this today?"

"Yes." Cameron massaged Olivia's shoulders.

"Hmmm. We'll do our best."

"Thanks a lot." Cameron sighed. "That's what you people have said every time we've brought you a letter. Curious what level of threat it needs to become before the law takes it seriously. He's been in our house!"

Olivia took a couple of deep short breaths, pulled back from Cameron and started to walk away. "I need to clear my head. I'm going for a walk."

"Why don't I come with you?" Cameron said.

She could hear the concern in his voice, but she just wanted to be alone. "No, that's okay. I may even decide to go to the Post and do some work."

Why hadn't Rex called her back yet? She needed him. A stroll around downtown D.C. often proved the best solution when she needed to sort things out. Besides, for the moment she felt safer out in public than in her own home.

She turned around and half-smiled. "I may be a while, okay? I just can't go back in there right now."

"Please be careful." His shoulders slumped. "I don't like the idea of you out there alone in this city when there's a lunatic on the loose."

"Don't worry. I'll keep to public places." She just wanted this nightmare to go away. Should she call her psychologist for an emergency session? No, she could handle this. Or maybe she'd call on Monday.

Olivia made her way down E Street to the Lincoln Memorial and sat on the steps, gazing into the reflecting pool. She wasn't sure how much time passed. Her mind was in another place. Olivia had to figure out a way to find out who was stalking her and why.

Eventually she got up and walked to M and 15th Street, where she worked at the *Washington Post*. She spent the next few hours attacking the endless piles of paperwork that cluttered her desk. The mindless activity helped soothe her nerves, and once her desk became visible again, she decided to head home.

The sun sat high in the sky. She was beginning to feel more serene until she walked through the center of Dupont Circle, and something stopped her cold in her tracks.

7

Olivia observed a young couple take their infant out of a stroller and cradle him between their arms. They looked so blissful. That was supposed to be Cameron and her with their baby right now.

Olivia walked home in a blur. Instantly she pictured Patrick's room... the baby blanket they'd purchased together, still hung over the railing of his crib...the stuffed animals sitting wide-eyed in anticipation of a new life...the walls smelling of fresh green paint.

Now all that remained was a room filled with baby things that she'd been unable to bring herself to change. It sat frozen in time from the way they'd left it six months before, when they'd thought they'd be bringing a baby boy home to fill it with life.

Cameron suddenly appeared from upstairs with a cardboard box in his arms.

"What are you doing?" Olivia's lips parted in surprise.

He stumbled back and corrected his balance. "I didn't hear you come in."

"Is everything okay?" She closed the door behind her and put her purse down.

"Yes, it's fine." Cameron avoided eye contact and placed the box on the floor. "I was hoping I would have heard from you by now. I was starting to get worried."

Olivia glanced at the box and saw some of Patrick's stuffed animals. "What are you doing with Patrick's things?"

Cameron hung his head and sighed. "When you left this morning, I made a few decisions. I got the locks changed, ordered a security system to be installed this week, and I went into Patrick's room to look for that cat and inspect the damage."

"And?" Her jaw clenched and nostrils flared.

"Nothing's been stolen or destroyed that I can see. But…well, I decided…" he hesitated, looking at her to gauge her reaction, "that it was time to let go."

Tears sprang to her eyes at the realization of what he'd done.

Cameron gently grabbed Olivia by the shoulders and looked her in the eyes. "I decided it was time to do something with Patrick's room."

"Without talking to me? I can't believe this. How could you do this?"

"This shrine has been here long enough, and it isn't healthy for either one of us to keep his room as if we're waiting for him to miraculously come home one day. We eventually have to move on."

"Move on. Move on?" She squirmed out of his embrace and took a few steps back. "Why is it fair for you to decide when *I* move on?"

Cameron had tears in his eyes. "I'm sorry. I know this is hard."

"You should have talked to me. You should have told me how you felt. This is crazy. First my stalker, and now I feel violated because you made all these decisions without me. What have you done?"

She raced up the stairs, around the corner and gasped when she saw the empty room. Everything was gone, even the beautiful little wooden crib.

How could he have done this? Changing her baby's room wasn't going to make her pain go away or make it any easier to forget Patrick. She braced herself against the wall and sobbed silently. The only thing left in the room was a stuffed animal on the floor that must have fallen out of the box he'd just taken down. She picked up the teddy bear and hugged it against her, sensing Cameron's presence behind her.

"I'm really sorry, Liv. I guess I thought I was doing the best thing for both of us. I knew you wouldn't be able to do this on your own."

"How could you be this insensitive, especially after the drama this morning?"

"He's gone. Patrick's gone." He stepped forward and then hesitated.

"You don't think I know that? I miss him every second of the day, even if I never got to know him." She placed the bear back on the shelf.

"I miss him too."

"I want his room back just the way it was," she said. "I want *him* back."

"I know, I know." Cameron rushed forward to embrace her, and they both wept out loud.

Olivia could feel Cameron's pain too and fought to keep her heart from imploding while her mind took her back to that dreadful day six months before. The silence that followed their weeping reminded her of the silence she'd heard in the delivery room when she'd given birth to her baby boy.

Hours after she'd gone into labor, she remembered the look on the doctor's face and the grave tone in his voice when he'd told her that the fetal monitors indicated her baby had died, but that she still had to help deliver him. The doctor had been so matter-of-fact about it.

"This can't be happening," she'd screamed. "I just felt him kick a few hours ago. No! No! I don't believe you! You heard his heartbeat too. How could he be gone?"

It had been surreal, and it wasn't until she pushed her baby out and heard nothing that she'd understood. He really *was* gone. Even with Cameron by her side, she'd never felt more alone in her entire life than when the nurse placed her quiet baby boy in her arms and walked away.

Patrick had been cleaned up and tenderly wrapped in a blanket. He had looked so peaceful, like he was sleeping. There had been a glimmer of hope in that moment. She had wanted so badly for him to open his eyes and cry, but he never woke up, even when she shook him ever so slightly.

At first Olivia had refused to let the nurses take him away. She pleaded with them to allow her just to hold him a minute longer each time they'd come. In the end, she'd held him for almost five hours. At least that's what Cameron had told her before he was finally able to remove Patrick from her clutches. She snapped back to the present and thought, *you took him from me then, and you just did it again.*

Everything that would ever remind her of her son was gone, and so was her heart. It might as well have stopped beating along with Patrick's because she knew it would never work the same. Not after all this.

8

Olivia came back to reality and looked around her son's deserted room. "What did you do with Patrick's things?" The space started to close in on her. "Where are they? Did you put them in storage?"

"No. I gave them to a family that needed some things." Cameron shifted his weight back and forth on the bottom of his feet.

"So, you've been planning this for some time?"

Cameron remained quiet.

"Well, whatever you sold it for, I'll pay double to get it back. How much did they pay?"

"Nothing. I gave it to them."

"What?" Tears stung Olivia's warm cheeks.

"We don't need the money, and they do. This couple is adopting a child soon, and they don't have anything."

"Fine. I'll give them enough money to go out and buy new baby things of their own. We need ours...or have you just completely ruled out the idea of trying to have children again too?"

"Olivia." Cameron reached out to her.

She folded her arms across her chest and stared at the blank walls. He'd even taken down the wall decorations and the mirror she'd loved so much. He must have worked like a mad man all afternoon.

"Give me the woman's phone number. Right now."

"Are you really sure you want to do this?"

"Absolutely," she said. "You tricked me."

33

He shook his head, left the room, returning moments later with a piece of paper in his hand. "Her name is Sarah Turner. She offered to pay, but I thought I was doing the right thing."

"You should have talked to me first." Olivia grabbed the paper. "I can't believe you went behind my back. I feel like I don't even know who you are right now."

"You're right. I'm sorry."

"You knew how important his room was to me."

"Liv, it's become a shrine…and it's not healthy."

"People grieve in their own ways," she said. "Isn't that what my psychiatrist husband is always telling me? Besides, it's only been six months. It's still raw."

"It is for me too, Liv." He raised his arms to the sky. "Ahh! Why don't you take a hot bath, and I'll make us some dinner?"

She narrowed her eyes, turned around and left Cameron standing there. On her way out the door, she grabbed her purse and cell phone and went in search of her car on P Street. She'd explain the situation on her way to meet Sarah. Surely she'd understand, and Olivia would have Patrick's room back to the way it was by this time tomorrow.

Sarah picked up on the second ring, and Olivia could hear the smile in her voice.

"Sarah, this is Olivia Penn."

"Oh, hello. Thank you so much for the wonderful baby furnishings. That was so generous of you. Everything is perfect."

"That's actually why I'm calling. Would you mind if I came by your house for a few minutes? I need to speak to you about something. It's important."

Twenty minutes later, Olivia was locking her car doors from the inside as she drove through a part of southeast D.C. she'd never ventured into before. She pulled up to the address Sarah had given her and looked around. The house was tiny and worn with paint peeling off the side paneling, window shutters that looked like pirate patches, and a lawn in great need of affection. What was she doing here?

Moments later Sarah welcomed her into her home.

"Thanks for coming, Olivia. It's a pleasure to meet you, and I can't tell you how thankful Rob and I are to have these special things of yours. When I started seeing your husband to help me deal with some issues a while back, I never dreamed my doctor would turn out to be such a life saver."

Sarah's blue t-shirt and khaki shorts were so tight, Olivia wondered if she'd ever be able to get out of them. Her blond hair was thin and wavy, but her countenance, so genuine and lovely, gave Olivia the impression that no matter how much life had burdened her with, Sarah was a gracious survivor.

Olivia looked around the cluttered house. Patrick's baby crib and things were already set up in the far corner of the tiny living room. They actually looked like they belonged, despite the chaos surrounding the space. The mess made Olivia's skin crawl. She liked order and for everything to have its place, even though that preference often times collided with the swells of an angry storm brewing inside.

"My husband said your things finally make the place look fit to live in." Sarah giggled. "Our son should arrive in the next two weeks, and we've just been trying to prepare. You've made our lives so much easier."

Olivia didn't know what to say. How could she possibly ask Sarah for Patrick's things back? Sarah clearly needed them, and she seemed so grateful for Cameron's gesture.

"I'm sorry. I'm going on and on, and you said there was something important you needed to talk about," Sarah said. "What is it?"

Olivia couldn't answer right away. "I don't really know how to say this, but I had no idea my husband was giving you all of Patrick's things."

"Oh."

"I lost my son six months ago, and we've kept his room untouched until now. I guess I'm still in shock." Olivia walked over and scooped up Patrick's blanket, running her fingers around the comfort. She wished it smelled of him, but it had never touched his skin.

"I'm so sorry about your baby. I can see how it would be hard to part with his things. I had no idea you didn't know we were coming to pick them up. You should take them all back. God will give you another baby, and we can find other things. He's always provided for us."

Olivia could hear the warmth in Sarah's voice, but inwardly Olivia's tension lessoned at the thought of having all of Patrick's things back. She looked around again at Sarah's modest home. Sarah had a baby who *was* alive. She needed Patrick's material possessions a lot more than Olivia did.

Olivia snapped out of her daze. "No, that's not the answer. At first I couldn't believe Cameron did this, and I'm embarrassed to admit that I wanted to come over here to pay you off just so I could have these things back."

Sarah smiled and touched Olivia's arm. "I completely understand."

Tears streaked across Olivia's cheeks. She wanted nothing more than to pack up her things and go, but there was another part of her that knew that Cameron was right. It was time to start letting go.

"After meeting you and seeing the kind of loving woman you must be and the warm home you want to provide for this new child, I feel strongly that Patrick's things belong right where they are. With you and your baby."

"Are you sure?"

Olivia conceded with a nod. "It's so odd, I didn't think I would ever be able to part with these things. Someday I want to try to have another child, but not right now." She gestured toward the little dresser and rocking chair. "I have a good feeling about this. Besides, I know I need to try and move on. I've been holding on to the past for too long." It was to time release the material reminders, even if it she wasn't able to completely cut off the pain.

Sarah walked over and gave her a hug. "I can't imagine how hard this must be for you. You've been through so much in the past two years..." Sarah pulled away and frowned.

"You know, I remember when Stacy worked with you at the Post," she continued. "She always had nice things to say about you, and she was right. Now that I've met you, I can see why she loved you so much. You did a good thing writing those stories about her when she disappeared. You've done everything you could to help."

Olivia's heart stopped. "You knew Stacy?"

"We were roommates in college but lost touch once she got her big break at the Post."

"So, you and Stacy were good friends?"

"We were great friends…but our lives grew apart. It happens. Although I still hope one day we find out what really happened to her." Sarah paused. "You know, I've never really told anyone this before, probably because I didn't think it was that important…but that night she disappeared, she called me."

"What did she say?" Olivia hung on every word.

"She said that if anything ever happened to her, her boyfriend wasn't to blame. But I'm sure you already knew that since you two were so close." Sarah shrugged. "Anyway, she sounded pretty drunk, so I just assumed it was the booze talking and not worth mentioning to the police. In fact, I'd totally forgotten about it until just now."

9

When Olivia returned home from visiting Sarah, she found Cameron passed out on the living room couch. He lay on his back snoring and still wearing his glasses. A half-empty tumbler of whiskey sat on the coffee table. She grabbed a coaster to put under the glass.

Spotting the cotton throw at his feet, she unfolded it and gently placed it over him. She hated it when they argued and knew he'd had good intentions, but it had taken her off guard. The worst thing was, he was right, and if he hadn't have done something drastic, there's no telling what it would have taken to break free of the reminders of what they'd lost. Patrick's room *had* become a shrine.

Realizing she was wide-awake, she walked into the kitchen and poured herself a glass of Merlot from the open bottle on the counter. She longed for pen and paper. Her work seemed to be the vital artery that kept her life worth living. It gave her purpose.

As she walked up to her office, something gnawed at her and tempted her to open up her file on Stacy to see if there was something else she'd missed, but she forced herself not to. She'd just file Sarah's comment away in the back of her head. Did it really matter anymore?

Stacy wasn't coming back either, and Olivia couldn't take any more pain tonight. Sipping her wine in her office, she flipped through her Miles Davis CD collection. Miles always helped her unwind. But even after sitting in her recliner and listening to him going at it on the trumpet, she still felt wired and distracted.

Olivia couldn't seem to stop the story that was unraveling in her head, as if it were trying to escape her. She needed to capture it, put it on paper. She walked over to her desk, grabbed a notepad and started jotting down questions and ideas as they came to her.

As an investigative reporter for the Post, she had developed good instincts. Ninety percent of the time, the solution to any problem was buried within information she already had. Now she needed to pay attention to her natural aptitude and the facts. Everything else she would block out. Patrick. Stacy. Cameron.

She attended to the questions that still haunted her: *What do I already know that I'm trying desperately not to believe? Get to the root of what is already there...the essence. I have the answers.*

Olivia's current story involved tracking a series of high-profile "suicide" cases in the metro D.C. area. She believed there was much more to the story. Something told her that these "suicides" were connected and were very likely the work of a serial killer. Admittedly, it could sound far-fetched. It wasn't a theory her editor would accept without a truckload of proof. So, that's what she'd get: proof.

What did all the victims have in common? If she could answer that, she'd be closer to knowing the killer's motive. Infidelity seemed a common thread. And, of course, just the fact that they were high-profile cases. But something else must link them all to one killer. For instance, how did he choose his victims? Randomly or did he know them? And, why had the police so easily labeled these deaths as suicides? Or had they? Maybe Rex knew more than he'd let on in the past.

Yes, in each case a suicide letter had been left behind. Rex had let her see some of them because she'd been in the right place at the right time...but he'd owed her. She'd helped catapult his career with the "Stacy Greenburg" case.

The letters all had one thing in common. The phrase: "I deserve to die." She suspected, since the FBI was involved, they knew these details. Why hadn't they caught this monster already, and why was the FBI keeping so much from the press? Why had the victims become victims in the first place? Were there more cases labeled suicides in other states that might be connected? If not, why were they all concentrated in the D.C. area?

Olivia reached for the crime timeline she'd put together over the last year. Case number one hadn't gotten her attention until six months after it had happened, when she discovered parallels in the suicide notes. Dr. Zachary Wilde, a psychiatrist at the Psychiatric Institute of Washington, supposedly had taken his life by overdosing on painkillers. Made sense. He had access to medicine, and overdoses happened all the time.

He had allegedly taken a bottle of Oxycodone while his wife was out of town on business and left her a note saying that he'd been having an affair with a co-worker and that he "deserved to die." Olivia remembered writing the story and interviewing the wife, never thinking much of it. She specifically recalled feeling sorry for the woman because she seemed so sad and naïve to the affair.

Case number two happened a month later. John Christianson had been a lawyer on Capitol Hill. He'd hung himself, leaving a note that said he "deserved to die," not only for his unethical practices but also for his elicit affairs. He left behind a grieving widow but no children.

Case number three was still very vivid in Olivia's mind. She had watched the victim, an ABC 7 news reporter, on numerous occasions. Victoria Ruiz was a household name in the District. Young, petite, charismatic, and wildly successful. Rumor had it that she was on her way to becoming an anchor. *Had* she really been having an affair?

Her husband also worked on the Hill. When Olivia interviewed him, he'd said that he and Victoria had been high school sweethearts, and he'd always supported her ambitions. She was fulfilling her dream of becoming a reporter at a top network.

He'd admitted having his suspicions of her unfaithfulness with all the long and late hours. One night she simply disappeared after her shift. Her body was found a day later floating in the Potomac, so it was natural to assume she had drowned. But, why had she even been down by the water?

Apparently she's also left a communication for her husband, which had come the same day, by way of telegraph, describing her failures as a wife and how she felt "she deserved to die." The telegram was an interesting twist. Especially since she probably wasn't the one who sent it, and normal people wouldn't bother with such a romantic but antiquated gesture.

Naturally, her husband figured the stresses of her job had gotten to her. Olivia quoted him in an article she'd written saying that he never really believed it was possible that she'd an affair because they were soul mates. It all boiled down to the hardships of her profession. Clearly he was in denial.

Case number four had shocked a lot of people. Nancy Ryan, the Deputy Chief for the Department of Treasury, had killed herself by overdosing on prescription pills.

Olivia switched positions from her desk chair to her cozy recliner and curled up to re-read the article she had written about Nancy's death. Very unexpected and sad, according to her husband. He had always thought his wife had a career she thrived on and loved.

"She was going places and had made many friends and alliances within the organization," her husband had quoted. He didn't understand the rash decision to end her life. Olivia recalled vividly that even though Nancy's husband hadn't admitted to knowing about an affair, he seemed unruffled by it. Was this what had disturbed her the most?

But if these were murders, as she theorized, and not suicides…how did the murderer know his or her victims were cheating? Most importantly – how had the killer picked his targets and gotten so close to them? It appeared that they knew him because, in most of the cases, the bodies were found in the victims' homes with no evidence of forced entry. They'd all trusted him. What professions would have lent themselves to this level of intimacy with their killer?

Case number five, David Russo, was a well-known condo developer in the D.C., Virginia and Maryland areas. He was found dead from a single gunshot wound to the head. And, like the others, his suicide letter also read, "I deserve to die."

The suicides all involved: an unfaithful spouse, high-profile individuals, no forced entries, and a note or telegraph with the key line, "I
deserve to die." Olivia had an impending sense of doom. There would
be more murders. More bodies.

10

The heat of the early morning sun beat down on Olivia as she stepped out her front door the next day. She'd stayed up half the night juggling her serial killer theories and got about two hours of sleep in her recliner before deciding to proceed with her Sunday. She needed coffee. Desperately. Cameron was still asleep on the couch, snoring away when she left. She left a note for him on the coffee table. Maybe they could talk about things later.

The cherry blossoms were out, which meant lots of tourists, but she didn't mind. Sometimes they made for interesting stories. She stopped at Starbucks and ordered a double shot of espresso and a grande black coffee. She didn't even remember the rest of her walk to the Post, and it didn't surprise her to find her boss, Duncan Smithe, hard at work.

He glanced up abruptly from his paper work. "Well, look who it is." He almost looked guilty of something.

"I just can't seem to pry myself away from this place," she said. "It's a compulsion."

He shook his head and frowned. "One I know all too well."

She couldn't help noticing a fresh coffee stain in the middle of his wrinkled, button down-shirt. The norm.

"You know, for an attractive woman, you look like an absolute wreck," he said. "Is everything okay?"

Olivia knew better than to take his comment as an overture. She instinctively pulled her wind-blown hair down over her ears, ignored his last statement and took a deep breath.

"Have you even been outside today?" she asked. "It's a beautiful day. The cherry blossoms are in bloom. People are out and about enjoying the city."

"I'm surprised you even noticed." Duncan sat up straight and sucked in his belly. "Actually, I have. Took a stroll down to the Lincoln Memorial earlier and had myself a hot dog…okay, I had two. Anyhow, I'm willing to bet you've been poring over a story for Monday, and you just can't help yourself. Am I right?"

She shifted uneasily on her feet. "Maybe."

"As your boss I would normally encourage that," he said. "But I'm going to tell you something as a friend. Maybe it wouldn't be such a bad idea if you took a day off every now and then."

"What? Why?" She eyed him. "In the eleven years I've known you, I don't think I've ever heard you say that before."

He shuffled papers then turned them over. "I worry about you."

"You worry about *me*?" She put her hand on her hip. "You're the one holed up in your office every weekend."

"Olivia, you're thirty-three years old, sharp as a whip, beautiful and enterprising…but you don't seem to have any life outside of the Post. You really *should*. I never hear you talk about friends or parties or anything else you're interested in. You can't hide behind your career forever, you know."

"I appreciate your concern, but I'm fine. Besides, you're the one who taught me that the news doesn't stop, even on the weekends."

"This job is going to kill you, you know that?" he said. "You have to find a balance."

"Like you have?" She knew he couldn't argue. "Dunk, I'm working on something big."

"You're always working on something big, and I have no doubt in my mind that it is, but –"

"But, what?"

He sighed. "You're too young to have already given up on the important things in life…like sanity."

"Where's this coming from? You sound like my brother." She began to pace the floor of his office.

Duncan didn't say anything for a moment. "I know what you're working on, this theory about a serial killer in D.C."

"How did you—"

"It doesn't matter," he said. "I think you've gone too far this time. You're becoming obsessed with the idea."

"I'm not obsessed," she said. "I've just been trying to gather everything together and do my due diligence before I talked to you about it."

He cleared his throat. "Look, do me a favor. Have Cameron take you on a long walk in the opposite direction of this place, and relax."

Relax? That was the last thing Olivia thought she could do. Not after the letter she'd just received and knowing some lunatic had been in her home. He even knew what kind of underwear she wore. "Is that all?" she asked.

Duncan looked down at his desk and was silent for a minute. When he finally looked up, he said, "This story you're working on…"

"Yeah."

"I think I understand why you're so passionate about it." He scratched his head and paused. "No matter what you do or how many brilliant stories you write, it's not going to bring Stacy back."

She stared at him in disbelief. "You don't know what you're talking about." Olivia turned and walked away. Away from the very idea.

11

Duncan's words had caught Olivia completely off guard. She floated through the newsroom to her cubicle and plopped down in her chair, dazed. Maybe he was right. She still thought about Stacy all the time.

After she disappeared, Stacy was all Olivia could think about. She desperately needed to know what happened that night after they'd parted ways in front of Stacey's apartment.

The next day when Stacy hadn't bothered to call in sick, Olivia went to her friend's apartment and found the door ajar, all the lights on, and Stacey's purse and cell phone on the kitchen counter. But no Stacy. She had never been heard from again. Olivia wondered if the truth would ever surface.

Questions haunted her over the last two years. Was there something she could have done to prevent it? She'd turned the note she'd found over to the police, but not before making a photocopy of it. The words came to her in dark dreams. *Stacy, it's over. Are you ready for what's next?* She eventually realized it hadn't been the content that alarmed her at first, even though it should have been. The most disturbing thing was, she recognized the handwriting. Unfortunately, she'd never been able to place it.

Sometimes she wondered if Stacy had just run away. Maybe she wasn't dead but was out there somewhere leading a different life with Price…or maybe she'd been kidnapped and was simply waiting to be found.

At the end of the day, Olivia wasn't sure what was worse – discovering the truth about Stacy, or living with a lie she had once mistaken as the truth. Or, just denying the truth all together. She had decided back then that she would write through the pain. She focused on that and nothing else. Her work had kept her sane for the most part. But she still felt she owed it to Stacy to find out what had really happened that night.

Fearing the worst for her friend had propelled Olivia into a state of chaos. She interviewed Stacy's friends and family, which helped Rex Conner with a few leads. But when the FBI learned of Stacy's connection to Senator Sterling Price, they took over the investigation. The Senator might have been a prime suspect had he not disappeared into thin air the same night Stacy had.

When it was all said and done, Olivia had won a Pulitzer Prize for her compelling stories. But as much as she valued who she was by what she had accomplished, winning the Pulitzer had been a bittersweet victory and not an accomplishment she reveled in. Especially since, her success had come by way of her best friend's disappearance...and possibly, her death. Regardless, other people seemed to value her more because of it, so maybe her efforts did matter.

Sitting in her cubicle on the fifth floor of the Post, she looked around. The newsroom was unusually, unsettlingly quiet. She spotted her co-worker, Emily Morgan, several stations over, who appeared to be hard at work. Emily made no secret of her hope to snag Olivia's job. Olivia suspected the other woman of only coming into the office on Sunday to be seen.

As she watched, a handsome, dark-haired young man walked up to Emily with papers in his hand. He suddenly looked up, saw Olivia and smiled. She wondered if he was Emily's new research assistant or perhaps a summer intern. Once again, Olivia weighed the odds that another reporter might have made the connection between the high-profile suicides and a potential serial killer. Emily? But to her knowledge nobody had come out with the story. Yet.

Whoever first broke the news would gain a ton of notoriety. It was news that the television stations and associated press would devour. But it meant taking a risk. This kind of story required fact checking and sources to back it up. It could potentially ruin a journalist's career. Especially, a Pulitzer Prize-winning journalist.

Rex would be the key to confirming her theory. He just didn't know it yet. They had been each other's sources for years, and it was a career relationship that worked in both of their favors.

Before she left, Olivia decided to check her MsgPost. She wondered what side notes Duncan might have left her about upcoming leads. To her surprise she only had one message, and the time indicated it had been sent only five minutes before. She didn't recognize the code name displayed. The message said, "Do you think the North Wall will approve of your theory? I'm watching you."

Olivia gasped and stood straight up out of her chair. The hairs on the back of her neck tingled. Her MsgPost was an internal Post resource. Whoever had sent the note was either in the building or had somehow gained access to an employee's password. Was this the same person who had been inside her home from the day before?

She gazed out across the expansive newsroom, which appeared to be the size of a football field. The cluttered cubicle walls hung low, but still she could see only a handful of heads at their desks. Olivia leaned to the right and looked around a stack of dusty books that she'd never read. She moved to the left, dodging boxes of old files, hoping to catch a glimpse of the person who had sent the message.

She tried to focus. If this person knew what Post employees referred to as "The North Wall," then he or she was most likely an insider. Olivia gazed in the direction of the large, glass-paneled offices on the far wall. The big cheese. The editors who had the power to run or kill a story in the blink of an eye. She could see a few of them gathered in one of their offices and wondered what they were talking about. Or plotting.

Suddenly, she felt someone's eyes on her and turned around to find Emily staring at her. Olivia made eye contact and abruptly sat back down in her chair, her heart pounding. *What had just happened?* She needed to tell Rex. Immediately.

12

FBI Special Agent Nathan Spencer received the call around eight o'clock that Sunday morning. He arrived at the scene in Dupont Circle fifteen minutes later, only to discover one of the most shocking crime scenes he'd ever seen. He had a feeling that everything he'd been working on for the past year was coming to a bizarre fruition.

Earlier that morning, a maid had discovered the corpses of two women. The bodies were not just *any* bodies. They belonged to Monica Habershamm, the world famous tennis player...and Sandra Schelbert, U.S. Secretary of State. The same Sandra Schelbert who Nathan had watched on television countless times, standing next to and advising the President of the United States. The same woman he'd put his trust in, along with many fellow Americans during the war. The same Sandra Schelbert whose husband and two children waited at home for her. And now it appeared that, not only was she having an affair, she had a gay lover. This was going to be one crazy day.

"Hard to believe, isn't it?" FBI Agent Steve Turner came up behind Nathan and put his hand on his partner's shoulder. They stood in the middle of Monica's living room while the D.C. Metropolitan Police CSU worked around them.

"Yeah," Nathan said. "It's tough to wrap my mind around this one. This case has racial prejudice, sexual hatred, infidelity, celebrity and political crime – all wrapped up in one."

"Fun and games, right?" Steve raised an eyebrow.

"Right," Nathan said. "It scares me for a lot of reasons. I see a magnitude of motives and hatred on many levels."

"Looks like our killer may be in it for fame based on who he took out." Steve stroked the stubble on his chin. "Maybe even a little revenge."

"Let's not jump to conclusions," Nathan said.

"But who would have guessed these two had secrets like this? Talk about skeletons in the closet."

"It's going to do a lot of damage to a lot of people when this hits the news." Nathan shook his head. "Not to mention some political agendas."

"Yep. Gay rights. Racism. Women in power. You name it. Can't keep it quiet though."

"True," Nathan said.

There was no way around the media circus that would follow. He had to make a statement to the press eventually, but first he needed to examine the evidence.

"Come on, let's take a look." Nathan slipped on a pair of gloves and saw Steve already had his on.

"I've already looked around the condo for a note but didn't turn anything up so far," Steve said. "Just in case it's the same killer as all the other high-profile cases."

"I have a feeling it'll turn up, but who knows. I just pray we don't have *another* serial killer on our hands." Nathan suspected they would eventually stumble across something possibly linking this to what the FBI was referring to as the "suicide/murder epidemic."

He tried to brace himself for what he was about to see as they rounded the corner of Monica's bedroom. The scene had more blood than he'd have imagined as he took in the grossly displayed bodies. Sandra lay face down in the naked lap of her lover.

The room smelled foul, and he fought the urge to vomit. It was clear that this was the work of a very disturbed person. He swallowed hard.

"Wow, looks like he decided to have a little fun after he killed them," Steve said.

Nathan put his hand up under his nose and breathed out his mouth. He noticed that Steve seemed to be unaffected by the smell and the scene. Had Sandra's husband found out about her affair and lost it? This didn't appear to be the work of a jealous husband's rage, though. The scene was clean, organized, well planned out. Meticulously staged.

The blood spatter on the wall beside the bed caught Nathan's eye, and he moved forward to take a closer look. He admitted that he wasn't an expert in forensics, but he did know some basics.

"Looks like there was a brief struggle of some sort," he said. "From the large quantities of blood and the direction of the spatter, I'd say one of them took a blow to the head before the perpetrator shot her." Nathan attempted to reconstruct the scene in his mind as it might have played out before the deaths. His instincts told him he was missing something.

"It's possible," Steven said.

Nathan got up closer to the bodies and examined the bullet wounds on both victims. "Both shot execution style based on the tattooing around the entry wounds." He could see the gunpowder particles had been driven into the skin, creating hemorrhages.

"Well, no matter how fascinating I find forensic science, there's a reason I'm a field agent, not a lab rat." Steve smiled.

Nathan decided his partner was right. It was time to leave the forensics to the CSI.

13

Nathan carefully scanned Monica's bedroom. He noticed a number of candles, and framed photographs of people he presumed were family and friends. In some photos she was holding trophies, drenched in sweat after a successful match. In others she was accepting her awards on the court or at fancy dinners. She had an expensive-looking glass window box of medals, photographs, programs and memorabilia from her career. Nothing out of the ordinary for an extraordinary life.

Steve began to go through her closet, and Nathan noticed how neat and organized it was, with all the regular things he would expect a woman to own. A very wealthy mega-star woman. Lots of designer labels, although he only recognized a few.

"Geez, her closet is probably worth more than three or four years of our annual salary combined," Steve said.

Nathan took a closer look. "No kidding." Gucci and Prada purses were carefully placed in the shelves, along with rows of stylish Italian shoes. The other side of the closet held a lot of athletic wear and tennis shoes, mostly Nike. There were some bigger boxes at the top.

"We need to go through these later," Nathan interjected. Inspirational books lined a portion of the top shelf. They looked new and un-read. "Let's take a look in the nightstand."

"What exactly are we looking for?"

"Anything that will give us more insight into her private world," he said. "Who she knew, where she went, what she did when she wasn't playing tennis."

"You mean who else she might be sleeping with that had a motive to kill her?" Steve raised his eyebrows.

"Somehow I don't think it was who *else* she might have been sleeping with that fueled this killer," Nathan said. "I think it was *who* she was sleeping with that set him off."

"Look, there's a little blood on the carpet in front of the nightstand," Steve said. "And someone knocked over a picture frame. I think you're right. This also suggests there might have been a struggle."

"My guess is that Sandra fought until the bitter end." Nathan opened the drawer of the nightstand.

Amongst the clutter were a few books, playing cards, random pens and pencils, a couple of dildos, some K-Y jelly and other assorted sex toys.

"Wow, you hit the jack pot." Steve smirked.

Nathan shuffled a few of the items around with a pencil until he spied a small leather-bound book. When he picked it up, he discovered it was what he'd hoped—a journal. The first entry dated 2003.

"The M.E.s are here," Steve said.

Nathan heard the medical examiners out in the hallway and quickly slipped the journal into the pocket of his blue windbreaker. He wasn't sure if it would amount to anything, but he wanted to comb through it for names of people she knew and their purposes in her life. Monica's personal world just kept getting more and more interesting.

"Let's move out of their way." Nathan bent over Monica's body. That's when he noticed it and picked it up with the end of his pencil. "What's this?"

"You mean the necklace around her neck?" Steve asked.

"Could be nothing. Could be something. I didn't see it before with all the blood."

Nathan removed the necklace around Monica's neck. "Looks like a locket."

"Either way, it's our evidence now. Bag it."

Nathan put the locket in a baggie and left the scene. Steve followed. As Nathan entered the living room, he tried to envision the scenario that had played out the afternoon before.

"Doesn't appear to be any signs of forced entry from what I can see," Steve said. "I checked all the doors and windows earlier."

"Yeah, I noticed that too," Nathan said. "I also noticed a set of keys lying on the kitchen counter earlier. "I'm guessing they're Monica's." He decided to do a test. He walked over to the table and riffled through the purse he spotted and quickly found Sandra's identification and her set of keys.

He took her keys, walked over to the front door and tried to open it with each one. The last key he tried worked. He checked the other set and found a match. "These have to be Monica's." But he couldn't help but feel like he was missing something that was right in front of him.

"What?" Steve said. "What is it? You have that look..."

"I was just thinking," Nathan paused. "If the perp didn't force his way in, maybe he also had a set of keys. Which would mean, he knew Monica."

"Or she let him in."

This killer was good. Not a force to be reckoned with. Nathan certainly had his work cut out for him with the precedent that had just been set. Murdering a famous athlete and a politico was something few famous killers had ever been able to accomplish in a lifetime, much less one day.

14

The only time he'd forgotten a detail as important as the locket was back in Los Angeles years ago. His thoughts flashed back to the day he'd met Candice Barretto.

She had been his first kill, his only impulse kill, spontaneous in every sense of it. It was odd how right he felt about it. Justice had been served then too.

After that he had meticulously plotted and planned and watched his targets for months at a time before making a move. He studied them, knew their vices, their routines, their habits, their professions, their families. He knew everything about them. He had the ability to get inside their heads.

At the age of twenty-one, Candice Barretto was already a big movie star with several hit movies. She was in every form of media, US Weekly, People, InTouch magazines...Entertainment Tonight TV, newspaper gossip columns, talk radio. She had made quite a little reputation for herself, un-becoming of course, but that was the Hollywood way.

He'd been shopping at Fred Segal's one afternoon when he spotted her across the room. There was no mistaking her. The tabloids reported Candice had recently announced her engagement to another famous actor. Out of the corner of his eye he saw her starting to walk his way.

Her long blond hair looked messy, as if she had just returned from the beach. As she got closer and they made eye contact, he could see that she was naturally beautiful, unlike a lot of stars who had make-up artists and stylists to salvage their average looks.

Her eyes were sea green, a color he could not have anticipated any more stunning. Her puffy lips turned down effortlessly in a pouty pose. He still remembered the blue jean mini skirt and the yellow tank top she wore that clung to her petite shape, leaving nothing to his imagination.

"These are my favorites." Candice picked up a handful of faded multi-colored casual shirts.

"Aren't they men's shirts?" he asked, at ease with the start of the conversation, his natural charm taking over.

"I think they're actually unisex, but maybe they *are* men's," she said. "I don't know…just know I have one in every color and I would definitely recommend them. They're *so* soft."

"I'm sure they suit you well." He flashed his million-dollar smile.

She had cocked her head slightly to the right and gazed up with him, still holding the shirts in one hand. "They're a must have, in my opinion…and you must have them. My treat."

"Okay," he said. *Sold.* "But only if you let me return the favor."

"What did you have in mind?" she said.

"How about a little champagne at the Skybar."

"Ooh, I used to love that place," she cooed, "but the Mondrian Hotel is so last year. I know a better place that's right around the corner."

"What about your fiancé?"

"You know the tabloids." She paused for a moment before continuing. "Can't believe everything you read. Besides, he doesn't have to know."

He was shocked and didn't know what to say to such a forward and somewhat flattering request. Stars, they certainly had a manipulative way of acquiring what they wanted just because of who they were. They seemed to think they lived in a consequence-free environment. Something stirred inside him, and the rage he felt for his first wife returned. He knew what needed to be done.

"Let's go have some fun," he said. "You're right, no one has to know."

Candice led him out the back door of Fred Segal's into an alley. He realized that he had not thought this through and worried about the paparazzi. If they followed them, his picture would be on the cover of every magazine in country. He couldn't let that happen.

"Relax," she said. "I know what you're thinking. You don't want your face to end up in the tabloids."

"The thought had occurred to me."

"I know somewhere private where we can go and not be disturbed. You'll like it, trust me."

Somehow they both managed to elude the paparazzi, and she took him back to her condo on Wilshire Boulevard. She was so young and full of herself. She was living on her own in her very own place. *How quaint,* he remembered thinking when they first stepped inside her condo. When she pulled out her private stash of cocaine, he became excited by the prospect of having a little fun before he killed her.

Candice's murder had been a turning point for him. It had happened naturally and proved effortless. When a friend found her body two days later, the police said it was an open and shut case. Overdose. No one thought anything different, and the media went crazy knowing Candice Barretto would never grace the big screen again. After that night he packed up and left Hollywood for good. He wanted to start fresh. Washington, D.C. had been Sam's idea.

15

He and Sam sat in his private quarters and anxiously awaited the breaking news. The television buzzed in the background. How long would it take for the bodies to be discovered? He knew it would be the top story for weeks, and the best was yet to come.

He poured himself another whiskey and drank it straight, attempting to calm his nerves. Then he paced the room and continued to wait. Another long swig, and a warm buzz settled over his body. He could feel Sam's curious eyes studying him from across the room.

Sam poured his beer down his throat and belched. "I know what you're thinking." He kicked off his Ugg flip-flops, unbuttoned his Seven jeans and got comfortable on the couch.

"Oh?"

"What if the press doesn't run the whole story?" Sam said.

The thought had occurred to him. "The whole story is bigger than a two-minute package on the evening news or even a front page headline." He sat down in his favorite green leather recliner. "It'll all surface one way or another."

"It's pretty shocking," Sam said. "I'd say you made history."

He smiled.

"Is there something you're not telling me?" Sam sat up straight.

"I made a decision after I killed them," he said. "I believe I deserve some credit for what I've done."

Sam's eyes got big. "Oh, no. I'm afraid to ask. What did you do?"

The recliner begged to be oiled as he leaned back further. "In a day or two when Sandra's husband opens his mail, he's going to find a message from his wife's lover. Then the world is going to know who's responsible for these killings."

"What!" Sam jumped up and walked over to the fridge for another beer. "I don't want to hear any more. Please tell me you didn't sign your name to that letter."

He laughed. "Of course I didn't." He sipped his drink and sank into the comforting arms of his chair. "But I did sign the name that I want the world to know me by."

"What's that?" Sam sat back down and popped the tab open on his fifth beer.

"The Punisher."

Sam took a sip and smiled. "Hmm...I like it. Has a nice ring to it. Plus, it makes sense." He rubbed his face with his fingertips. "So, we're really doing this? Again?"

"You in?"

The two shared a quiet moment while the television remained on mute.

"You took care of everything else at the crime scene, right?" Sam didn't look worried.

He didn't want to tell Sam he'd forgotten the locket. "Of course."

"Good. Can't afford to get sloppy now."

"You know me. I always cover every detail." He cleared his throat and looked away.

"Count me in then."

He felt his stomach sink when he thought about his oversight. He'd have to figure out a way to take care of it. Would he or was it already too late?

"So what's next?" Sam asked, wide eyed. "Someone bigger? I know you have a plan. You always do. What role do I get to play?"

"Slow down," he said. "I'll let you know when the time is right. Be patient." He needed to buy some time. A look of disappointment clouded Sam's face, and he slumped back into the couch and pouted.

He tried to be mindful of Sam's sensitive side. A boy at heart, when he felt played, he knew Sam would retreat inside himself and into the past. They'd only talked about his past once, but it had been enough to help him understand who Sam really was. Deep down.

Growing up in Texas had been rough for Sam at times, but his mother had always been there for him. At the age of twenty-six, his father had become a washed-up actor and shot himself, leaving a note of his confessions and detailing all the wrongs he'd done, including abusing his own son. In some ways, Sam still seemed more like an eight-year-old boy than a man.

Sam gasped. "Tell me you got photos of the tennis chick and the secretary!"

He smiled. "I may have gotten a few. I know how you like them." To Sam, photos were always the most important detail. That and not getting caught.

"You did, didn't you? I knew you would. I knew you wouldn't forget, even if you hadn't planned on killing them. Can I see them? When can I see them? Oh! This is going to be good."

"Perhaps. But not now."

"Why not?"

"Because I said so."

"I really need to see the photos. You always do this. Why do you like to tease me?" Sam crossed his arms in front of his chest.

The Punisher let the next sip of whiskey linger in his mouth. "Good things come to those who wait, Sam." Besides, he planned to have a little fun with the photos first.

16

After Olivia got the tip from Duncan that afternoon, she was in hot pursuit. Even though she'd had a feeling something big was on the horizon, she'd never imagined anything *this* big. Cameron had found her in her office with her nose buried in her work, and she told him about the breaking news. He walked her downstairs and sat her down on the couch.

"Just promise me you'll be careful, Liv." She and Cameron sat beside each other. He swept her hair behind her ears, and she immediately pulled it back. He shook his head and frowned. "Sometimes I really hate the type of work you do. It's dangerous, and I don't like that you're out there every day putting your life on the line for your next big story."

"I know you don't." She cupped her hands gently around his cheeks, leaned in and kissed him. "But I promise to be careful."

"I just don't want anything to happen to you because of one of your hunches."

"It won't. Please don't worry." The truth was, she was very concerned. And something about the fact that he sensed it too disarmed her. She wasn't sure whether to tell him about the text. She didn't want to worry him even more. She needed her work to get her through the pain of everything else. It proved a good distraction. He couldn't take that away from her too. Plus, she was meeting with Rex later that night to discuss things. He'd know what to do.

"How can I not worry?" Tears swelled in his eyes. "You're my wife, and I love you."

"I love you too." She wrapped her arms around his neck and hugged him tightly. "Everything is going to be okay."

He pulled away. "For once would you *please* just listen to me?"

She swallowed the knot in her throat, squared her shoulders and put on a brave face for Cameron. She was determined to find the person who was terrorizing her, no matter how hard she had to fight. But that meant researching, writing, putting herself out there and watching her back. Even if she was scared out of her mind at times.

He sighed and pinched the bridge of his nose. "I'll take that as a no."

"What do you want me to do? Quit my job?"

"Maybe that's not such a bad idea." He stood up and turned away.

"You know I can't do that." She stood up, slipped her arms around his waist and hugged him from behind. "My job is who I am. It's my life." She could feel his body tense.

"I just keep wondering what role I play in your life." His voice caught. "Ever since Patrick died, you've kept me at a distance…you don't even want to make love to me any more."

"That's not true." She released her embrace and held back tears. "You don't understand."

"And your work always comes first. It always has." He paused. "I lost him too, you know." He sighed and left her standing there while he walked upstairs.

She let him go. And then she wept silently. Was he upstairs doing the same thing? She didn't mean to be distant, but she still wasn't over the fact that he'd cleaned out Patrick's room without telling her. How could he expect her to ever be the same? How could he ask her to move on so quickly? She was doing the best she could.

She pulled herself up the stairs and tried not to think about her job, determined to make things right with Cameron. She knew he was hurting too. And he was doing the best he could too. She knew that. Why did she have to be so stubborn?

It had been some time since she'd tried "make-up sex," but this seemed like a good time to try. Anything to make things better.

17

The Old Ebbitt Grill was one of Olivia's favorite destinations in the city, even if locally it was considered something of a cliché. Past presidents, including Cleveland and Roosevelt, had dined there on many occasions in its various locations. But that didn't really impress her. Nor did the fact that it was the oldest restaurant in D.C.

What she loved most was the comfortable setting and the delicious crab cakes. No matter what time of day, she could always count on the place being packed, but her green velvet booth in the back corner of the main bar was always reserved for her. At least that's what the wait staff always made her believe.

She arrived early, as usual, to meet Rex. She didn't mind having to wait a few minutes for her "regular" table and decided to order a drink at the bar. The crowd at Old Ebbitt's never disappointed. She sat down on the dark, leather-covered stool and ordered a Sterling Merlot. Looking around, she realized how easy it was to pick out the tourists from the locals.

The tourists were the best behaved, as if they felt it was a privilege to be at such an establishment. The locals simply did as they pleased. A group to her left carried on singing military chants and songs after taking shot after shot. Empty glasses surrounded them.

Olivia sipped on her wine and made eye contact with a handsome gentleman at the far end of the bar. If she hadn't known any better, she would have thought it was Clint Eastwood. He tipped his well-groomed, graying head of hair and signaled for his ticket.

She didn't want to stare, but she could have sworn she'd seen him somewhere before. She looked back to the group of singing drunks but when she tried to sneak a peek at the gentleman once again, he was gone. When the hostess came over and told her the table was ready and that her glass of wine had been "taken care of," she became suspicious.

"He told me to tell you he was a fan." The waitress smiled and shrugged her shoulders. "Did you see him? He kind of looked like a movie star."

"A fan?" Olivia took the last sip of her wine and followed the woman.

The two women weaved through the rustic, mahogany bar, candle lit tables, and brass railings until they reached Olivia's favorite spot.

"Actually, I think he said he was one of your biggest fans." The woman placed a menu in front of Olivia as she sat down. "Your server will be right with you, Mrs. Penn."

Olivia couldn't speak. Had she just seen her stalker? The man who had been in her home? Or was the choice of wording just a coincidence? She sat with her eyes closed for a moment, trying to steady her nerves. Breathe, she told herself. Breathe.

She tried to put the incident out of her mind. Told herself she was overreacting. Remembering that Rex had said he'd be pressed for time, she went ahead and ordered the crab cakes and a black coffee for herself, and Rex's usual. She was on her second refill of coffee when he finally showed up.

He was perspiring. For a tiny man with short red hair and scholarly-looking spectacles, he was not at all what she envisioned the average cop to look like, but he was the best cop she'd ever met *or* worked with.

"I ordered you a burger and fries," Olivia said.

"You told them to hold the tomatoes, right?" His eyes grew as big as his glasses.

"Of course." Olivia laughed. "How could I possibly forget the last time the waiter messed up and left a tomato on your plate? Whew…let's just say that's a side I'd prefer to never see again. I guess it was your 'bad cop' persona."

He made himself comfortable in the booth. "Listen, can we make this quick because it's been a long day, and I still have a lot of work to do."

"I would imagine. Pretty crazy, isn't it?"

Olivia tilted her head sympathetically and played with the napkin in her lap. She considered mentioning the man at the bar, and immediately dismissed it. She was probably just being paranoid.

"Thanks for meeting me," she said. "I know this has been a huge day for you, and you have a million things to do."

"You have no idea." He rubbed his forehead with his fingertips.

Rex looked tired and defeated. Dark circles were beginning to show under his eyes and his shoulders slumped forward. He was a tiny man to begin with, and she could tell that the day had really taken a toll on him.

"It's really bad," he said, "All of this. I just can't believe it happened."

"I know, it's shocking." She sipped the warm drink and instantly felt rejuvenated. "It's just so disturbing and raw."

"That's a good way to describe it."

She already knew as much about the double murder as the media was privy to. "What else can you tell me besides the official details?"

"I don't know." He clasped his hands behind his head and leaned back. "I'm just so tired right now, I can't even think straight to be honest. Plus, seeing something like that this morning has really done a number on me. And, I've seen a lot of bad things. I just need some time to let it all sink in."

"You're a good cop, you know that Rex?" He was candid, open and honest. He didn't have the "small man's syndrome" behaving as if he needed to demonstrate his power or be the "tough guy" cop.

"Thanks."

"You have a lot of admirable qualities," she said. "And you have feelings, which I respect."

They sat there in silence for a few minutes, sipping their drinks.

"You should know that this story you're investigating has been turned over to the FBI."

She pressed her lips together. "Actually that doesn't surprise me."

"Shouldn't you be more concerned by the email you received yesterday?" He shook his head. "This person sounds dangerous. You need to take it seriously."

"I'm hoping you can help. Honestly, I can't believe this is really happening. What should I do?"

"For starters, be careful."

"You sound like my husband."

"You should listen to him," Rex said. "I also want to try and trace the message. If this guy really is connected to Stacy's disappearance, there is no telling what he's capable of."

18

A waitress walked over and set their food on the table, but Olivia had lost her appetite. "I know you've been consumed with this suicide slash murder case, and so have I," Olivia said. "I can't stop thinking about it, and I need your help. It's important. I'm starting to wonder if Stacy's disappearance, my stalker and these murders are all connected."

Rex looked as if he were carefully choosing his next words. He untied his napkin from his silverware and placed it in his lap. "We've known each other, for what? Five years now? In that time, it's no secret how much you've helped my career. If *and when* I become police chief someday, it will be in big part because of you. I haven't forgotten that."

"Rex, I didn't ask you to meet me here today to stroke my ego." Although, Olivia did feel flattered by his comments.

"Let me finish." He took a sip of his water and looked around to make sure they were still alone. "I admire your passion and your instincts when you tell a story. Not only are you a good reporter, you're an even better detective."

"Thanks, I think."

"So, I believe you when you say that this case is consuming you as much as it is me. It's maddening and frightening, and it's not going to go away. It's gotten too big for the MPD. I'm almost relieved that the FBI is involved."

"But now it's out of your control."

"It always has been." Rex stared off across the restaurant, looking as if he was reflecting.

Olivia wondered what Rex meant by his last statement.

"I'll help you as much as I can," he said. "You know that. Whatever is in my control."

She nodded and caught his eyes. "I have a theory."

"Why am I not surprised? Go on." He grinned and leaned back in his chair.

"Well, in the last six months that these supposed suicides have taken place, I've been tracking anomalies between similar cases that I've researched over the last year, all within Virginia, Maryland and D.C. These are well-known individuals who are allegedly taking their lives. Washington needs to sit up and listen."

"I agree."

"There has to be something else going on here, and I'm going to find out what it is," she said. "Why would someone want us to believe these deaths were actually suicides? From what I've read, most serials want credit for their work."

"You seem convinced it's a serial killer." Rex poured ketchup over his fries and strategically began to cut them up one by one and place them into his mouth.

"Yeah, I am. Who knows how long it's been going on? It might have gone undetected, but there are clues. The killer left a calling card."

Rex sat in silence. Olivia knew that he could potentially lose his job and credibility if anyone found out he had "leaked" information to a reporter. But, as he had pointed out, she'd helped further his career with the Stacy Greenburg case. Stacy's disappearance had catapulted both of their careers, *and* it had changed Olivia's life forever.

But the price she'd had to pay was that her best friend's disappearance would always haunt her. She also knew that Rex didn't always leak everything he knew. He couldn't afford to be that obvious. He needed to use the media to his own advantage just as she needed to use the police to hers. He actually told her more when he kept quiet because it indicated she was on to something.

"My gut tells me that these killings are only the beginning. They are much bigger and bolder than the ones before. He's trying to get someone's attention."

Rex placed his last fry in his mouth and chewed deliberately. Finally, he made his way to garnishing his burger with more ketchup. He devoured his burger in five deliberate bites. More silence.

"The story I'm writing is going to expose this for what it is," she said. "And of course, it would be advantageous to include your name as a source. This is a powerful story, and it's going to shake up the nation."

"Boy, that's a bit grandiose, don't you think?" Rex folded his napkin on his plate and rubbed his pitiful excuse for a belly.

"No, I don't." She took a bite of crab cake and swallowed. "He just killed our Secretary of State. This is bigger than anything I've ever written about."

"Yeah." Rex wiped his face.

"I can't just ignore this. Just like you, I need to know what's going on."

"What do you have so far?" he asked.

Olivia pulled out her notepad. "I realize that I wasn't there at all the crime scenes, but I'm aware of what most of the suicide letters say, from the copies you showed me."

She had Rex's full attention and couldn't tell if he was holding back or just wanted to hear what she had to say to confirm what he already knew. So she stopped talking for a minute.

"Look, I've seen it before," he said. "The press decides to take the lead in giving the police a voice for something speculative."

"I know you understand what I'm suggesting here," she said.

"We need three confirmed murders with the same M.O. to consider a serial killer."

"I have six. Actually eight if you count the last two high-profile murders."

"Or you think you do."

"I'm hoping you'll confirm that, even if it is only 'on background.'"

"You know I can't confirm anything at this point," he said.

"Why is it that the police have gone to extravagant lengths to convince the public that there isn't a serial killer at work in the Washington area? Is it all about politics? I can't believe that even *you* can just sit here and withhold any shred of the truth. What is it that you're not telling me?"

Rex looked her straight in the eye. "You know you can trust me. You're the only reporter I choose to talk to. Period."

"Then you know that this isn't a circulation ploy," she said. "I don't own the Post, I just work for it. But the public has a right to know. I just can't believe that the authorities have gone to the extreme of allowing friends and family to believe that these deaths had anything to do with drug overdoses or freak accidents." Olivia sat in silence for a moment and reflected before continuing.

"I deserve to die," she said, breaking the silence.

"What are you talking about?" Rex looked around the neighboring tables in the restaurant, as if to make sure no one was listening to their conversation.

"The phrase 'I deserve to die' is the one consistency in all the suicide letters. It's the killer's calling card. Why can't you just admit that I'm on to something here, Rex?"

"Look, my hands are tied for now with this case. You need to contact Nathan Spencer with the FBI. I'm sure he'll be interested in what you have to say, and I'll give you a good referral."

"Thanks." She had her crab cakes boxed up and picked up the check. Mission accomplished. This was one story that wouldn't be a labor to write. It had already written itself.

19

Olivia's story ran on the front page of Monday's *Post*. The headline read: SECRETARY OF STATE FOUND MURDERED WITH TENNIS CHAMPION.

The Associated Press also picked up the lead article, which was now circulating in every major and minor market in every newspaper across the country. It had to be one of the most shocking stories the country had ever read.

This kind of news was what publishers lived for. It kept newspapers alive. Some might call it sensationalism at its finest. Olivia didn't know any other way to spin the truth. And it was the truth. Sensationalism would have been to assume the two were lovers, but she knew she couldn't go that far. Not yet anyway.

The Post was in its usual hyper state when she arrived at 1150 and 15th Street. Her first phone call of the day was to Terry Carson, an ex-FBI agent with a reputation for solving "unsolvable cases." She'd never met him in person but he remained well respected, even though he'd been dismissed from his duties at the FBI almost a decade before. This still remained a mystery to her.

She suspected Terry would help her because she had a feeling that they might have something in common. She'd heard that even though he was officially retired he still liked to "unofficially" track down cold cases. She'd be willing to bet that he was following this case and figured he was her best shot at digging up the truth. It was the third time she'd called, but so far he hadn't returned any of her messages.

Her co-worker, Emily, slithered up beside her desk and looked her up and down. Her broad frame towered above her. Emily looked like she should be playing football, not chasing news.

"Well, that was quite a little story you wrote." Emily stood with her hands on her hips and peered down with a patronizing grin.

Olivia felt three inches tall and wondered what Emily was up to. "Thanks."

"You know, Duncan called me too."

"Oh."

"Lucky for you, I was on my way back from New York. I told him to let you cover the story."

Olivia had to fight to contain her amusement. "How generous of you."

"Well, I just thought you should know that."

"I guess so." Olivia shifted a sheet of clean paper over the notes she'd made.

"So what are you working on now, Olivia? Anything big?"

"You know how the news works. It's out there, we just have to find it."

"Wow, that's profound." Emily rolled her eyes. "I just thought if you were working on something newsworthy, you might want to return the favor by giving me the lead. You know, a little give and take."

Emily had some nerve. "I have work to do," Olivia said. "You should really speak to your editor regarding your stories. That's the way it works."

"Fine." Emily turned and stomped back to her cubicle.

Olivia shook her head in amazement at the exchange. Although she shouldn't have been surprised. It was typical Emily. Olivia had zero respect for her, but if there was one thing the woman was, it was confident. It was no secret that Emily had slept with more than one of her editors, thinking that's how she would make a name for herself. She had certainly done that. In more ways than one.

20

The next day, Duncan appeared to be waiting patiently for Olivia to arrive, his feet propped up on his desk, cup of coffee in hand. She was sure he had already devoured his usual half a dozen doughnuts, his morning ritual.

"Good morning, Dunk." She took a seat across from him.

She noticed he had combed the little hair he had left neatly over to the left side of his head instead of to the right. An odd choice for a style change, but that was Dunk. He liked to keep people guessing, especially her. His short-sleeve button-down shirt looked ready to burst at any moment from his pregnant belly. He clumsily shifted his feet from his desk to the floor. Then he took a long sip of coffee, unaware at first as it dribbled down the front of his shirt.

"Never fails." She shook her head and pointed to his shirt.

"Blast it!"

Olivia handed him a napkin from his desk. She had never actually heard Duncan utter true profanity, and that cracked her up more than anything. Some days she would pay good money to hear him swear. Just once. Even though they gave each other a hard time, they both knew they needed one another. They had been through thick and thin for the past eleven years. She knew Duncan well, and he knew her even better.

"Nicely done on your story," he said after he finished dabbing the coffee stain.

"I couldn't have done it without you." She settled back into her seat.

Duncan grinned. "Yes, you could've."

"We make a pretty good team, don't we?"

"We do." He rubbed the top of his head with the palm of his hand. "I did feel a bit guilty after my lecture on Saturday, telling you to enjoy your weekend and relax. The next thing you know I'm hunting you down to do a breaking news story."

"But that's what I call enjoying my weekend."

"You'll never learn, and I know I'm not the best influence." He seemed nervous as he began to straighten items and papers on his desk. "Why don't you take the afternoon off? You deserve it after breaking this story."

"Are you kidding – and miss Emily Morgan's dramatic antics? No way."

"Actually, I was kidding, but what do you mean?" He raised an eyebrow.

"She mentioned that you called her yesterday about the lead." Duncan looked a bit bewildered. "I did call her, but not about the lead. I wonder what would have given her that idea. It was about something un-related. Besides, she's not seasoned enough to handle a story like this."

Olivia knew she never should have questioned Duncan's integrity or loyalty.

"I've got work to do," she said. "Is there anything new I should work on?"

"I'm serious about taking some time off at some point," he said.

"I can rest when I die." She winked. "Besides, I have a feeling there's a suicide letter that's bound to surface from these latest murders, and I want to be around when it happens."

"Oh, for crying out loud," Duncan said and then looked up at her. "But seriously Olivia. Good work."

Olivia's cell phone buzzed with a text message. She stood up and took her iPhone out of her pocket. As she read the words, the room sud-denly started to spin, and she had to brace herself on the chair to keep from falling.

"Are you okay," Duncan asked. "You look like you've just seen a ghost."

She didn't say anything. She couldn't. The message was clear. It said, "I'm watching you…just like I did Stacy."

21

Olivia felt relieved to have a friend like Rex. He'd taken her last call very seriously, had her computer hard drive scrubbed and SIM card on her cell phone downloaded to try and trace the text. She anxiously awaited any results.

The very next day, another "suicide" letter appeared, just as she'd expected. She was thankful for the lead and the distraction. Jordan Schelbert's phone call to her that afternoon had Duncan in a frenzy.

He was pacing the cluttered space around her cubicle as she spoke with the grieving husband of the former Secretary of State. Duncan hung on every word. Jordan received the suicide letter in the mail that morning that was apparently signed by Monica Habershamm. The tone in his voice was sad and angry. He was ready to talk.

"I'd like to give an interview," he said. "But only to you, and I'd like for the Washington Post to publish this letter."

Olivia couldn't imagine publishing something so disturbing. She was curious what the letter said. "Are you sure about that?"

Jordan sighed. "I just really need the opportunity to tell my side of the story, before the tabloids run their own twisted version."

"You realize that's more than likely going to happen either way." She twirled the phone cord between her fingers.

"I guess. Look, I've spent the last three days denying any type of statement to the press."

Olivia listened while he stated his case.

"I'm ready now," he said. "This is absolutely mind-blowing and devastating for my family. I want to know the truth. I want America to know the truth. No matter how much it hurts. And I want this killer caught."

She madly scribbled down every word. She could hear the tears in his voice as he spoke.

"Frankly, I'm a fan of your writing and was even before the Stacy Greenburg case. I'm confident in your ability to tell the story fairly and accurately, and I believe that you're the only one capable of telling this one."

"Thank you, Mr. Schelbert. I'll do my best. When would you like to meet?"

"How about now?" he said. "I'm packing a few things and heading to my sister's home in Silver Spring. I just can't stay at the house with everything that's happened and the media swarming the place day and night. I'm sure you understand."

Olivia tugged at the collar of her shirt that threatened to cut off her air supply. She peered down at her watch as she held the receiver. "I can be there within the hour. Why don't you give me the address?"

Duncan tripped over a crumbling box of files when she ended the conversation with Jordan. "Well, what did he say?" he demanded.

"Jordan Schelbert requested an exclusive interview with the Post."

"That's fantastic."

"Apparently he's declined to make any statement to the press so far."

"But he wants to talk to you?"

"Sounds like it," Olivia said. "I should go. He wants to talk right now."

"What else did he say?"

"Well, he got a letter in the mail today from the killer…and he wants us to run with it."

Duncan was speechless, for once.

"I'll be in touch after the interview," she said.

Duncan certainly had a nose for news, and over the years he'd helped her find her own unique voice for telling it. But the only other time in her career that she'd felt reluctant to tell a story, was Stacy's. For a moment, something reminded Olivia of the instinct she'd had the night her friend had disappeared. Only now, *she* was the one in danger.

22

Typically, Olivia felt a little nervous when she arrived for a big interview. Usually she took the time to prepare her thoughts and questions. But this interview was different. Jordan Schelbert had tracked *her* down. Her plan was simple. Allow him to do most of the talking, and he would probably end up answering all of her questions without her having to pry. The letter would really be the key.

Jordan was a physically strong man. He was well over six-feet-tall and fit. Up close, though, she could see old acne scars and a feeble attempt at covering a receding hairline.

Emotionally, she guessed he was a nervous wreck, but he appeared to be good at pretending, despite what was going on around him. Olivia stepped into his sister's home and almost tripped over a toy truck and a miniature scooter. She heard the laughter of little boys in the other room.

"Your children?" she asked, attempting to ease the awkwardness as he led her through the home. She quickly realized at that point that it was only awkward for her. Jordan seemed deep in thought.

"Oh, yes…those were my kids…I mean are my kids, Chase and Cory."

"How old are they?"

"Seven and eight. They really do miss their mother," Jordan said. He led Olivia through a small kitchen out onto a wrap-around porch. It amazed her to think how children seemed so resilient, even amidst a tragedy like this.

"Do you like tea?" he asked. "I like tea. Although on days like these, I sure would appreciate something stronger…"

"Tea will be fine, thank you." She realized that Jordan was out of his element and possibly out of his mind with grief and shock, so she was patient. The furniture on the wrap-around porch was comfortable and gave her a chance to survey her surroundings. The backyard contained a grill, a weathered-looking hammock, beautiful, overhanging trees that reminded her of a Southern plantation, and the remainder of a small vegetable garden, long forgotten.

Jordan returned with a piece of paper in his hand. "I'll cut to it," he said. "I can't believe this is happening, to me, to our family. I'm so angry at Sandra…" He paused before continuing and looked down at the ground. "This part is off the record."

"Please, go on."

"How could Sandra have done this? What was she thinking?" The pain resonated deep within his expression and his eyes. She felt sorry for him as he spoke, realizing that celebrities, political people, athletes, and anyone in the media were real people with real problems too. Unfortunately their problems got magnified because of who they were. She gave him an encouraging nod.

"I just want the maniac who did this caught," he said. "But a small part of me also wants to know how *he* knew and *I* didn't. I guess it really doesn't matter any more. What's done is done, and that's why you're here, right?"

"I'm here because you called me," she reminded him politely.

"Listen, I think with this letter you'll have more than enough to write your story." Jordan seemed numb to the words he was saying as he handed her the opened letter.

Olivia eagerly absorbed the last words of Monica Habershamm, even though she had a feeling that they weren't actually *Monica's* words. The world famous tennis player had written a very interesting suicide letter to her lover's husband. It read:

I have loved your wife for three years now. I was
deeply in love with her. I am sorry for the pain I
have caused you. What we have done is wrong, and I
deserve to die. I know now that she did not love me.
She was using me. According to The Punisher, justice will be served over and over again. Be aware.

Finally, Olivia had proof that her theory was correct. She couldn't
believe the last two sentences of the letter. This confirmed everything
she knew in her heart to be true about these murders, but this was
the first time the murderer had chosen to reveal who he was and his
motive.

Jordan stood over her as she read the letter through several times. "I
think you should take it to the police," he said.

"I agree. Probably even the FBI." This was certainly bigger than the
local police.

"I just don't want to deal with it," he said. Jordan started to wring his
hands and swayed slightly side to side. "Olivia, would you please do me a
favor and pass it along? I just can't deal with the media any more. When
they catch wind of this, they'll never leave me alone. Please."

"I'll be more than happy to help." She almost couldn't believe her
good fortune.

"I'm planning to leave town for a while after the funeral," he said. "I
won't be granting any further interviews beyond this one. I have to figure out a way to move forward, and I can't do it in Washington."

Was he running? Was he using her to obtain what he wanted in the
same way she was using him? What *did* he want? A frightening thought
suddenly occurred to her. *Did Jordan Schelbert kill his wife?* And, if he did,
he certainly was an incredibly convincing actor. A million questions
started circulating in her head. She reacted quickly.

"Do you have the envelope the letter came in?" she asked, curious if
he had received it by mail as he'd claimed.

"No, I must have thrown it away," he said.

How could he have thrown important evidence away? Or did he? What was he thinking? She was careful not to let her fear show, but there was only one question running through her mind at that point. *Was she sitting in front of a killer?*

23

By the time Olivia returned to the Post from her interview with Jordan, she had finished writing the story in her head. She just needed to get it down on paper before it escaped her. She still had tons of questions and couldn't lose the uneasy feeling that Jordan might be involved in everything that was happening.

It took her an hour to write the first draft of her story and another hour to polish it before she emailed it to her boss. Duncan was on pins and needles expecting it. While she waited for his comments, Olivia called her psychologist.

Mimi Stone answered on the first ring. "Olivia? How have you been? I haven't seen you in a while."

"Any chance you could see me first thing tomorrow morning?"

Mimi cleared her throat. "Is everything okay?"

"Actually, I was hoping you'd be available for an emergency session."

"Okay, okay. Let me see what I can do." Mimi was quiet for a moment then said, "Can you be here at eight a.m.?"

"That's perfect. Thanks. I'll see you then."

It had been a long day, and Olivia decided to go home a little early after she wrapped up her story with Duncan. She was relieved to see her husband waiting for her.

He gave her a huge hug and said, "I'm taking you out to dinner."

Even though she wasn't over the fact that he'd cleaned out Patrick's room without bothering to consult her, she figured she'd punished him enough for now with her silence, so she didn't bother to argue with his suggestion. She didn't feel like being angry at him tonight.

Cameron looked very sharp in his pinstriped pants and fitted black button-down shirt. They hopped in his silver Jaguar and drove north on Connecticut Avenue toward Cleveland Park. Olivia loved the restaurants in that area, especially Sorriso.

They had met the owner a couple of years back and always enjoyed the true Italian flair of Sorriso's homemade pasta and a bottle of the Chianti from his family's Venetian vineyard. Cameron found a parking place two blocks down on Macomb Street.

"This feels like one of our first dates." Olivia took a deep breath and smiled. He took her arm and placed it in his as they walked down the block.

Forgetting her pain for a moment, she reached up and pecked him on the cheek, grateful for his concern. He had suffered as much as she. In some ways, it was amazing their marriage had survived Patrick's loss. She hoped they could both relax and enjoy this evening.

Just then something caught her eye. It was only a movement, but it struck her as familiar. Olivia quickly turned around and saw the back of a woman's head as she crossed the street a block in front of them. That walk. The swish of her hair. Her body.

It can't be. *Stacy?*

Olivia pulled away from her husband's arm and broke into a full sprint. Her high heels caught on the pavement and slowed her down, but that didn't stop her. *Stacy! Stacy! Is that really you?* Olivia thought. She ran as fast as she could, dashing out in front of oncoming traffic after the light changed. She was losing her. Car horns blasted all around her. The woman was rounding the corner of the next block. *Wait! Wait! Don't go.*

"Excuse me!" Olivia yelled and almost trampled an older woman with a cane. "Please wait, Miss...Stacy, it's me." The woman kept walking, not hearing her.

Olivia ran faster. She had crossed the street and was catching up, when her heel caught in a crack in the sidewalk, and she fell to her knees, twisting her ankle. She winced with pain and looked up as tears streamed down her cheeks.

"Please, someone," she pointed, "that woman – I need to speak to her."

A short, older man reached out to the woman as she passed him, got her attention, and pointed back at Olivia.

Olivia could hardly catch her breath. She looked down and noticed that her heel was broken and her knees were bleeding. Her ankle throbbed. The woman she'd been chasing turned and walked back toward Olivia, a puzzled look on her face. Olivia wiped her tears away.

"Stacy?" Olivia gasped.

The woman made a funny face. "No. My name is Amanda."

Suddenly her face became clearer, and Olivia gasped, realizing her mistake. She looked just like Stacy, except for her nose.

"I...I'm sorry," Olivia said. "I thought you were someone else."

The woman frowned. "Are you okay? Here, let me help you."

"No, I'm okay. Really." Olivia nodded and waved her away, humiliated by her impulsive behavior and for making a scene. What was she thinking? She rested her forehead in the palm of her scraped hand. The woman shrugged and walked away.

"Liv! Are you all right?" Cameron ran up beside her and reached for her hand. "You scared me." He pulled her up beside him.

"I thought I saw Stacy. I was sure it was *her*." She sobbed into her hands and allowed Cameron to wave away onlookers who had gathered.

"I'm sorry," Olivia murmured, her knees buckling even as Cameron supported her.

"It's okay. Let's get you steady on your feet." Cameron held her in his arms for a moment before stepping back. "What's going on with you? I can't believe what just happened. You're really starting to scare me."

"I don't know," she said. "I don't know."

"Stacy's gone." He looked into her eyes.

Olivia lowered her head. She really had lost it. "I know." She smoothed out her shirt and pulled herself together. "It's just so hard to believe sometimes, especially when she visits me in my dreams. Then, when I think I see her on the street…" She shrugged. "I could have sworn that was her. Even after all this time."

24

He scanned the comings and goings on O Street in Dupont Circle, patient with his plan. Adrenaline exhilarated him. He ventured out behind the bushes when he heard voices behind him but was careful not to be seen or look suspicious. He blended in, like a lion stalking his prey. Ready to pounce at any moment.

Olivia approached, arm in arm with her husband. She was so close he could almost reach out and touch her. She didn't see him of course. But someday she would. *Someday she will realize just how important I am. Then she will love me as much as I love her.* He needed her like he needed air to breathe. He watched the couple walk down the street as they approached their home. He stayed as close as he dared, without giving himself away.

He watched Cameron fumble with the keys at their front door, turn and smooth the hair away from Olivia's face. He enjoyed eavesdropping, but their affection made his blood boil. He longed for Olivia's touch.

"I'm concerned about you," Cameron said.

Olivia turned her face lovingly into her husband's hand. "Don't be."

"I can't help it." He placed both hands around her shoulders. "I think you're in over your head at this point. With this story you're chasing...and tonight. I want you to stop living in the past and let the FBI do their jobs."

"Let them do their jobs?" Olivia backed away. "I have a job to do too, and I could use a little support here. The public has a right to know that there's a serial killer out there."

"You know I support you." He sighed. "I always have. I admire your passion and commitment to finding the truth. I just don't want to see you get hurt in the process."

"I'm fine."

"No, you're not. You behaved like a crazy person tonight, running after that woman. First your stalker breaks into our house, and then this? I think the stress is getting to you."

Olivia removed her husband's hands from her shoulders and said, "You forgot one thing. It certainly hasn't helped that you cleaned out our son's room without telling me. I wonder if *that* has anything to do with how *crazy* I'm feeling. But since you're a psychiatrist, I'll let you figure that one out."

As he listened from the bushes, unable to believe what he was hearing. He *did* have an impact on her life. He was getting to her, and Cameron. His plan was working. It wouldn't be long now before he'd put his plan in action.

25

Benjamin Funkhouser was enraged at the article in the Post that morning. The byline read Olivia Penn, but he already knew who had written it from the content and style, and the fact that it was above the fold once again. He felt entitled to let Ms. Penn know when she wasn't doing her job. It had become his hobby or rather his obsession. The article was pure sensationalism, publishing the last words of dead woman. A letter so personal could only have been meant for the Secretary's husband to see.

In the words of Eugene Meyer, who back in 1935 had published the seven principles establishing what he believed made a newspaper truly great, the first mission of the newspaper was to depict the truth as accurately as possible. This article wasn't the truth!

A journalist's job also included writing material that fit the reader young or old. This article was x-rated and an embarrassment to the newspaper. How could they have published such blasphemy? Benjamin was furious at the woman's editorialized version of the murder investigation. Mr. Meyer would roll over in his grave if he could see it.

It was true that Benjamin had been Olivia Penn's biggest fan for a long time, and he had praised her on many occasions. But this morning he felt the need to remind her of her journalistic duties to the newspaper, to the public…and to him. He thought it a good idea to send her a copy of the principles that the employees of the *Washington Post* should adhere to.

For the last year, he had followed the attractive young reporter's career. He admired her talent for telling a story. He'd even begun to fantasize about her and the life they would share together someday. He'd done things for her, made sacrifices and gone to extravagant lengths… all because he loved her. He wanted to give her a purpose, something to write about.

That was why he was certain that she would appreciate his concern, criticism, and discipline. He cared about her, and she needed to know that. But, she needed to be reprimanded. She needed to understand his power and influence, as well as his wrath.

He typed in her email address on his computer screen and began to write. He savored the idea of his thoughts being instantly transported to her. Soon she would be reading his words, his carefully phrased advice. This excited him. When he finished with the email, he read it over several times, reveling in his turns of phrase, his instinctive writing style. He was important. The world would soon see that. This time he signed the email, Benjamin Funkhouser.

26

Olivia took the Metro to the Farragut North stop on the red line at 7:30 a.m. the next day. Her commute usually fell much later in the morning, missing the morning rush hour. She wiped the sweat from her upper lip while she waited on the platform with a hundred or more commuters before cramming into the metro car. Standing room only. Even though she wasn't obsessive compulsive, she hated the idea of grabbing the filthy, cold metal pole everyone held on to, but she had no choice.

Luckily she was only one quick stop from Dupont Circle. When the doors opened, she pushed her way out of the car, up the escalator and onto the corner of 17th and K Street. A street musician was playing, "Somewhere Over The Rainbow," on his saxophone, and the music lingered in her ears long after she'd made her way into her psychologist's building.

Olivia greeted George, the doorman, and signed in at the front desk. She made her way to the second floor where she smelled Mimi's incense as soon as she walked off the elevator. The scent clung to her as she walked down the long hallway to Suite 2027.

She took deep breaths while she waited. She was early, but she need-ed a few minutes to gather her thoughts. The only sound in the waiting room was the ticking of the clock on the wall.

There were so many things she needed to discuss with Mimi, but she didn't even know where to begin. She looked around. The walls in the wait-ing room were stark white and the overhead light was bright and warm.

Olivia was thankful when Mimi emerged and beckoned to her. Olivia followed her down a narrow hallway and transitioned to a different environment. The bright waiting room was a vast contrast to Mimi's office, which was dim, with the exception of two small lamps on opposite ends of the room and a lit blueberry candle that created a subtle glow.

Mimi sat in her floral-patterned, high-rise chair, and crossed her legs. Olivia never sat on the couch across from her chair, but chose the more comfortable chair parallel to Mimi's.

Today her psychologist was dressed in a navy blue skirt suit. If it weren't for her long legs and torso, her petite frame would barely be able to fill it out. The suit looked like it had come from the sale rack at TJ Max, but she still appeared professional and put together.

Mimi had perfect ebony skin and a short, stylish haircut. She always appeared calm and collected. She spoke like the well-educated woman that she was, and Olivia liked her. For a moment, Olivia got lost in the smell of incense and blueberry. It had been two months since she'd seen Mimi. But she wished she could spend the next two months filling her in on all that had happened just in the last week.

"I'm glad you're here, Olivia." Mimi smiled and re-crossed her legs. "It's nice to see you again."

I'm sure it is for a hundred and fifty dollars an hour, Olivia thought. "Thanks for seeing me on such short notice."

"That's what I'm here for."

Olivia suddenly felt nervous and wondered how Mimi managed to always look so calm. "I'm feeling uneasy about calling now because I'm not sure how to explain everything that's been happening recently."

"Okay. Why don't you just start with what's on your mind right now?"

"I don't know." Olivia sighed. "I don't know."

Mimi sat patiently.

The sweet aroma of blueberry filled Olivia's nostrils. She told Mimi about the letter her stalker had left and how he'd broken into her home. And about the disturbing text message that mentioned Stacy.

"I just feel so helpless and vulnerable right now. I don't like being a target and having no control over what's happening." Olivia pulled her hair down around her ears.

"You mean about this stalker?"

"Yes, but it's not just him. The day I found the note from this creep, my husband decided to clean out Patrick's room without telling me. He gave all our baby things away. I couldn't believe it. We had made a pact to leave the room the way it was. Then he decides it's time for ME to move on."

"How do you feel about that? Do you think you're ready to move on?"

Olivia noticed that Mimi squirmed in her chair after her last question. Did she understand?

"Maybe," Olivia said. "I'm not sure I'm ready to forget Patrick, even if there wasn't much of him to remember. Keeping his room the way it was the day he was supposed to come home from the hospital has been my way of keeping him alive somehow. At least in my heart."

Mimi stayed silent.

"I'm not sure how I feel about it exactly. I'm still upset with Cameron for doing it without first talking to me, but I understand why he did it now. And when I went to visit the woman who had taken Patrick's things, I realized she needed them more than I did. I agree with my husband, it *is* time to try to move on. I'm just not sure how."

"It sounds like you've already made some good progress, Olivia. These are all positive things you're saying."

"I want to have another baby again some day, but I'm afraid to get pregnant. What if he dies again? I wouldn't be able to handle that."

"Do you think this fear has affected your relationship with your husband?"

Olivia thought for a moment. "Sometimes I don't want to have sex because I'm afraid, so I make up excuses. When in reality all I want to do is be with Cameron, but there's something holding me back."

Mimi paused. "Do you think any of this has to do with losing Stacy?"

Olivia's jaw dropped. She stared at Mimi. "What do you mean? How does my being afraid of getting pregnant again have anything to do with Stacy?"

"I didn't mean to upset you." Mimi reached over to the end table and extended a box of Kleenex.

Olivia grabbed one, only then realizing tears were streaming down her face. "What does Stacy have to do with any of this?"

"You've lost two very important people in your life. You didn't know Patrick outside of your womb, but you knew him for nine months and the promise of who he was. He was a part of you, and you loved him, even if you never got a chance to watch him grow. On the other hand, you knew Stacy very well. From the way you talk about her, it's obvious you loved her very much too. You haven't had any closure on either one. They left you, and you had no explanation as to why. It's understandable that it's affecting your life."

"Oh." Olivia buried her face in her hands and wept. "Sometimes I feel like I'm going crazy."

Mimi let her finish crying before she answered. "How do you mean?"

Olivia wiped her eyes and sat up straight. "Last night, I was walking down the street in Cleveland Park with Cameron. We were on our way to dinner...and then I could have sworn that I saw Stacy walking in front of us. This woman had all the same mannerisms. I ran after her, tripped and fell, only then realizing it wasn't her. I made a huge spectacle of myself. I could see it in his eyes. Cameron thought I had lost my mind. He told me he's concerned about me. And maybe he should be. Apparently, I'm seeing things now."

Mimi looked down at the floor, deep in thought.

"How do you explain that?" Olivia rubbed her breastbone.

"I think you're in crisis mode." Mimi looked in her eyes. "I'm glad you came in today. I'd like to see you do some journaling about what's on your mind. I actually think that at the moment you're haunted more by Stacy's disappearance than by Patrick's death or your stalker. All three seem to be surfacing again now for some reason, but the part of your nightmare that seems to upset you the most is Stacy. Write it down and get it out. You might be surprised what your writing will reveal."

"I don't know how much more I can take of re-living all of this." Olivia shook her head. "Part of me wonders if Stacy's still alive. That hope is why I can't let her go."

Mimi frowned sympathetically. "For some reason, I have a feeling she may be the connection to everything that's happening in your life."

When Olivia left Mimi's office, she wondered how her psychologist was so perceptive…unless she knew something Olivia didn't know.

27

Olivia got to the Post around 9:30 that morning and sat in her cubicle with her latest story in hand. By most reporters' standards, she was in early. The newsroom was still waking up. She still found it hard to believe that Jordan had really wanted Monica's letter published. He was admitting to the world that his celebrity wife had been cheating on him. With another *woman!* Olivia found it difficult to understand his motive. Unless it simply wasn't true and the affair had been manipulated by the killer himself.

She shook off her concerns, and tried to turn her thoughts to work and her email inbox. She scanned the list of messages. There it was, marked with an "urgent" flag:

My dear, sweet Olivia,

Consider this a warning! You are dangerously close to angering me beyond a point of no return. Haven't you learned anything yet? Why must you be so greedy? You already won your Pulitzer Prize! Why must you exploit the truth?
Your latest article was absolute sensationalism. Perhaps that is all your work amounts to these days. I feel compelled to remind you of your roots. I am very disappointed in you. You're wasting your

talents. I know more about this investigation than anyone else. I should be writing these stories, not you! In fact, I even know the killer's next move. Do you?

I remain your biggest fan, Benjamin Funkhouser.

She only had to read the message once before she frantically called Rex. He'd agreed to meet her for a late lunch at the Round Robin Bar at the Willard hotel. If she hadn't been totally convinced before that her life was in danger, she was now.

Rex and his team had been studying the emails for months and even had a copy of the letter left at her house. But still, no leads. Now she had a name for her stalker: Benjamin Funkhouser. If that really was his name. She also called and left a message for Nathan Spencer at the FBI. She had a feeling he would respond quickly.

This communication was different. Benjamin was clearly upset, and he'd finally revealed himself by signing his own name. But why? Did he want her to find him? Didn't he realize what this would mean for him? *Was Benjamin The Punisher?* How else would he know the killer's next move?

Olivia didn't understand the message or his intent. She didn't even want to think about the possibilities or the fact that she had ignored him for so long. Why was he so angry? She tapped her fingers on her desk and tried to organize her thoughts. She grabbed the nearest notepad and started jotting down all the questions that were racing through her mind. She was on question ten when her phone rang. It startled her, and she jumped in her seat.

"This is Nathan Spencer," the voice on the other end said. "I'm a special agent with the FBI."

Olivia relaxed. "I've been expecting your call, Agent Spencer. I'm sorry we weren't able to connect sooner. I have some information I'd like to turn over to you that I'm certain you'll find very interesting."

"I'm presuming it's Monica Habershamm's letter that I read about in your article this morning," he said.

"Actually, yes, that's a huge part of it. The killer supposedly mailed the letter to Jordan Schelbert's house. Jordan contacted me yesterday after he received it, requesting an interview. He said he would only talk to me. When I saw the letter, I advised him to turn it over to the proper authorities, but he asked that I do it for him."

"That worked out nicely for you," Nathan said.

"I guess it did," she admitted.

"Well, as you can imagine, I'm anxious to get my hands on that note so that our labs can examine it. Are you free to talk about this more?"

"Certainly, any time," she said. There was something about Nathan's voice that she instantly liked. She couldn't really put a finger on it. He sounded very down to earth and professional.

"I'm actually right down the street," he said. "How about fifteen minutes?"

She suddenly realized that she was smiling. "That would be just fine."

28

When Olivia met Nathan, he was not at all what she had expected. He looked younger than she had pictured him, probably in his mid to late thirties. With his boyish features, he could have passed for mid to late twenties. He was tall and fit and looked as if he had played football in school. His sandy brown hair stuck up half an inch all around his head, resembling a hair cut a ten-year-old boy might sport.

Nathan wore khaki pants, brown loafers, and a t-shirt. No blue FBI windbreaker to draw attention to himself. He flashed an awkward smile in her direction and shook her hand. "Thanks for seeing me on such short notice," he said.

She pushed a few cardboard boxes out of the way, pulled an empty chair over from the cubicle next to hers and motioned for him to have a seat.

"From what I've read in the paper and what your friend Rex tells me, we have a lot to talk about."

"Yes, we do." She pulled out the letter he'd come for, which she'd carefully placed in a plastic baggie.

He took the baggie from her. "Nothing like the FBI being the last to know about something like this." His raised his eyebrows in a friendly manner.

"I wanted you to have it as soon as possible, and I'm sorry you had to learn about it in the newspaper."

"Me too," Nathan said, with an edge to his voice. "As you know, this is a high profile murder investigation. Getting the bad guy should be highest priority. Your story could've waited."

"I understand your position," she said. "I really just want to help. I felt I had no choice but to do as Jordan asked. He said he only wanted to talk to me, so I went. You might not have gotten the letter at all if I didn't play by his rules."

She sat down again and continued. "The funny thing is, when I asked him about the envelope that it came in, since it was allegedly mailed to his home, he said he must have thrown it away. So, I guess there is really no proof that it was actually mailed unless someone can analyze the handwriting to confirm that it's Monica's."

"The envelope could be very important." He examined the letter through the plastic. "I plan to contact Mr. Schelbert about this."

"You may want to call him sooner than later," she said. "He's staying with his sister in Silver Spring and told me he's leaving town directly after his wife's funeral. He didn't say where he was going."

"Did he say anything else?" Nathan scratched his head.

"He just said he needed to move forward and couldn't do it here in D.C. But he has two young kids, so I thought that was really strange. Plus, why would he have thrown away a piece of important evidence like the envelope?" She paused. "I assume he could be a suspect, given the nature of the crime and possible motive."

He seemed to tense up. "I'm afraid I can't say at this point."

Back off, Olivia. You're pushing too fast and too hard. Let him talk. Let him come to you. But she just couldn't help herself.

"Look, I'm not sure if Rex told you, but I've been researching a string of high-profile suicides that I believe are actually murders. It's always been my feeling that they were connected somehow, and I think this latest case proves the link."

His expression darkened. "How do you figure?"

"There were always notes left behind," she said. "These murders were different though. The killer finally identified himself as The Punisher…

almost as though all the deaths before were just practice. I think he's just gearing up to strike again. And he seems to choose victims who will get him the most attention. Next time I think he'll strike someone even more important."

"You know I can't talk about an open case."

"Is it safe to say we've got a serial killer on the loose in D.C.?"

"I'm not at liberty to comment." He looked away from her.

"Okay." She really wanted to build a relationship with Nathan, but it wasn't off to a great start.

He smiled with a sudden gleam in his eyes. "I've been told you have the instincts of a street detective. Is that true?"

"I don't know. You'd have to tell me." She went to retrieve the emails that Benjamin Funkhouser had sent her. "Agent Spencer…"

"Please, call me Nathan."

"Okay, Nathan. New topic. I've been receiving what I thought was just an annoying form of fan mail over the last six months. The emails seem to come from the same person but from a different email address every time. This morning I received another one, but this time the writer mentions that he knows what your killer's next move is." She handed him the print outs and gave him a minute to read them over.

He looked up at her, frowning. "You didn't show these to the police?"

"I originally gave them to Rex, but so far we have no idea who this could be. The reason I'm showing them to you is because it mentions the killer's motives." Goosebumps raced up her body as she spoke. She rubbed her arms, forcing them away. "I'm wondering if my fan might be your celebrity killer. I'm particularly worried he might come after me."

Nathan shifted in his chair. "This changes things. Tell me more."

"He's already been in my home and sent me a text message that links him to Stacy Greenburg's disappearance," she said. "Stacy was a very dear friend. And now I wonder if the author of these messages is trying to make me his media puppet."

"How so?" Nathan stared at the messages in his hands.

"The text he sent said he was watching me, just like he did Stacy. And, the more I think about it, it isn't a question of *if* this killer will go after someone again. It's only of question of *when*. I think he wants me to break his story. I think he likes the idea of causing panic, becoming famous."

Nathan shook his head and placed the evidence in his lap. "I'll be honest with you," he said. "I do believe your life may be in danger due to your involvement in this case. I can assure you the FBI will look into this. I would hate to see you become the killer's next target."

29

Rex had never stood her up before. It wasn't like him. Olivia wondered if he was tied up at another murder scene and couldn't get away. She waited in the Willard's Round Robin Bar and sipped on a glass of Merlot. The Willard was known as, "the residence of presidents," since every president since 1850 had stayed at the hotel. At least once.

The historic watering hole reminded her of photos she'd seen of the Oval Office, only it had regal green walls and a circular bar anchored in the middle of the room. Olivia could almost feel the ghosts of Lincoln and Grant, sitting nearby with a brandy and cigar. The original bar top, although raised over the years, was still intact. She gazed down at it and ran her fingers over the uneven surface of the cool marble.

The walls were covered with sketches of important people who had once been guests. As she studied the faces, she remembered why this was one of her favorite places to frequent. To think that Martin Luther King had written his famous "I Have a Dream Speech" in one of the upstairs rooms. And that the words to "The Battle Hymn of the Republic" were inspired by an incident at the hotel.

The mystery of the place and what it represented was what drew Olivia back each time. The hotel had hosted events that had helped shape the country. If only the walls could talk, she thought, what stories she'd have to write about.

Rex showed up thirty minutes late. The lunch crowd at the bar still hadn't thinned. Sweat dripped down the sides of his face from his forehead. "Sorry I'm late, I had an emergency," he said.

"Is everything okay?" Olivia asked. She moved her purse off the empty barstool next to her to make room for him.

"Yes," he said.

For some reason, she didn't believe him and wondered what was really going on. "Would you like to eat?"

"Actually, I don't have much of an appetite." He wiped the sweat away with the back of his hand.

"Okay, a drink perhaps?"

"I'll have a Jack on the rocks," Rex told the approaching bartender.

Olivia had never seen Rex drink during the day. Actually, she'd never seen him drink period. She studied him for a moment, and he avoided her gaze.

"On second thought, let's order some food." He reached over the side of the bar and grabbed two menus.

An hour later, Rex had polished off two more Jack Daniels, and Olivia wondered if he'd even remember half of what she'd just told him about the latest stalker email and her meeting with Nathan.

"I've gotta--" He fought back hiccups."—run. Check, please." Rex held his breath. "My treat."

Why was he acting so strange? Something seemed different about him. Maybe the stress of this case was starting to get to him. Or, maybe he was having marital problems again.

"Well...thanks for meeting me and for lunch," she said.

"No problem." He scribbled his signature on the receipt the bartender placed in front of him. "It's always—" he belched "—good to see you, Olivia."

"Yeah, you too," she said. "Although one of these days it should be under normal circumstances."

He smiled, kissed her on the cheek, rushed out of the entrance and hung a left toward the lobby.

Olivia sat there for a minute. She hoped Rex was all right. He seemed so distracted. She looked up and watched a middle-aged couple across the bar get up to leave. They giggled and looked too smitten with each other to be married. She noticed their empty champagne glasses. The woman wore pearls, a blue sleeveless dress and a Burberry overcoat. The man, a dark blue business suit. When they walked away, Olivia noticed an attractive gentleman across the room who sat alone. He looked familiar. Where had she seen him before? He suddenly looked up and met her eyes.

It was *him*. The man who'd bought her a drink at the Old Ebbitt Grill that past Sunday before disappearing. This was too much of a coincidence. He *had* to be her stalker. What should she do? How long had he been there? Where was Rex when she needed him? She grabbed her purse and rummaged around inside it for her phone, although she wasn't sure what she was going to do with it once she found it. Her hands touched her wallet, hairbrush, keys, lip gloss...where was her phone?

"Hello, Olivia."

Startled at the deep male voice, she looked up from the depths of her purse. *He* was standing right in front of her. She caught her breath.

"I didn't mean to frighten you," he said and smiled.

"I'm here with a police officer." Don't let him see your fear, she thought.

"I saw him leave a few minutes ago."

"He'll be back," she lied. "I'm sorry, who did you say you were?" She tried to stay calm. "Have you been sending me fan mail for the past six months?"

He laughed. "Fan mail? I guess I thought it was the other way around after all the messages you've left me. I believe your last message was on Monday. I decided to answer it in person. Hope that doesn't make me a creep."

She exhaled, feeling like an idiot. "You're Terry Carson?" Olivia asked.

"Yes. It's nice to finally meet *the* Olivia Penn in the flesh. Would you care to join me? I was just about to order dessert."

Olivia looked at her watch. Why not? She'd been trying to meet the man for months.

Terry was well known for his involvement in a notorious serial murder case ten years earlier. She'd heard that, although he was retired, he followed ongoing cases as a hobby. And he sometimes did consulting jobs with local police departments. She suspected her hunch that he might be following this case was right.

But why he'd decided to follow her around and do his homework before he finally introduced himself or returned her calls was beyond her. She studied him for a moment. The waitress at the Old Ebbitt Grill had been right. He did look like a movie star. Olivia followed him to his table, curious to hear his explanation for why he'd been following her. Did she have two stalkers...or just one?

30

"Dessert?" the waiter asked. The Round Robin Bar at the Willard Hotel had cleared out. It was three o'clock in the afternoon.

The only thing Olivia was hungry for was information from Terry.

"Yes," Terry said. "The lady here will have a Merlot, and I'll have another Maker's Mark."

"Fine, sir." The waiter smiled at Olivia and scurried away, only to return two minutes later with their drinks. Olivia didn't protest to the order.

"You know, Ms. Penn, I'm officially retired. Have been for a long time." He sipped his drink, the clinking of the ice cubes seemed to fade into the walls.

"Yes, I'm aware."

"I have to hand it to you though," he said. "You *are* persistent."

She could hear the amusement in his voice.

"I've been dodging your calls for some time now," he continued. "Then I discovered you have the kind of gumption most reporters I read don't, so I decided to do my due diligence and find out more. Just what is it that you feel I can do for you? And more importantly, why should I?"

"I'd like to talk to you regarding the rash of suicides in the city." She lowered her voice and took a sip of her wine. She took another sip, and a slight buzz settled over her. "You and I both know, that suicide has nothing to do with it."

He kept a straight face. "Do we? Suppose I were to agree with you, that we're talking murder here, not people offing themselves. What's in it for me?"

"Knowledge," she said.

"Knowledge?"

"Yes. Knowledge."

"What makes you think I care…or that you can give me anything I don't already have?" He still looked amused.

"I guarantee, I know things you don't," she said. "And, what's even more intriguing to me, I'm certain you know things I don't."

"Ah." He nodded and took a long sip, peeking out the window.

"You like games, Mr. Carson? Well, here's one for you. Why, after being retired for almost a decade, would an ex-FBI profiler still be following a case? Excuse me, working a case, as if you're still being paid to work eighty-hour weeks."

He shrugged.

"I'll tell you why," she continued. "Because you can't let it go. Which is why you're good at what you do – notice I said that in the present tense."

"Your point, Ms. Penn?"

"You've been profiling The Punisher, haven't you?"

"That's what they're calling him?" A flicker of interest lit his eyes.

"That's what he's calling himself." She'd heard that he'd become a recluse, obsessed with solving cold cases until the unique "hot" case fancied him. Someone in the department must be feeding him information, but apparently it wasn't as up to date or complete as what she had.

"Well, I see why you won a Pulitzer." He smirked. "You're not afraid to seek the truth. That's good. That's how you find it."

"Then I guess we have something in common, don't we?"

"I suppose we do."

"And, I think we'd make a good team." Olivia raised her glass.

"Perhaps." He didn't raise his glass. Yet.

"When can we meet again to discuss things further?"

"I'm going out of town for a long weekend. Tomorrow is the only day before I leave. You could stop by my house in Alexandria, say three o'clock?"

"That'll work." She lowered her glass and took a sip. Olivia considered the situation for a minute. *This could be the start of a beautiful friendship*, she thought.

31

The next afternoon Olivia made her way to Alexandria. She rolled down the windows in her Mini Cooper and let the breeze play with her hair. She was curious to see what Terry's home would look like. Why did he retire from the FBI? *Were the rumors true?*

She'd heard from one reliable source that he'd gotten fired for a profile his superiors believed was way off. Problem was, the Bureau later found out that *they* were the ones who had been wrong. But by then office politics kept them from rehiring him.

Maybe this was his motivation. Maybe he felt like he needed to prove himself again. Show the world he was the best. An ego thing. But that didn't jibe with other facts. She knew that for years, universities had sought after him as a speaker for criminology courses, but he had declined them all. Terry remained a mystery.

Olivia pulled up in his driveway, the sound of gravel crunching beneath her tires welcomed her. Somehow she'd had no trouble finding his back road. She wasn't surprised to find that he had no close neighbors. She parked, grabbed her purse, notepad and pen and made her way to his front porch.

The former FBI agent sat in a rocking chair. He looked relaxed. Rocking back and forth. A tumbler of what appeared to be whiskey in one hand and a folded newspaper in the other.

"Good afternoon, Ms. Penn." He stood and put the newspaper down.

"Let's not start this game again." She smiled. "Please, call me Olivia."

"Works for me." He chuckled. "Personally, I found it kind of sexy being referred to as Mr. Carson. But Terry works too."

"Good." She liked his ornery side.

He led her through his front door, and she finally got a glimpse into his soul. His home was nothing like she'd pictured it. He didn't appear to live like the bachelor that he was. The living area and dining room flowed together and featured a magnificent floor-to-ceiling wall of windows overlooking the Potomac.

Dark wooden bookshelves on the far wall displayed books, picture frames and other decorative artifacts. A world globe stood in the right corner next to a modest fireplace. A burgundy rug blanketed the majority of the hardwood floors and comforted a dark green leather recliner and a black leather couch. The rest of the furniture was eclectic but matched. The telephone table and coffee table looked like antiques, but she couldn't be sure. All she knew was that the room was exquisite.

An ornate wooden staircase promised to lead somewhere even more interesting. But the one thing that captured her attention the most was the shiny black grand piano that made a sophisticated statement in the left corner of the room. It was either well dusted or well played, she noted. Sheet music stood at attention. She felt in awe of her surroundings.

"You've got a gorgeous home," she said. "You play the piano?"

"Since I was a kid." He looked at the instrument. "It keeps me honest."

"What kind of music do you enjoy?" Olivia walked over to the window.

"A little bit of this, a little bit of that?"

She turned around and saw him blush, but she wasn't sure if it was from the alcohol or if he was actually embarrassed by her questions.

"It's such a nice day, I thought we could sit outside if you'd like," he said.

"Sure." She followed him past the long rectangular dining table and high backed chairs through a side door that led to a wrap-around porch.

He motioned for her to take a seat on a cushioned wooden chair. "Would you like something to drink? I have wine, soda, fruit juice…"

"Do you have any coffee?"

"Sure do. I pegged you as a coffee drinker and made some before you came. I'll be back." He took his tumbler with him and returned a few minutes later with extra inches of whiskey and a steaming cup of black coffee.

"Thank you." Olivia took a sip and savored the aroma of strong coffee. Just the way she liked it. "I'll get straight to the point. You know why I'm here. I want to find The Punisher. Meanwhile, I want to continue writing stories about him."

"Who knows, maybe you'll even win another Pulitzer?" He winked.

"Believe it or not, I've never been driven by the possibility of awards or fame," she said. "Getting to the truth is what motivates me. I just want to understand what type of person could do these things to people and why he or she is targeting high-profile individuals in the Washington area. My guess is that you might have an idea."

"What makes you think that?" He took a big gulp of his whiskey, swirled the glass making the ice cubes rattle, then took a second swig.

"The way I see it, the FBI screwed you over ten years ago on the Jackson Myer's serial case." She looked him straight in the eyes. "So you refused to give speeches or teach because, in your opinion, you lost a part of yourself when the bureau decided not to admit their mistake. You can't bear to be seen as anything other than what you were when you were at your peak. The best."

Terry rolled his glass around on the tips of his fingers, watching the ice cubes tumble around like dice he was about to toss.

"I'm right, aren't I?"

He set his glass down and smiled politely. "So you think I've holed up in this house and I'm trying to prove something to myself by following this case?"

Olivia leaned forward in her chair. "I think what you don't realize is that you don't have anything to prove. You used to make death your life, and you loved it. It's time to do it again."

32

A warm afternoon breeze swept through Olivia's hair, and she pulled her hair down over her ears. She had waited until she saw Terry's face relax, as if he'd made a decision. When he set down his glass and didn't go for a refill, she decided it was time to get started.

"What do you think this killer's motivation is?" She grabbed her pen and paper, ready to take notes.

"You mean, who do I think The Punisher is?" he asked. He seemed to be back in his element now. Leaning forward in his chair. Animated. His expression intense. She could hear the passion in his voice as he spoke about the subject he knew best.

"Most serials want a stimulus," he continued. "You have to be ready to test them. They're normally highly intelligent, attractive, charismatic, and smooth talkers. They are master manipulators, always on the hunt. I think this killer is a man, somewhere between late twenties to mid-thirties. And, more than likely, he experienced some form of abuse in his childhood."

"Really?" she replied. "But you just described a third of the population."

Terry saw the humor in her statement and chuckled. "Funny thing is, people aren't born to be serial killers. They become a product of their environment, which usually develops from an early childhood trauma."

"That's sad," she said.

"This killer's murders have proven geographic stability, which indicates he lives nearby," Terry said. "But because Washington has such a transient population and the killings, to our knowledge, started about a year ago, I would say he moved here from another part of the country."

"Which probably means, he's killed before in another area."

"Right," he said. "And we may never know how many more victims he has."

"You mean you know of other murders besides Monica and Sandra's?"

"I think so," he said. "I've been keeping a crime timeline."

"So have I," she said, surprised but also pleased that he was confirming what she already thought she knew. She was mesmerized by the way Terry's brain worked. He had certainly done his research and had been tracking the case just as carefully as she had. Maybe he was closer to the truth than she realized. She pushed away the fleeting thought that maybe he knew so much because he was involved somehow. Surely not.

"Another thing," he continued. "He's not a disorganized killer. He's methodical. His M.O. seems to be the suicide letters he leaves behind, but it has evolved, even though the emotional reasoning that triggers this type of signature stays the same."

"Why do you think that is?" she said.

"Because the letters he writes, or has his victims write, satisfy a need that sets him apart and is unique. Whereas the method he chooses to dispose of the bodies has no particular significance to him. In the past, he's made the deaths look like suicides, but he didn't take any credit."

"I'm not really sure I follow you." The last sip coffee lingered on her lips.

"He's playing out some sort of fantasy, but I haven't been able to figure it out yet," he said. "Most serials fantasize all the time."

"Do you think he knows his victims?" Olivia continued taking notes. "A lot of evidence certainly suggests this."

"It's important to determine why each individual was targeted." Terry picked up his tumbler and twisted the rim between his fingers. "They were all high profile, some political figures but all successful and wealthy. I don't think our killer seeks the random opportunity murder. I believe he has had a relationship with each of his victims, which implies pre-selection.

It also suggests that, perhaps, he is a high profile person as well or runs in their circle. And, there's no telling how long he's planned the murders."

"Or maybe he resents their wealth?" she suggested. He nodded. "Do you think you can find him?"

"We all have our habits, don't we?" he said. "Just as victims die because of theirs, killers' habits often give them away. Their routine activities dictate their behavior. Generally speaking, people are slaves to their psychology. The Punisher will leave behind clues because every human contact with each other leaves a trace."

"You mean DNA?"

"Yes, but the problem with DNA testing is that it usually takes weeks or months, sometimes even up to a year to get results sometimes." He rubbed his temples.

"Really? I didn't know that. I thought you could get results within a day or two."

He laughed. "That's because television shows only have an hour to solve a crime. In real life, detectives have to rely on other clues to guide them along. But DNA can be useful in aiding convictions once a case goes to trial."

"How does it work?" she asked.

Terry smiled. "Let's see...the easiest way I know to describe it is that every state is required to establish a DNA database for law enforcement. Then, when police recover DNA from a crime scene, the crime lab generates a DNA profile. They then try to match it up to determine if the DNA sample matches a convicted offender. If it does, it's a hit."

"What happens if police don't find a match?" Olivia leaned forward.

"At that point the DNA profile is compared against DNA from unsolved crimes," he said. "And this is important because it can link crime scenes that might have been considered unrelated."

"So, that means that a criminal could be linked to who knows how many crimes, before their identity is ever known?" Olivia asked. "And, if a person has never been convicted of a crime, their DNA wouldn't be in a DNA database. That's how people get away with murder."

"True," Terry said. "See why it's hard to rely on DNA?"

"I always assumed that as long as the police found DNA, they could find the killer. That's interesting." Olivia put her pen down. "So, what else can you tell me?"

Terry stared off into the distance and stroked his chin. He sat thoughtfully for a moment before answering. "You have very good instincts, Olivia."

"Thanks, but I didn't think instincts really mattered that much. I thought they weren't as reliable as experience."

"True, but they do come in handy." He sat back in his chair and folded his hands behind his head. "Plus, I think you have good experience. I could tell that right off the bat when you were investigating the Stacy Greenburg case."

"Really."

"You knew where to look and you asked the right questions," he said.

"You followed my career?" She raised her eyebrows.

"I followed the case," he said. "And I'll tell you something else. For the longest time I thought Stacy was still alive and had run off with Senator Price since they both disappeared at the same time."

"How did you link the two of them?" Olivia couldn't believe he knew something like that.

He frowned, as if maybe he'd said too much. "It doesn't matter. What I'm trying to tell you is that now I'm not so sure either one of them are dead."

His statement took her completely off guard. "How can you know that?"

She couldn't believe what she was hearing and fought back tears.

"There is another possibility you may not have considered," he said.

"What?" She felt her stomach turn.

"What if Stacy or Price, or both of them, disappeared with a purpose in mind."

"I don't understand," she whispered, barely able to speak over the lump in her throat.

"What if they're getting back at all the people who did them wrong, taking them out one by one? Do you think there's a possibility your friend is still alive, calling herself, The Punisher?"

No. No. Olivia refused to entertain the theory. It simply couldn't be possible. Or could it?

33

When Olivia returned home that evening, she was happy to see Cameron waiting for her. Despite what she assumed had been a long day at the hospital with psych patients, he'd still made time to come home and prepare a meal. He had a messy apron tied around his neck and waist but still gave her a big hug and kiss on the cheek.

She peeked over his shoulder at the lit candles scattered throughout the living room and kitchen. A beautiful arrangement of yellow roses sat on the dining table. The smell of garlic enticed her. He'd prepared spaghetti and had even decanted a bottle of red wine.

"What did I do to deserve this?" she asked and pulled out of his embrace.

"I know it's been a rough week for you, and I hate that I've had something to do with that?" He frowned. "I just wanted to do something nice for you."

"Thank you," she said, meaning it. She was deeply touched. "This is perfect. I'm famished, and I can't wait to tell you what I did today. She walked over to the roses and noticed the table had been set and a bowl of salad and steaming garlic bread were ready to eat. "These are beautiful. I love you."

He walked up and hugged her from behind. "I love you too."

"Let's eat while it's hot," she said.

"So what is it that you wanted to tell me about?" He grabbed a bowl of spaghetti and meat sauce from the kitchen counter and joined her at the table.

Olivia served herself and enjoyed the moment. "You're never going to believe who I finally spoke to."

"Who?" Cameron put his fork down. He grabbed the decanter of wine and poured them both a glass.

"Terry Carson," she said, eyebrows raised.

"Who?"

"The ex-FBI profiler who was famous for the Jackson Myers case about ten years ago." She twirled a mouthful of spaghetti into her spoon.

"I'm not sure why I would know him," he said, biting into a piece of bread.

Olivia chewed slowly and swallowed. "Anyway, I went to talk to him about this psychotic that's running loose here in D.C."

"You mean The Punisher?"

"Yes." She savored her wine and frowned, unsure how he was going to react.

"Sounds like he'd actually be classified as a psychopath to me," Cameron said. He grabbed the tongs, tossed the salad and filled up her empty bowl.

"Thanks, that's good. Everything is delicious." She forked a piece of lettuce. "What's the difference?"

"You mean the difference between a psychopath and a psychotic?" Cameron put his fork down and looked her in the eye. "Well, for starters, a psychotic is usually out of touch with reality, but a psychopath is obsessed with power. Plus, he's aware that what he does is criminal. And he's very smart."

"I still don't see much of a difference." She swirled the spaghetti around her fork.

"The difference is knowing right from wrong." Cameron closed his mouth and sucked in a loose strand of spaghetti.

"Hmm..."

"A psychopath will usually hold a job below his intellectual level, which fuels his anger," he continued. "He strongly believes that the world does not appreciate him or know what he's capable of."

"That's interesting." She reflected on a thought that she'd had earlier but had forgotten to ask Terry. Her husband caught her eye from across the table and smiled seductively. Sometimes she regretted having a one-track mind as she continued to probe.

"What are your thoughts on depression and mental illness?" She was curious what her husband's thoughts were on the subject since his expertise was psychology.

"You know, it's funny that we're talking about this because it's a subject that I've been wanting to write about. In fact, I was just reading an article yesterday about the 'deception of happiness.'"

"Really? What did it say?" She wiped her mouth with her napkin and focused all of her attention on Cameron as he explained.

"It suggested that mental health relied on self-deception, which implied that depression is based on not being able to deceive yourself."

"What?"

"Think about it. If this is true, then lying to ourselves is a good way to maintain mental health and remain engaged with life's pleasures."

"That would mean that people who suffer from depression actually deceive themselves less than the average normal person does." Her lips frowned, but her eyes smiled.

Cameron looked away, deep in thought.

"Is this what you're telling your patients, to deceive themselves as much as possible?" She asked, poking fun.

"I think it's a good theory that can actually be beneficial."

"Well, I think my brain is overloaded with theories today." She sighed and rubbed her stomach. "I'm not sure how much more I can take."

They finished their meal in silence. When she looked up from her empty plate, Cameron had an expression on his face she couldn't read. "I've got a surprise for you, and I hope you're going to like it."

"What is it?"

He reached across the table for her hand. "Follow me." He led her upstairs and stopped in front of Patrick's door. "Even though Patrick is gone, that doesn't mean we have to give up our dream of having a baby." He beamed.

Olivia backed away. What had he done now? She was afraid to go in the room. She remembered how empty it had felt the last time she was in there. What could he possibly do to make up for that?

"I bought a few new things…and I thought we could finish the room together. I left the walls green since it works for either sex."

When he opened the door to what was once a room filled with hope and love, she felt her knees go weak.

A brand new crib sat in a different corner of the room, along with a rocking chair, and a few stuffed animals. Other than that, the room was still bare.

"Let's try again," Cameron said. "When you're ready. But in the meantime, we can dream about it and believe it will happen again some day. We can make a new start."

Olivia walked over to the crib and looked down. Empty. Patrick was gone. He was never coming back. And she wasn't sure she believed another baby would either. She wasn't sure she wanted to take the risk of getting her heart broken again. It was too painful.

"Olivia…say something, please." Cameron's voice sounded shaky. "I thought you'd like it. You've shown me that this room doesn't have any other purpose but to be filled with our baby."

She walked over to the rocking chair and picked up a stuffed animal. Mickey Mouse? He had a ridiculous smile on his face. A price tag stuck out from one ear. She noticed all the new stuffed animals still had tags on them, and they were different from the ones they'd bought for Patrick.

"Did you buy him a blanket?" She asked. "I don't see one."

"What?"

"He'll need a blanket...to keep him warm." The last thing she remembered was feeling Cameron's arm under hers as she fainted and fell to the floor.

When she woke up, she was in bed and Cameron had his arm wrapped around her, holding her, protecting her.

She rolled over and looked into his eyes. "What happened?"

"You fainted. Oh, Liv – I'm so sorry. I meant for it to be a good surprise."

She'd fainted? Olivia frantically searched her memory for the last one. Terry. Spaghetti. Cameron's surprise. The new baby's room... "Stop. Please," she said. "It's just too much right now. What you did is very sweet, and I love you for it. I *do* want to make another baby together. There's a part of me that's really scared."

He smiled and stroked her hair. "Okay, I understand." He leaned forward and kissed her on the forehead. "Whenever you're ready. Get some rest." He rolled away. "I'm going to clean the kitchen."

Something in her awoke. "Don't go," she whispered. "Stay."

She reached out for him in the darkness and pulled him on top of her. Slipping her hands under his t-shirt, she felt the hardness of his flesh and the tenderness of his lips. She wanted him. "Make love to me," she said.

Cameron held her. He was slow and gentle, taking off her clothes, kissing her all over as they made love. She felt more connected to him than she had in a long time.

34

Thursday night at the Hawk 'n' Dove bar down in Capitol Hill always attracted a crowd. FBI Agents Spencer and Turner sat in the corner, next to a dark fireplace, and relaxed after a long day. For being the oldest Irish bar in D.C., it certainly set a different standard for a historical setting.

It wasn't a place where powerhouse people made important business deals, but it did serve as an outlet for the staffers on the Hill who came to gossip about Senators or other politicians. For other government employees, it proved a good place to blend into the background, like a groove in the dark wood that encompassed the place.

Nathan took a long swig of his fourth beer for the night and rubbed his eyes. His fingers smelled like the greasy cheeseburger he'd just devoured. "Ahh…it's been too long since we've been out."

"Yeah, too much work and no play." Steve grinned. "It's no wonder I don't have a life. Thirty-five and single because all I do is chase serial killers."

"Somebody's got to do it." Nathan downed the rest of his beer and turned his head to check the score of the Wizards game.

Steve motioned to the waiter for another round. "I wouldn't know – don't remember the last time I caught a game."

"That's what ESPN is for," Nathan said. "It's all I need." Nathan thought about what he'd just said for a moment. It had been seven years since he'd joined the FBI, and it had certainly taken a toll on his personal life. Recently divorced, he'd spent all his free time trying to solve cases. He was *always* on call. That had bothered his ex-wife. "I take that back. I also need sex, sleep and food."

"Those are the staples." Steve raised his glass and took a gulp.

"Yep." Nathan stared at the bubbles in the new beer the waiter set in front of him. His mind wandered back to the case. He'd read through Monica Habershamm's journal twice in the last few days but hadn't turned up anything that would help. Sandra Schelbert's name wasn't even mentioned.

"There's something that keeps bothering me about this case," he told Steve. "How did Monica know her killer? I just have a feeling that's the key."

"I don't know." Steve took a huge swig of his beer. "Maybe she was bi-sexual and he was screwing her and wanted in on more of the action."

Nathan coughed and felt beer tingle in his nose before he was able to swallow. Sometimes Steve surprised him by some of the things he said. "The killer entered without forcing his way in and, more than likely, he or she even had a key to Monica's condo."

He went back over the crime scene in his head again. The blood. The way the bodies were staged. What was he missing? Then, he remembered the locket he'd found hanging around Monica's naked neck. It was the only piece of jewelry she'd been wearing. Why? What was its significance? What was the connection?

Inside, he'd found two photos. One was of Monica at a much earlier age. The other one was of a woman who also looked familiar but he couldn't place her. The only thing he was certain of was that it wasn't Monica's lover, Sandra. Who was this other woman? He knew her face. She was white, had dirty blond hair, and her cheekbones indicated she was in her early teens.

The pictures had not been generous in detail, but the images of the two young girls were still engrained in his memory. He would figure out who the other one was and what role she had played in Monica's life. Clearly, a significant one for Monica to still be wearing a locket with her picture in it.

Steve sighed. "Can we please take a break from the case tonight?"

Nathan shrugged his shoulders. "I wish it didn't consume me."

"Yeah, I know." Steve's attention shifted to the two women who sat down at a table in front of them.

This case was really wearing on Nathan. Especially with no new leads on The Punisher. Two reluctant, but Steve-insistent-shots-of-Tequila later, Nathan decided to take a long walk home to clear his head.

His thoughts returned to Olivia Penn and their meeting the day before. Instinct told him to protect her, although he wasn't sure why. She seemed to know a great deal about The Punisher investigation. The one thing she didn't know was that the bureau suspected a female serial killer.

35

The next morning there was no place Olivia would rather be than Mimi Stone's office. The familiar smell of incense and her signature blueberry-scented candle comforted her. Olivia had shown up unannounced at Mimi's office that morning. She hadn't really thought it through. She'd just arrived and walked through the door.

"Olivia, I have an appointment scheduled in twenty minutes," Mimi said. "Do you want to tell me why you're here?"

Olivia didn't remember how she'd gotten to Mimi's office. She'd just woken up from a nightmare or so she thought. The night before had been a blur. The last thing she recalled was being in Patrick's room, but it was no longer his room. It looked different and felt different. Then, had she dreamed it, or had she made love Cameron?

"At first, I thought it had been a dream," Olivia said.

"You thought what was a dream?" Mimi looked at her watch.

"Being in my baby's room, a space that was so familiar at one time. Now it just seems like a foreign place. The furniture and things were all new. All traces of Patrick were gone."

"So you weren't dreaming? I'm trying to follow."

"No, Cameron bought some new things and said he wanted to create a new life." Olivia looked up from her daze. "He wants to have another baby. How could he expect me to be ready for that right now?"

Olivia noticed something had changed in Mimi's eyes. "I understand...I mean, that's understandable that you feel this way."

"Do *you* understand?" It was the first time in a long time Olivia felt a glimmer of hope.

"I don't usually tell my patients this," Mimi began, "but I think it might be helpful for you to hear. I lost a baby too once. In fact, it's probably the reason I never married."

"I'm so sorry." Tears welled up in Olivia's eyes, and she felt instantly connected to Mimi. "Then you must know what I've been going through."

"To some extent." Mimi looked away as if to gather her thoughts. "I tripped and fell down a flight of stairs and miscarried about a month before my due date."

"That's terrible." Olivia forgot about her own problems for an instant.

"I was supposed to have a little girl, but it wasn't meant to be," Mimi said. "One minute life was good, and the next, it had changed forever. Losing her was like watching a passing train. At first glance it was a passenger train headed for an exciting destination. I watched as it flew by... until I spotted a face in the window, staring back at me, and that moment seemed frozen in time as our eyes met. I couldn't help but wonder who that person was, where she was going...and I remember thinking to myself that maybe I'd like to go with her. But then it was too late. And the train was gone. And, even though the moment was gone, I kept living in it, yearning to return to it time and time again, and wondering what might have been if I'd been on that train too."

"Wow," Olivia said. "That's it exactly. How have you gotten through it?"

"Just like you will," Mimi said. "By living in the present. Without Patrick. And when you're ready, you'll have another child. You don't have to rush into things. It sounds like your husband is only trying to help and that he loves you very much. You have to remember that he's hurting too, and his method of dealing with things may be different than yours, and that's okay."

"I'm so confused," Olivia said.

"That's normal. You're grieving, and you've got a lot going on right now in your life. Have you been journaling like I suggested last time?"

Olivia shook her head. "No."

"Try to write it out if you can."

"Okay." She grimaced and rubbed her chest.

"You're going to get through this," Mimi said. "Trust me."

Olivia didn't know what to think. All she knew was that there was a piece of her life that was missing. From the time she was in Patrick's room the night before to the moment she realized she was in Mimi's office that morning. And, it wasn't the first time she'd experienced black outs, if that's what they were. It had happened the week before on her walk through the city. The only other time she recalled it happening was the night Stacy had disappeared.

36

Olivia went home and put on a pot of strong coffee. On her drive back from Mimi's she'd called Duncan to let him know she'd be at the Post a little later. There was something she had to do first while Cameron was at work.

She walked up to Patrick's old room and sat down in the beautiful, new, wooden rocking chair her husband had bought for her. She held Mickey Mouse and the other stuffed animals in her lap and rocked, trying to get used to the possibility of having another baby.

Closing her eyes, she visualized the room filled with life, and love. It made her smile. Someday, she'd find joy again. For now, she just wanted to find peace after Patrick's death and make a new start. Maybe part of the reason she'd had trouble letting go was because she'd felt guilty for moving on without him.

Mimi was right. Olivia had to live in the present. Without Patrick. She wrapped her arms around herself and took a deep breath. When she opened her eyes, she didn't feel as afraid. One day, she would help Cameron finish decorating the new baby room. When the time was right.

Her thoughts shifted to Stacy. It was almost impossible to get her out of her mind lately. She kept flashing back to the night she disappeared. Olivia had been there, right before it had happened. Why hadn't she made sure Stacy made it home safely? She couldn't erase the image of

Stacy stumbling out of the cab that night. Why hadn't she followed her instincts?

She kept hearing Stacy's voice in her head. "You know what I like about you, Olivia? I like that I can be myself around you." But Stacy hadn't been herself, or had she? She'd been distraught that Price had stood her up...and about the note she'd received.

Olivia had turned the note over to the police, but she could still remember the handwriting and what it had said. "Stacy, it's over. Are you ready for what's next?"

The question that burned in Olivia's head remained, what had been next for Stacy? What had really happened that night? And who had written the note?

"We're in love," she had told Olivia. *No, you're in love...he's in lust,* is what Olivia had wanted to tell her friend.

Olivia still had a box of Stacy's personal things that she'd packed up from Stacy's apartment and had never gotten around to sending to Stacy's parents. It was in her basement. She suddenly felt compelled to go through that box again. Maybe there was a clue there she'd missed before.

Olivia got up, walked across the bare nursery and closed the door behind her. She told herself she wasn't closing the door on a dream, just saving it for another day. If she was going to live in the present, that required that she delve into the past first. Just to make sure the present was all it presented itself to be.

Olivia walked back downstairs and poured a fresh cup of coffee before heading down to the basement. The doorknob felt cold and sent chills racing down her body, but the hot coffee helped to warm her. She hadn't been down in the basement in months. It was more of Cameron's thing. She wasn't even sure what she had stored there any more.

The rest of the area had been turned into a wine cellar. Cameron's pride and joy. He'd gotten into wine right after they'd married and had started collecting from different wineries when he traveled. He'd gotten a wild hair to turn the space into a wine cellar around the time Stacy went missing.

Olivia hadn't been involved or appreciated the project since she'd been so preoccupied with her friend's disappearance. In fact, the majority of the time she forgot it was even down there until he brought out a delicious bottle to share.

The wooden stairs creaked beneath her as she searched for a light and flipped the switch. The temperature had dropped significantly. She spotted Cameron's inventory log perched on the end of a big wooden table in the middle of the room. On three walls, wooden beams criss-crossed half way up the wall to provide a resting place for aging wines.

She ran her fingers over a few bottles and wiped off the dust. It was a rustic and charming room but very underutilized. It was set up to entertain, but to her knowledge, the space had never served its original purpose. She shivered and took a sip of her coffee. Strange, it had already turned cold.

She shrugged and moved to the back part of the basement where it didn't take long to find the small, cardboard box she was looking for. Seeing Stacy's name scribbled on the outside of it brought back a wave of painful memories of helping Stacy's parents clean out her apartment. Olivia pushed the thoughts away, picked up the box and took it upstairs to her office.

She plopped the box down on her desk, and the cardboard lid popped open. Olivia didn't even remember what she'd put in it, if any of it were significant or why she still had it. She spied her Miles Davis collection out of the corner of her eye and put in the first CD she grabbed. Miles was a good distraction for what she had to do. Travel back in time.

37

Stacy had always worn Coco Mademoiselle perfume by Channel. It was the one thing she'd been willing to spend a little extra money on. "Price likes it. He says it reminds him of me," Stacy had told her once. "I like it too. Makes me feel sexy."

The familiar scent still clung to Stacy's fake Gucci bag she'd carried that last night. Seeing her purse on her kitchen counter the morning after she'd disappeared was Olivia's first indication that something was terribly wrong. It was the first item Olivia pulled from the box. She'd been with her when Stacy had bargained with the street vendor and gotten him down to twenty dollars from thirty.

"Do you think Price will be able to tell the difference between a real or a fake?" she recalled Stacy asking at the time.

"Depends on if his wife likes Gucci," Olivia had responded. "If so, then I guarantee he's a savvy consumer because it affects his pocket book."

Stacy had handed the vendor a twenty-dollar bill before grabbing her new purchase. "I guess I'll take my chances." That had only been a month before she'd disappeared, and Olivia had never seen her friend without her pet "Gucci."

The next item in the box was a photo album. Olivia closed her eyes and swayed to "Embraceable You." There was something about Miles and his trumpet that put her in a safe place. She sat down in her recliner and opened the album in the middle, flipping through photos quickly. Olivia recognized images of Stacy's family and some of her friends.

Her stomach wrenched when she came across one of the two of them not long after they'd first met. They were young, naïve and full of life. It had been taken on New Year's Eve, right after Stacy started her affair with Senator Price.

They were dressed to kill, and Olivia remembered asking a stranger to take their picture at the event they were attending at the French Embassy. They'd had some wine at Stacy's apartment before they'd arrived. "How'd we get into this event again?" Olivia asked. Not that she cared at the time. She was having a great time.

"Don't worry about it," Stacy had laughed. "I've got connections."

Little had Olivia known at the time, her friend's connections were of a political persuasion. The night had been a blur of mingling with snooty drunk people and lots of cocktails. When midnight rolled around, Stacy was nowhere to be found.

Olivia had waited until the place cleared and shut down before she finally took a taxi home, alone. Stacy had apologized the next day but hadn't offered a logical reason for where she'd disappeared to that night. Olivia realized later on that she'd ended up with Price somehow, despite his wife having been at the event.

There was nothing Olivia hadn't already seen in the photo album. Until she got to the end, and found a large photo turned upside down and stuck to the back page. When she pulled it free, Olivia saw that it was Stacy's sixth-grade class photo. The first thing she noticed was a boy's face that had been rubbed out with what looked like a pencil eraser. He could no longer be identified. Why had Stacy done that? Who was he?

She searched for her friend in the group and recognized an adolescent version of the Stacy she knew. She'd grown up in a small town in Texas. So Olivia didn't find it odd that there had only been one African American student in the class.

She skimmed the photos of the rest of the students before she noticed the names printed at the bottom. She ran her pointer finger along the line until she found the name of the boy whose face she couldn't see. His name was Sam Camp. She didn't know anyone by that name, and she'd never heard Stacy mention him. But then again, sixth grade had been ions ago. Maybe she'd just had a crush, and he'd rejected her.

Olivia got out of the recliner, put the photo down, and walked back over to the box. She found a book Stacy had been reading called, "Blink," by Malcolm Gladwell. She noticed Stacy's bookmark was on chapter three. Ironically, the chapter was called, "The Warren Harding Error: Why We Fall For Tall, Dark, and Handsome Men." Oh, Stacy...

The only other item in the box was a Miles Davis CD that Olivia had loaned Stacy. She'd totally forgotten about it.

Olivia opened the CD case, but Miles wasn't there. Instead, a generic looking CD marked "Holiday" in black permanent marker and a small post-it attached to it said, "Don't Blame Me," in Stacy's handwriting. Had Stacy left it for her? What was on the disk?

She popped the CD into her laptop and waited for the files to open. Opening the files was like opening Pandora's box. She double-checked to make sure she had paper in her printer and got chills when the document opened and Stacy's words appeared on the screen.

The first sentences read, "I fell in love with a U.S. Senator, and he promised to love me forever and run off with me if I promised to kill his wife." Shocking. This was a Stacy that Olivia had never known. Had Stacy written a memoir? Had she been planning to blackmail Price or had she actually considered killing his wife? Olivia's mind was spinning with questions. Perhaps she'd finally found the reason Stacy disappeared.

38

Olivia walked over to pick up the pages of Stacy's memoir as they rolled off the printer. She paced back and forth in her office while she read. She skimmed through as fast as she could, desperately searching for answers to who her best friend really was. Stacy talked about how she'd met Senator Sterling Price and worked for him before she became a reporter at the Post. One excerpt Stacy wrote, read:

I'd worked for Price for almost two years before he talked to me about killing his wife. At first I thought he was joking, until he brought it up again and had all the details worked out. He wanted me to take a vacation – with the two of them, only he and I would be the only two coming home. He'd even been so confident as to buy me a ticket on their Alaskan cruise.

"Do you know how easy it will be?" He told me. "I'll take her out for a romantic dinner, slip some of her own Valium in her wine…take her out for a late night walk…and the rest is up to you."

"What do you mean the rest is up to me? What do you want me to do?" I honestly couldn't believe he was serious.

"You're a smart woman." He'd smiled and kissed me on the cheek. "Just push her overboard, and I'll look the other way. People get drunk, and sometimes they fall overboard and drown. Accidents happen. When this one does, then we can finally be together."

That's when I'd known he was truly insane. Although there was a small part of me that actually considered what he'd proposed…so I agreed to go on the cruise. It was a free vacation if nothing else. I never intended to kill Mrs. Price. I just wanted to be with Price, and if that's where he was going to be for a week, then that's where I wanted to be."

Olivia could hear Stacy's voice, as if she were speaking directly to her through her writing. Stacy had always been a good writer, especially when she was honest. Something made Olivia pick up the CD case again that the memoir had been in. She scrolled down the back cover until she saw the title of number nine. Her heart stopped when she realized the clue that Stacy had left: "Don't Blame Me" was the name of the Miles Davis song she'd referenced on the post-it. But why?

What was Stacy trying to tell her? Or was Olivia reading too much into it? She picked up Stacy's purse again and stuck her hand inside one more time to make sure it was empty. The cool satin interior felt soft on her fingertips. Then she touched something. It felt like a book of matches. She pulled the object free and read the cover. Sonoma Wine Bar. An urge made her flip the cover open, and when she did, Olivia discovered a name and phone number. Sam. Should she call him? Who knew how old the number was, but she decided she didn't have anything to lose.

She raced downstairs and got her cell phone out of her purse and then headed back up to her office. The number was a local one. She dialed, not even sure what she was going to say if Sam picked up. Was it the same Sam as in the sixth-grade photo who Stacy had rubbed out of her life? Or was this just a coincidence? Seconds later she received a message saying that the phone line had been disconnected.

She put the book of matches aside. The only thing she wanted now was to put the box away. Stacy's memoir had finished printing, and Olivia grabbed and straightened the pages. She got distracted by the photo album, and decided to take one last look at the class picture.

Who was Sam? She desperately wanted to know what he looked like and why Stacy had never mentioned him if he had been a part of her adult life. She couldn't help but notice the black girl again too. She was a tall, skinny girl with a confident smile. The longer Olivia looked at her, the more she became real.

She quickly scanned the students' names one more time. Nothing could have prepared her for the connection she made when she saw the name, Monica Habershamm. She felt her eyes almost pop out of her head and fear race up her spine. This couldn't *all* be a coincidence.

39

Olivia shifted gears when she got a phone call from Duncan.
"It's after one, and I was just wondering when you were planning to show your ugly mug around here?"

She appreciated his poor attempt at humor and grabbed her purse, her keys and rushed out the door. "I'm on my way," she said, pushing all thoughts of Stacy far from her brain.

On the metro ride, Olivia began to reflect. She hadn't heard back from Nathan regarding the stalker emails, and she wasn't sure how long she was supposed to wait. It surprised her that this didn't appear to be more of a priority to the FBI at this point, especially since the writer had mentioned the high profile murders and knowing the murderer's next move. What was really going on?

She understood that the Bureau's main focus right now was solving the Schelbert and Habershamm murders, but she also felt that the emails might provide a compelling connection. Perhaps so could her findings in Stacy's belongings. She wondered if Nathan had ever gotten in touch with Jordan Schelbert before he left town. Had he played a part in the murders? There were lots of possibilities at this point.

She stopped off at Starbucks for a treat before she faced her boss. It didn't matter that it was a Friday, Starbucks was packed any time, any day of the week. She needed another cup of coffee and something special for Duncan, along with a good cover. The last thing she wanted was him to worry about her. She was fine.

She stopped by Duncan's office on her way to her cubicle. "Got you a cup of coffee." She sat down in the chair across from him and placed the steaming cup of Starbucks coffee within his reach. "Even bought you a muffin - one of those black bottom ones you like so much."

"Wow, what's the occasion?" He went for the coffee, and they both laughed when he accidentally spilled it down the front of his tie and shirt.

"You're so predictable," she said. "But you may be onto something here."

"What's that?" He picked up the tail of his tie, assessed the damage, and grabbed at the closet napkin he could find.

Olivia couldn't stop laughing. "You should really just start your day off by pouring a whole cup of coffee down the front of your shirt. Then you won't have to worry about whether you spill again the rest of the day."

"Sounds like a great idea." He suddenly looked a little frustrated with his own clumsiness. He kept dabbing at his tie, desperately trying to wipe it clean. "I should just give up coffee altogether."

She remembered he had an important meeting later that afternoon with the publisher. "Right side, top drawer of the cabinet at my cubicle, there's an extra one of Cameron's you're welcome to borrow for your meeting later. Go out for a late lunch and buy a new shirt. Maybe the dry cleaners can salvage that one."

Duncan didn't have to say anything. The relief on his face said it all.

"Speaking of great ideas," she said, as she pulled out copies of all the emails and set them in front of Duncan. "I've got a big one. Get ready to request a big budget line. I think I'm going to need at least thirty inches for this next story."

"Oh? Tell me more."

"What if we publish all the emails my stalker has sent me?" She held her breath.

Duncan looked at her in disbelief. "What?"

"I know what you're thinking, but I've weighed the idea pretty carefully, and I think it's the smartest thing I can do at this point."

"It's crazy." He shook his head, which usually meant he'd consider it.

"Just hear me out." She put her hands up in protest. "Look them over and tell me what you really think then."

"I don't understand," he said. "Why would you want to exploit yourself?"

"First of all, it bleeds. Secondly, I think it'll draw this person out, appeal to his ego and when he contacts me again, he may be less careful." She couldn't believe what she was hearing herself suggest.

"Olivia..."

"I think I should be the one to pitch the North Wall. Don't you agree?"

"I'm not sure about this." Duncan sighed and closed his eyes. "Let me take a look and think about it. If it's worth pitching, I'll talk to them. That's protocol."

"Every other story has been about me and my fame. This time the story will be about The Punisher or someone who may be connected to him."

"What do you mean? I still don't follow."

"I'm going to write what I think he wants me to say." Olivia looked Duncan square in the eye and raised her eyebrow. "I'm going to use his words to communicate directly to him – to draw him out."

"You mean you're going to dance?" Duncan asked.

"That's right. If this stalker or The Punisher...or whoever he is, wants a media puppet, then that's what I'll be. This is our one chance to bait him."

"What exactly has gotten into you?" He leaned forward in his chair and frowned.

"Stacy Greenburg," she said. "I need to find out if the two are connected, and this is the only way I know how."

"Ahhh!" Duncan slammed his fists down on his desk. "I know the North Wall will approve of your idea because it'll definitely sells papers. I just can't believe that I'm actually willing to back you on this wild idea of yours. I know you well enough to know that you won't back down until you get to the bottom of this. Just promise me, you'll be careful. And, be honest with me. No more games."

"Deal. No more games. Thanks, Dunk. I don't know what I'd do without you in my corner." She winked and left his office.

40

Sunday morning, Nathan reluctantly made his way to the Hoover building, better known as The Bureau. The government-owned building maintained a massive presence. It encompassed an entire block. Inside, the long, dismal, hospital-white hallways always reminded him of the movie, *The Shining*.

Steve was waiting for Nathan when he got to his cubicle. The first question out of his mouth was, "Did you see this morning's Post?"

"No, haven't had a chance to look at it yet," Nathan said.

"Well, I was going to ask you if you'd turned up anything new on the emails Olivia Penn handed over to us, but it seems she's taken matters into her own hands."

"What do you mean?"

Steve pulled the folded newspaper from behind his back and slapped it down on the desk. "See for yourself."

Nathan glanced down at the front page. The headline read: POST REPORTER'S STALKER LINKED TO PUNISHER MURDERS. His eyes grew big. He kept reading. "She published the emails?"

"Every word," Steve said. "Good stuff."

"What was she thinking?" Nathan skimmed the article.

"Not convinced she was…"

Nathan thought about it for a moment and suddenly understood. "Oh yes she was." He looked up at his partner and smiled. "She's trying to communicate with him by empowering him. Here, she writes…'the emails have gotten the FBI's attention and its full resources. The author of these emails is powerful and a force to be reckoned with. Although the FBI is unable to comment at this time, it is possible the emails were written by the same individual who is responsible for the murders of the Secretary of State and Monica Habershamm.'"

Steve furrowed his eyebrows. "I don't get it."

"She's trying to draw him out, see if he'll contact her again in response to this article," Nathan said.

"Oh, it'll either make him angry that she put two and two together or it'll make him swell with pride. But either way she figures he'll contact her again to set the record straight, at the same time revealing more clues as to who he is."

"Nice work," Nathan mumbled.

"Not to mention gutsy." Steve gave his partner the evil eye and laughed. "Are you sure this woman doesn't have a penis?"

"Easy." Nathan shook his head. "And you wonder why you're single."

Steve ignored the jab. "Seriously, anything new on these emails?"

"We subpoenaed the Internet provider for the identity and address of the subject. The emails were set up under alias names and addresses. Each email had a new account with completely random information."

"Have you been working with the Cyber Division on this?" Steve leaned on Nathan's desk.

"Yes, and they discovered that the emails were sent from various computers within the library at American University."

"Great, there must be hundreds of computers in use there, right?"

"Not sure of the exact number," Nathan said. "Could be anyone who has access to the library. Anyone from an employee, to a student, professor, a volunteer or even a homeless person off the street."

"So where do we go from here?" Steve asked.

Nathan stroked his smooth chin and thought for a moment. "Here's what I know so far. The library policy requires students to scan their library card before entering. Pretty standard…and photo ID's are asked for but not enforced, which could make it fairly easy for anyone to gain access to the computers."

"Like finding a needle in a haystack." Steve sat down on the corner of the desk. "Here we go again."

"The good news is that I do have the times the emails were sent, as well as a list of students who are entered into the library's system as being present that day. The bad news is that the system only reflects when the person entered, not when they left or how long they stayed."

"I'll start cross checking the list to see who was logged in during the times the emails were sent," Steve volunteered.

"Good idea...course there's always the possibility that the person could have used or stolen someone else's identification." Nathan shook his head. "This person may not even be in the system if they worked there or don't have to check in. We'll need to check the employee's schedules as well."

"Guess we need to go down there and interview some of the staff and watch the flux and flow," Steve said.

"I plan to have surveillance there by the end of the day, just in case this Benjamin Funkhouser, or whoever he is, decides to send another email. I just don't want to cause any hysteria. We need to keep this discreet."

"Got it," Steve said. "Listen, do you really think the writer of these emails is a threat?"

"You mean because of the reference to the other murders?" Nathan said. "Yes, I do. In fact, I think it's possible that this person could even be The Punisher."

"Really?" Steve sat up straight and seemed to come alive.

"I've requested surveillance on Olivia's home and activities. She's not aware we're watching her. I don't want her spooked and changing her usual routine. We have two agents on her now."

41

After Steve left to go to American University, Nathan began reviewing the Funkhouser emails again. He had his own theory about the writer's identity but was curious what Daniel Pratt, the FBI Linguistics Specialist in Stylistics, would say about possible characteristics of style in the email language. Nathan was right on time for their appointment. So was all of six foot and well-over-five-inches-of-human-muscle of Dan.

"Hey Dan, how's it going?" Nathan asked.

"Fine, Nate. Not much time to spare though today." Daniel showed Nathan into his office and they took seats across from each other. "I'll get right to it. I don't know what case you're working on, but I can tell you from reading these emails that the author means business. In my opinion, he sounds ready to snap. The language I've identified doesn't lead me to believe he's from another part of the country. There's no distinct dialect in his tone or geographic idiosyncrasies."

"How do you know?" Nathan asked.

"I look for clues pertaining to spelling, capitalization, abbreviations, punctuation, word choice, content and grammar – all of which appeared to be perfectly manicured. This guy seems fairly well educated."

"I'd have to agree," Nathan added. "So have you put a profile together yet?"

"Yes, I have." Daniel scratched his head. "Let's start with the first email he writes to Olivia. It says...*allow me to introduce myself, without technically introducing myself. I am your number one fan. Sometimes I feel so connected with what you write and how you say it, that I feel I may know you better than you know yourself. I've been following your career for a long time. You are the best writer I've ever read, which says a lot because I read everything. I look forward to the day that we meet in person. Until then."*

"What do you deduce from this?" Nathan said.

"Well, he says he reads everything, which could indicate that this is an older person or someone seasoned beyond his years."

"Okay…go on," Nathan said. "The first one seems harmless enough, but the trail started six months ago and has continued on average about once a month…all anonymous until now. Anything from the second email?"

"He says, *I continue to study your talent. You always amaze me with your gift. I wonder how you learned such a skill – but then I realized that it comes naturally for you. Your endowment is not something that can be taught. Someday I hope to be as good as you.*" Daniel paused. "My guess is that this person is an aspiring writer. Maybe a professor or student."

"That makes sense since the emails came from American University," Nathan deducted.

"I wasn't aware of that," Daniel said. "Interesting. The third email makes me wonder how he views his connection between their writing. It reads: *you bring such joy to my life. Your article today stirred something inside me. You are my muse. You inspire me to greatness. I look forward to reading your articles. Each and every one of them is special to me. I still remain your number one fan.*"

Nathan scratched his forehead. "I think this is at least confirmation that it's still the same writer, despite the different email addresses he uses. It contained the same style and tone as the other two. I found out the three email addresses have already been terminated. It looks like the writer opened a new account, under a false name and personal information, used it once and then discontinued it."

"Let's keep going," Daniel stated. "The fourth email was soulmates@ hotmail.com which reads, *I feel a strong bond between us. I think we have a lot in common. Did we know each other in a former life? I sense that we did. We are made of the same material, I'm sure of it. My words have become your words. Your words have become my words. How can you be so close yet so far away?"*

Nathan sighed and shook his head.

"The fifth email from iamasgoodasyou@hotmail.com reads: *do you ever catch yourself thinking of me…your biggest fan? Do you fantasize about me? I am special, just like you. I am great, just like you. I am talented in many ways, just like you. I know you must sense my presence at times…you know – that feeling you have when you feel a pair of eyes watching you from somewhere. That's me, your biggest fan."*

"This gives me the creeps." Nathan raised his shoulders and rubbed his upper arms. "It's almost as if somewhere along the way, the writer gained some confidence. He alludes to being a writer himself. Did he win an award? He all of a sudden begins to feel equal to his mentor, as opposed to just a student. So I wonder what happened. He now feels like he is in a position to criticize."

"Well, the emails progressively get more threatening and aggressive. The sixth email from listentome@hotmail.com reads: *I think it's time to meet properly. You still have a lot to learn. Give me the attention I deserve."*

"The writer was asserting himself and beginning to become impatient and restless with no response from Olivia," Daniel said.

Nathan wasn't sure he understood why Olivia had ignored these emails for so long. He figured maybe she was just too preoccupied to realize the potential danger. "Dan, who do you think this person is, based on the language in these emails?"

"Well, in my opinion he's an older student or a professor with an ego, someone who would never normally stoop so low as to write such pathetic emails. But he's infatuated. I think you're looking at a middle-aged loner who decided to go back to school, someone with a lot of time on his hands and a job that's beneath his intelligence, or at least he thinks it is. Maybe this guy had a child but was never able to father it and that's where he feels this entitlement to scold Olivia."

Nathan sat back in his chair in silence. "You got all *that* from those emails? How do you do that?"

"It's just an opinion, but I have been doing this a long time."

"So it's not just a hunch." Nathan gave him a sly look.

"No, I learned a long time ago to ignore my hunches," Daniel said. "They're usually wrong."

"In the seventh email the writer identified himself as Benjamin Funkhouser," Nathan said. "So why now? This email interested me the most. It's the longest and most aggressive, stating he knows the killer's next move." *Think, Nathan, think.* "Would this be possible if he weren't the killer? Maybe the writer was just bluffing to get attention."

"Either way," Daniel stated, "the message is clear, and this lunatic shouldn't be ignored any longer."

42

After returning from a nice dinner at Bobby Van's steakhouse, where they'd shared a prime rib and a bottle of wine, The Punisher sat in his private quarters with Sam, sipping cocktails—Lithium and Valium washed down with a Maker's Mark whiskey. For some reason, he still couldn't relax. His mind raced with ideas, plans, rage. And the past.

"You okay?" Sam put his feet up on the couch and rubbed his belly. "You look sad."

"I'm not sure. I have a lot on my mind."

"What are you thinking about?" Sam asked. "Wanna talk about it?"

"It's all Annie's fault," he said. "I don't know how she still has a hold over me after all these years. It's still so painful."

Sam half smiled. "You have to let your wife go. She took off, and you're never going to see her again."

He knew it was true, but he couldn't help dwelling on the rejection that had become the catalyst for his killing spree. He closed his eyes, leaned back in his recliner and reflected.

The day his wife had left him had actually started off as a very nice one. They'd woken up and made love. He'd almost forgotten that he'd caught her in bed with his best friend. But she still loved him, and that's what had mattered.

He was certain he could forgive her, now that she'd come back to him. But the image of walking in on her with his best friend continued to haunt him. He'd come home early that day from work, with flowers. He'd wanted to surprise her. He'd even made reservations at their favorite place in Newport Beach, and had taken a bottle of 1985 Mouton Rothschild by the restaurant five hours earlier to have decanted. It was the wine they'd been fortunate enough to indulge in the night they'd married.

He wasn't the only one who was surprised when he'd walked into his home to find the two of them in bed. It had sounded like someone had broken in and was watching porn, until he realized that the primal noises coming from the bedroom were from his wife. Then he'd seen Clint. Positioned comfortably on top of his wife.

Moaning in ecstasy she'd turned with a look of horror after seeing him standing in the doorway. He could still see Clint's face, frozen as he rolled off of her. Neither of them had known what to say or do, it seemed. He'd run out of the house.

Of course, Annie had wanted to talk. But she hadn't come home for three days after that, and he'd known deep down that it was over. He'd still wanted her back. How could she have done this to him? With his best friend? How had this happened? He recalled thinking that it had probably just been a one-time thing and meant nothing. He'd beat himself up for everything he could have possibly done to drive her into the arms of another man.

Had it been his possessiveness? Had he not given her enough space to follow her dreams? Was she just not attracted to him any more? What was so wrong with him that she'd want to hurt him like this?

And then she'd called. Sounding all sweet and innocent. And sorry. He had agreed to meet her. They hadn't really talked about the affair when they saw each other. Instead, they'd enjoyed a wonderful day together.

Looking back he still wasn't sure if he'd just chosen to forget or block out the past because he had been so afraid of losing her. What he remembered most about that day was waking up and feeling that she was back. He hadn't wanted to think about her with anyone else, much less his best friend.

"Will you make me one of your special omelets?" He remembered her asking in a pouty way that he couldn't resist. He had gladly obliged. He'd even give her a back rub.

"I think we should buy some new furniture," she's said. "Make a new start. What do you think?"

He'd smiled. "I think that's a nice idea. What did you have in mind?"

"I'm not sure."

They hadn't had much luck at the three furniture stores they'd visited. It had gotten late, and he could tell her patience was wearing. She was hungry.

"Why don't we stop off for dinner somewhere?" he suggested.

"Sure." She shrugged.

"I know just the place." He'd driven to their favorite restaurant, Spazio, valet parked and opened the car door for her.

Spazio had never failed his expectations. The tables had always been candle-lit, the room dark with deep green curtains pulled away from the windows – just enough to give a glimpse of the outside world, but allowing the diner to forget it too, if one wished.

He was in the moment that had changed his path in life. A Frank Sinatra classic had been playing when they'd arrived. Just The Way You Look Tonight. He couldn't remember ever having felt so happy. Annie was back, and she loved him. He savored the smell of lamb with a wine reduction sauce and conflicting aromas of pasta with clams and mussels as they'd passed by each table. His senses enticed and delighted him.

But Annie had gotten quiet throughout dinner and didn't say much, until their main course was served. That's when a new reality set in. And he knew he'd never be the same.

"I can't do this any more," she'd stated, matter-of-factly. No tears. "I'm in love with Clint, and I'm pregnant with his child."

He dropped his fork.

"I did the best I could, but it's just not working," she'd said, very matter-of-factly, as if unscathed by how heartless she was.

He wanted to jump across the table and strangle her.

"I'm leaving you," she'd said. Just like that.

He pictured her with Clint again. And now she was pregnant? How could he have been so blind? But why had she said she wanted to buy new furniture and make a new start? And she'd even made love to him? She'd lied to him.

"I know what you're thinking...about this morning. I just wanted to make sure I wasn't making a mistake. You have to understand. I tried. I really did."

The waiter who approached their table had no idea what he'd interrupted. "Would you care for dessert?"

After he'd gotten past the knot in his throat he managed to say, "No thank you, just the check." Then he'd looked around the room for a sharper knife than the one in front of him to put through Annie's heart.

Thinking back now, he wished he'd acted on his impulse. But that had been the beginning of his desire, when he'd been able to question it enough to control the compulsion.

"I think this would be easier if I just left," she said. "Let's just leave things like they are."

He'd paid the bill and remembered thinking that he'd have a chance to kill her later. That's why he'd let her walk out. She'd be at home when he returned. But she hadn't been. In fact, all of her things were gone, and he was left to wonder if she'd planned it from the beginning. He never saw her again after that night. She had simply vanished.

43

Sam was staring at him when he finally opened his eyes and returned to the present.

"If you want my opinion, you have to let go of Annie's mistakes," Sam said. "They were her mistakes, not yours."

"That's mighty mature of you, Sam. But, you're right."

"You can't control the past, but you do have control over the future. You're The Punisher."

He sometimes couldn't help living in the past. He looked at Sam and raised his eyebrows. "You understand why I do what I have to do. Don't you?"

"Of course." Sam sat up and nodded. "Better than anyone."

"So you don't think I'm crazy?"

Sam laughed. "Of course I do. But so am I. Ain't it great?"

The Punisher laughed, and his mood lifted immediately.

Sam sipped his drink. "I also think you're bored. You've grown restless with the thrill of this game because you aren't fully being appreciated for what you've achieved. You are The Punisher, a god!"

The killer sat upright in his chair with a new burst of energy, despite the influence of the drugs. Sam was right. He *was* doing a noble and honorable thing. And, he had the power to punish those who deserved it.

"Let's have a little fun," Sam said. "I think it's time to make another move, shake things up a bit and throw the FBI off track. And Olivia Penn."

"I know what to do." The Punisher smiled, his instincts coming alive again. "I have the perfect target. We *will* make history once again."

"How's that?" Sam asked.

"The next murder I have in mind is one I've been contemplating for a long time. It's never been done before."

44

Brendan Campbell took an extra fifteen minutes getting ready in the bathroom that morning. He stood sideways and sucked in the slight remnant of his belly and thought, *not too bad*. He had a lunch date with a co-worker later, but not just any co-worker. Cynthia Jameson, a hot new intern he'd had a hand in hiring. She'd been so eager to schedule a lunch to talk about her "goals" and "aspirations." *I can think of a few of her "aspirations" I'd like to see.*

Brendan took one last look in the mirror and smiled confidently. *He was a winner. He* could have any woman he desired, he told himself. He chose his favorite suit and hippest tie. He was dressed to kill and pleased with himself.

"Honey, are you almost finished in the bathroom?" His wife yelled from their bedroom. He rolled his eyes and got out of her way. He would meet her in the car.

The drive to the "slug" or "casual carpool" line in Virginia was always the same with Carla. While he was grateful for the ride, some days he would have preferred the inconvenience of taking the bus, so as not to hear her endless nagging and whining. He usually just tuned her out and day dreamed about his latest fling.

Most days, Brendan really enjoyed his experiences as a "slugger" because it was free and got him to work faster than taking a bus or the Metro. He managed to always abide by the "rules" and reaped the rewards as a commuter.

Understanding "slugging" was simple. It had originally come about to help reduce gas consumption and pollution. When a driver didn't have enough passengers for the HOV lane, he or she pulled up to a designated slug line and called out the destination. A minimum of two or more occupants was needed. Money was never exchanged because of the mutual benefit to the driver and riders.

The most amazing phenomenon of slugging was that hitching rides with strangers actually proved to be quite safe. At least for the past thirty years. Brendan found it surprising that no crimes had ever been a part of the efficiently run, government-free operation.

45

At the slug location in Crystal City, The Punisher watched from a distance as Brendan Campbell leaned over and kissed his wife goodbye before exiting their car. It appeared to be an obligatory gesture on his behalf. She abruptly sped away in the opposite direction as soon as he shut the door.

Little did she know that would be the last time she would ever see her husband alive. But once his sexual misconducts were exposed, she'd understand why he had to die.

The Punisher reflected on the ideal situation before him as his car pulled up to the slug line where he found Brendan waiting. He knew this would probably be the riskiest kill of all because there would be witnesses, even if they didn't realize it at the time.

Plus, there would inevitably have to be a sacrifice. He almost pitied the other person who would accept a ride with him today. He anxiously anticipated the shock the slugger community would experience, after they learned what had happened. His plan would change everything once again. He rolled his car up beside the line and called out to his friend.

"Hop in. You're going to the Pentagon, right?"

"Oh, hello there." Brendan appeared pleasantly surprised, and began to make his way toward the car. "Yeah, thanks. You have a good memory."

"Great, then we just need one more person," the killer said. "Pentagon," he yelled out the car window. A distinguished-looking man in a tailored business suit, who appeared to be in his late-forties, jumped in the backseat, and they were on their way.

The killer smiled to himself as he thought about Sam, hiding in the trunk. What a surprise Brendan was in for. He needed Sam to come along to eventually help him dump their bodies.

"How are you doing?" Brendan asked.

"Fine…and you?" The killer gripped the wheel.

"Couldn't be better. What have you been up to since I saw you last? Man, it must have been at least several months ago."

The killer peered in his rearview mirror at the passenger in the back seat. He was staring out the window as they passed the Washington Monument.

"Primarily a lot of research."

"Oh?" Brendan was staring at his profile, and the killer hoped he appeared calm, despite the heavy traffic. Cars were merging in and out of lanes around them.

"Yeah."

"What about? Anything interesting?"

"Well, I don't know. You tell me," the killer said in a patronizing tone and without even realizing it had accelerated up to seventy-five miles per hour. "I have discovered a lot of interesting things about a certain individual who's been cheating on his wife."

The man in the back seat suddenly perked up and seemed a little more interested in their conversation. Brendan looked bewildered and gripped the armrest as the car veered through unsafe merges.

"Really? Anyone scandalous? Anyone we know?" Brendan asked.

Adrenaline shot through his body. He was thoroughly enjoying this. "As a matter of fact, I think we both know him very well."

"Now you've got my attention. Are you going to tell me who or do I have to guess?"

"I'm surprised you had to ask." The killer pulled out a gun. "You're the one who's been cheating on your wife. And now you're going to pay for what you've done. You deserve to die."

46

The Punisher could sense the tension in the car after he revealed his intentions, and he loved every minute of his passengers' fear. Had the man in the back seat realized his fate as well? He could see the "suit" shift forward to the edge of his seat, wide-eyed, staring at the back of his driver's head in confusion. Brendan also looked shocked by the words he'd just heard.

"You didn't think you would really get away with it, did you?" He laughed.

"Why are you doing this? What do you want from me?" Brendan demanded to know.

The Punisher didn't respond.

"Did Carla put you up to this? Is this a joke? It's not funny!"

The car slowed down a bit and sank back into the right lane.

"This isn't a joke," the killer said. "You deserve to die for what you've done. And you will."

"What's going on here?" the man in the back seat demanded. "I want out of this car right now. Pull over and let me out!"

"I don't want to hear another word from you. This doesn't concern you."

"Yes, it does. You just threatened to kill him." The man looked out the window, perhaps realizing they had just passed the exit for the south parking area drop at the Pentagon. "That's my stop. You missed my stop!"

"Stop yelling," Brendan said.

"That's it - I'm calling the cops." The man reached in his jacket for his cell phone.

The Punisher swerved the car violently into the left lane, nearly ramming into a Ford Explorer. The driver of the Ford leaned on his horn. The man in the backseat dropped his phone and scrambled to retrieve it from under the front passenger seat. As he leaned over, the killer swerved the car back into the right lane, causing the man to hit his head hard on the door. At the same time a loud thud sounded in the trunk area.

"What's that noise?" Brendan yelled. The weight shifting in the trunk actually moved the car a little. A muffled groan sounded. "Is there someone in the trunk?"

The Punisher thought about Sam. He hoped he was okay back there. In his rear-view mirror he watched the man as he weighed his options silently. He couldn't find his phone. It had been thrust too far to the front or wedged between the metal pieces holding the seat in place.

He had to act fast before the situation got out of his control. He pulled out his gun and pressed it into Brendan's temple, steadying the wheel with his left hand.

Suddenly, to his surprise, the man in the backseat did the unthinkable. He flung open the door and jumped. Brendan gasped and turned to look back. The door slammed shut again from the force of the speed and wind.

The killer hadn't counted on this move. He watched in his rearview mirror as the man rolled across the pavement. He wondered if he should stop. After all, the man could identify him. He should have shot him while he had the chance. He just never expected him to jump. *Crazy!*

He checked his mirror again and saw that the momentum of the jump had caused the man to roll into the middle of the right lane where an oncoming SUV swerved to miss him and rammed into traffic in the left lane. The Punisher watched as several other cars screeched to a halt, but not before slamming into each other first. As he sped away, he felt a moment of panic and thought, *surely the idiot couldn't have survived the fall.*

47

hree hours later, the ABC 7 News report remained on mute on the television across from him. The Punisher made sure to DVR two of the other major networks to capture the highlights of his masterpiece. He had told himself that his passenger's jumping to his death provided the perfect distraction for Brendan's murder.

The massive pile up, caused by vehicles trying to avoid the body sprawled across the highway, gave him the time he needed to continue with his plan before anyone could figure out what had just happened. But Sam was angry with him.

"I can't believe you just kept driving. What were you thinking?" Sam asked as he paced the living room. "Witnesses! Witnesses…that's all we need at this point. And plenty of them."

The Punisher had never seen him this angry. Perhaps he should be worried that someone might have identified him. He sat very still in his chair and watched his friend stomp around in circles. He wasn't worried like Sam. They had done a good thing, a marvelous thing. He quickly grew tired of Sam's ranting and took the sound off mute. Alexis Latham's voice elated him as she reported from the tragic scene.

"Police are on the look out for what they believe to be a white Honda Civic after the driver allegedly fled the scene of a six-car pile up earlier today." She stared bright-eyed into the camera.

"Witnesses tell us they saw a man jump out of a moving vehicle, right here where I'm standing." The camera zoomed in on the highway behind her where rubble from the pile-up was still scattered. "Doctors are saying it's a miracle he survived."

"What?" The Punisher yelled. He couldn't believe what he was hearing. "How is this possible?"

"I don't believe this," Sam said. "I knew I never should have listened to you. This was too risky."

The reporter continued, "Witnesses also say they noticed the vehicle in question to be driving recklessly just moments before. The man, whose name police haven't released yet, remains in a coma at GW Hospital this evening in critical condition. At this time police have no other leads. If anyone has information that could help, please contact the D.C. Metropolitan Police Department. We know of no other serious injuries resulting from the multi-vehicle accident at this time. Reporting live from the Pentagon, this is Alexis Latham. Now back to you in the studio." A phone line for tips ran across the bottom of the screen.

"Are you even listening to me?" Sam cried over the sound of the television. "I told you there would be witnesses!"

"Of course I am, Sam. Get a hold of yourself. You have to trust me. We have nothing to worry about. For starters, the car was a rental and it was a white Acura, not a Honda."

"Nothing went as planned," Sam said. "This has never happened before."

"Relax. Our witness is in a coma, and I'll see to it that he stays that way."

"I don't have a good feeling about this," Sam said. "This was sloppy, despite what you think. This was your first mistake."

Actually, it was his second. The locket was his first, but he still didn't want to tell Sam about that. Especially now. All he wanted to do was enjoy the moment and bask in his brilliance.

He refused to listen to Sam's negativity. He smiled to himself and replayed the crime scene once more in his head, reliving the satisfaction of a deserving death. He was a genius. Pure and simple and anxious for the fame he was about to receive. It was only a matter of time.

48

Sandi Starr needed a break. She'd been working the corner of K and 23rd Street in northwest D.C. all morning and hadn't brought in anywhere close to her normal income. Usually by this time, she'd made enough for a gourmet breakfast at the Ritz, a Café Mocha at Starbucks and a nice lunch at The Palm. Not that she ever took advantage of any of those luxuries, looking like she did.

After all, she was dressed like a bum - because that's what she wanted people to believe she was. Today she wore a loose fitting camouflage t-shirt and a pair of baggy brown corduroys. Bumming was how she supported herself – one hundred thousand dollars a year to be precise, sometimes more.

She wasn't blessed in the looks area. She was Olive-Oil skinny, no matter how much she indulged in rich foods. She had a pointy nose and a clumsy-looking way about her that some people might interpret as being handicapped. But she always came across as friendly and likeable, which was why she did so well on the streets.

Today was different though. People seemed preoccupied, rushing blindly off to their jobs, rarely sparing her a glance. She decided, since she wasn't taking in anything on her usual corner, she'd try over by the Lincoln Memorial. When she got there, she made her way up the exaggerated steps. Lincoln's head crested into view. That was when she noticed the man.

He looked like he'd run out of breath on his way up the steps and stopped to rest for a moment. She kept going and when she reached the top of the stairs, she looked out across the Mall. Sunlight danced across the reflecting pool. She stood in the bright light for a moment, letting it warm her.

Sandi looked down again at the man and noticed a jogger giving him a second look. Something didn't seem right. She hurried down the steps to get a closer look. He wasn't breathing. She touched her fingertips to his throat but felt no pulse. Sandi knew what she had to do and reached for her cell phone. She scrolled down her list of contacts until she found Olivia Penn's name and dialed. She had no doubt that this news was going to pay off.

49

Olivia planned to catch up with Rex over breakfast at the Luna Cafe in Dupont Circle. He'd agreed to meet, even if it was his day off. Plus, it was one of his favorite places to eat in the city.

Breakfast was going beautifully, that is until Olivia's phone rang. She peered down at her iPhone, which had already instinctively made it to the palm of her hand, but out of sight beneath the tablecloth. She was more than a little surprised to see the name that appeared on her caller ID.

"I've got to take this, Rex. It could be important." She put the phone to her ear and recognized Sandi Starr's voice immediately. She sounded excited. "What can I do for you today?"

"It's not what you can do for me," Sandi said. "It's what I'm about to do for you."

"Well, you've certainly got my attention." Olivia watched him shut his menu. She silently mouthed an apology and held up her pointer finger to signal to give her a minute.

"I just discovered a dead body," Sandi continued.

"What? Where?" She grabbed a note pad and pen from her purse to write down details.

"At the Lincoln Memorial. Come quick."

"The Lincoln – right out in public?"

"Yeah, it's pretty crazy." Sandi paused. "I haven't called the police yet."

"Don't worry, I'll take care of that. I'm on my way now."

"You better hurry before some fame-seeking tourist spots him."

Olivia glanced at her watch. "Has anyone else noticed him? Can you tell what happened? Gun shot wound, stabbing?"

"No, there's no blood," Sandi said, almost in a whisper now. "In fact, at first glance I just thought he was passed out. But I'm sure he's dead. He isn't breathing!"

"Are you going to be there?" Olivia picked up her purse and car keys.

"Yeah, just hurry. I'll tell you more once you're here. I wanted you to be the first to know."

"I know, I know, Sandi. I owe you big time." Olivia knew exactly what her intentions were, but she didn't care. Time was of the essence now. Losing this lead was not an option. It might be a murder connected to The Punisher.

Olivia had a decision to make. And, it wasn't until she was in her car driving toward the crime scene of a dead body that she questioned whether she'd made the right one. She had to see this for herself. As she frantically weaved her Mini Cooper in and out of traffic on K Street, she mentally replayed the conversation in her head with Rex. She needed to justify her recent actions and the indecision she felt mounting in her heart.

"Olivia," he'd said, shaking his head in disappointment. "When are you ever going to learn? There will be another front-page story to chase tomorrow."

"I'm sorry, I've gotta go. There's a dead body at the Lincoln Memorial." She got up from the table and gathered her things.

"Then I'm glad it's my day off." He shook his head. "You should let the Park Service Police handle this. It's not a good idea to get involved."

Olivia hadn't known what to say. Why did Rex disapprove so adamantly?

"In the end, this latest news article of yours…it's just more words on a piece of paper," Rex had continued. "Paper that will be thrown out in the next day's garbage. You do realize that, don't you?"

"Thanks, I appreciate your support." Olivia rolled her eyes.

He grabbed her arm. "I don't have a good feeling about this."

"Please don't do this," she pleaded. "Not now."

"One day I hope you understand. I mean really understand."

As Olivia sped toward the Lincoln Memorial, she couldn't help wondering what Rex's words really meant. What was he really trying to tell her? *Had she* been wrong to leave? A sense of dread and regret instantly washed over her. Silently, she cursed the career and the passions inside her that continued to push her husband and personal life further away. She couldn't help herself when it came to this job. Rex of all people should understand that. She loved her job, and it loved her. It remained her strongest weakness.

50

Olivia's thoughts returned to Sandi. They shared a bizarre, mutually beneficial relationship. She had met the "bum" several years back while writing an article on the homeless and mentally ill population in Washington, D.C. Since then Sandi had become a key contact, a source in Stacy's case and various other leads. Sandi saw a lot on the street, had a lot of secrets, some of which Olivia had paid dearly for.

To her credit, Sandi was also a master at being in the right place at the right time. Olivia could understand why some people claimed Sandi was responsible for keeping some crime off the streets, despite the fact that she was technically "stealing" money from innocent bystanders each day. She owed Sandi, and she was thankful to have her as a friend.

Olivia spotted a parking place, very small, but the Mini didn't fail her. She bolted from her car and sprinted across the grassy lawn leading up to the steps of the Lincoln Memorial. Her heart raced in anticipation when she spotted Sandi, guarding the crime scene.

"What took you so long?" Sandi shifted from one foot to the other, speaking rapidly. "You know this is going to cost you."

"I'm fully aware. Name your price, and I'll see what I can do." Olivia approached the spot where the body lay and felt the color drain from her face. She feared the Park Service Police might stumble upon the body at any moment. Why hadn't they noticed it already?

"What do you think happened?" Sandi asked.

"I have no idea," Olivia walked around the man. *Focus, focus. Don't think about the dead body. Time is precious.*

"Did you notice anything strange when you arrived?" Olivia asked. "People lingering around? Is there anything else you can think of, even if it's just an instinct or fleeting thought?"

Sandi didn't answer. She put her hand over her eyes to shield the sun.

"Listen, if it eases your mind, this is worth seven hundred, all right?" Olivia said. "Which is more than I've ever paid you."

"Eight hundred."

Olivia frowned. "Seven and that's final. You should know you're in no position to bargain now. Didn't they teach you that in Homeless Haggling Tactics 101?"

"Oh, come on." Sandi said. "This is big, and you know it."

"I said seven hundred, and that's it. That's more than fair. Don't get greedy on me."

Sandi stepped away, attempting to pout.

Olivia looked the woman up and down, squinting against the bright sunshine. She could feel the sweat begin to bead on her upper lip. "Nice outfit," she stated, taking note of Sandi's semi-expensive rags that were made to look worn. "New?"

Olivia laughed under her breath and continued to examine the scene. The first thing she noticed was the man's twisted expression. "You didn't mention on the phone that his face was all contorted. That wouldn't be from drinking or drugging." She'd read books on poisoning and lethal injections, which could explain the distortions.

"I guess I didn't look too closely." Sandi glanced away.

Olivia tried to push away her thoughts of revulsion. She actually thought she might throw up and was glad she hadn't eaten breakfast yet as her gag reflexes started to kick in. *Keep your focus, you need this story,* she kept telling herself. But something deep inside, no matter how disgusted she was, could not pull her away from this scene.

She wondered why she couldn't just walk away. Her need to write her stories had always taken over her life. *Why? Why?* Once again, she was already sucked into the mystery of it all and knew she wouldn't stop until she found the answers. She suspected that, despite the suspicion of foul play, there were other forces at work here. It was no suicide that was for sure.

51

Olivia kept an eye out for the police, and against her better judgment pulled her tiny tape recorder from her pants pocket. She took a deep breath, ignored the nausea, and began dictating notes. "Male, age estimated to be in his forties," she said, holding the recording device up to her mouth. "Check missing government officials. Looks familiar."

She moved closer to the body. "Man is wearing an expensive looking dark gray suit, pink striped tie, nice quality button-down, probably Brooks Brothers. Gold wedding band on his left hand. He is slumped against the....one, two, three, four, five, six, seventh step from the top of the Lincoln Memorial. Could this placement bear any significance to the crime? Sandi Starr discovered the body at approximately noon today."

"What's this?" A tiny piece of white paper stuck out from the man's pants pocket. She bent closer and tilted her head. The paper appeared to have handwriting on it, but she couldn't quite make out what it said. She decided to take the law into her own hands. Something that could ruin her career and get her thrown into jail, but she pushed that reality aside.

Olivia quickly looked around until she saw what she was looking for. She walked down a couple of steps and picked up a soft, greenish fallen leaf and brought it back to the man. The leaf was not crisp enough to splinter, so she folded it in half between her fingers and plucked the piece of paper out of the man's pocket, careful not to leave any fingerprints.

"Wow," she said out loud when she realized her instincts were correct. She turned her attention once again to the tape recorder and spoke, almost mechanically now. "The note in the victim's pocket appears to be a link and another murder by The Punisher.

The note reads, "Dear Carla Campbell, I'm sorry to be the one to inform you that your husband has been unfaithful. He has cheated repeatedly on you. Don't waste your time mourning him because you deserve better. I made sure he suffered. He deserved to die. The Punisher."

Quickly, she wrote down every word of the letter in her notepad as a back up, in case the tape recorder shorted or something unforeseen happened. She noted the detail of the handwriting, describing how it slanted. She looked up and saw Sandi staring at her.

"A deposit in the amount of seven hundred dollars will be in your account by the end of the day. Okay?"

"That's all I needed to know," Sandi said. "I'm out of here. Let me know if I can be of further service. Always nice doing business with you."

"Be sure and buy yourself something presentable next time we meet," Olivia called out to her. "You look like a *bum*."

52

Olivia knew she needed to call Nathan at the FBI and figured she had some explaining to do as to how she ended up being the first person at this crime scene *and* had tampered with evidence. But then again, she had a story to write. And that was what she planned to do. The story instinctively unraveled in her mind as she took in all the details of the scene.

With Sandi out of the way, the realization of exactly what she was dealing with hit her hard. A dead body on the steps of the Lincoln Memorial. How did he get there? Her heart raced. Something didn't make sense. Why the public display? Now, as she peered down at this lifeless body, she had an overwhelming desire to find out what had happened to him.

There was something she couldn't quite place yet that still bothered her. *What was it?* She looked down at the note in her hand again, hesitating about what to do with it. Was it the stationery? It did look familiar. Where had she seen it before? Then it hit her. The handwriting looked similar to the writing in Stacy's note the night she'd disappeared. Something about the way the letter "D" was formed. Then, something else struck her. When she flipped the piece of paper over, the other side contained another message. Had the killer intentionally left a clue?

It was a quote, neatly printed in all caps. "What lies behind us and what lies before us are tiny matters compared to what lies within us."

"What does this mean?" She held the tape recorder close to her mouth and spoke excitedly, repeating the quote. "Are these the killer's own words or a quote from someone? It almost seems as though he's playing games and is fascinated by his own fame and power. Who is he?"

She turned off the tape recorder and pulled out her iPhone. Biting her lip she dialed. Nathan picked up on the first ring, as if he was expecting her call.

"Olivia, I was just about to call you. I have some…"

"Listen – there's no time right now," she cut him off. "There's been another murder, and this time The Punisher left a note in his own hand-writing. I'm at the Lincoln Memorial with the victim."

"What? I'm on my way." The connection went dead.

She found herself staring into the phone as if she could see where Nathan had suddenly disappeared, feeling a little sick to her stomach when she realized she'd just told him she found the note. Bad move on her part.

53

Olivia needed to wrap things up and return the note to the man's pocket before the police or the FBI arrived. While she adjusted the leaf in her hand to make sure she hadn't accidentally left her fingerprints on the note, she glanced up in the direction of the reflecting pool, and that's when she saw him.

A Park Service officer. He looked like a hungry bulldog. His scruffy jowls swung back and forth across his face as he walked, and his meaty limbs would have given the impression of muscular power had it not been for his bouncing belly that appeared to have eaten his belt.

She had a terrible feeling about what was about to happen. Quickly, she slipped the note in her pocket, without thinking, and the leaf fled the scene. She only hoped the bull dog hadn't seen her do that. Even from the distance between them, she could sense his fury.

He stopped to catch his breath on the second step and rested his chunky hands on his knees, hunched over like he was examining the ground below him. She slipped the tiny tape from the recorder in her other pocket, but it was too late to hide the machine. He'd seen it as he gathered himself and continued his trek up the next several steps.

"What exactly do you think you're doing?" He whipped a radio out of his back pocket and requested back up. "Looks like we've got a tourist here who thinks she's in some sort of CSI episode." Static stuttered. "Just caught her stealing evidence from a crime scene. How about that,

177

Johnson? Do you read me? I need you here pronto so I can secure the scene."

"Roger that," came a voice on the other end. "I'm almost there. Over."

Olivia held her breath. Should she run? She hadn't even thought about the possibility of all the other implications of her being there. "I'm a reporter for the Post, and I'm the one who called the FBI about this body. I was just waiting until they showed up."

"A reporter. Oh. Well, that's just great." He shook his head. His jiggling jowls threatened to fly right off his face. "Lady, I don't care who you are. You just messed with my crime scene." He began to focus his attention on the body and dismissed her with a wave of his hand. "Reporters. What? You didn't have anything to write about today, so you thought you'd just kill someone for kicks? Story makes the front page and all. Brilliant."

He paused. "Makes sense, doesn't it? You kill him, you bring the body to a public place, you risk being seen, so when you are, you go and pretend you found him." His patronizing tone did nothing for her. If there is one thing she couldn't stand, it was suffering fools. "Now, wait a minute, officer. I didn't kill this man."

He turned his head sideways and looked her square in the eyes, ready for an attack. "Well, I guess we'll never know that, now will we? Seeing as how you've contaminated the evidence."

"Why do you say that?" She realized she was on thin ice.

"You must think I'm pretty stupid, or blind." He put his hands on his hips and spread his legs apart. "I saw you, that's why."

The officer squinted from the bright sun. For a moment his eyes had disappeared. His face appeared to devour them. When he finally did open them again he wasn't subtle about looking her up and down. "I'm going to need your tape recorder and any other evidence you've stolen. Including the notes you've made that you're holding." He began to walk toward her.

"Look, the person responsible for this is probably somewhere nearby, watching," she said. "Maybe you should focus your energy on that."

She was trying her best to distract him but knew she was digging herself deeper and deeper.

"Lady, that's it. I don't have time for you to tell me how to do my job."

"Please don't call me lady. My name is Olivia. Olivia Penn."

"Well, then. Olivia Penn, you're under arrest for disrupting this crime scene. You have the right to remain silent..."

She didn't hear the rest of the rights he read as he placed the cuffs around her wrists. Olivia couldn't believe what was actually happening. What a disaster. She'd gone from eyewitness...to potential murderer... to a common criminal.

54

The ride to the police station gave Olivia time to think. She didn't mind being stuck in traffic, if it meant not being in jail. How bad were things? Once Nathan found out, he would help her sort everything out. Wouldn't he? When she arrived, the guards allowed her to make a phone call. Cameron didn't answer his cell phone, so she left a message.

She hated to tell him over voice mail she was in jail. Instead of being sent straight into a cell, she was detained in a questioning room for an hour before the FBI showed up. Olivia took a deep breath when Nathan entered the room.

"I'll make this brief." He looked at her, and she sensed his awkward position. His stress. She glanced in the direction of the two-way glass and wondered who was behind it. Watching them. "You mentioned that The Punisher left a note...so I'm assuming you have it on you."

"I'm sorry, I just thought – "

"I'm sure you did," he began, "but the fact is, you broke the law. I like you, and I do believe for whatever reason you probably think this was your job."

"I did." Her eyes pleaded with him to believe her. "I swear."

"That's beside the point right now." He shook his head. "I have a job to do, and your actions almost got me fired today."

"What do you mean?"

"When my boss found out you'd called me with the lead, and I didn't put a stop to your being at a crime scene, he said I didn't follow protocol. He considers me responsible."

"I'm sorry." Her shoulders sank.

"I appreciate that, but the best way you can help me is to hand over the note and whatever other evidence you have. I've got to get it to the lab right away. I just hope the integrity of the crime scene hadn't been so seriously compromised that we end up with no useful evidence."

She nodded and handed over the note. And the tape. "It's a recording of what I observed at the scene," she said. "If it helps at this point."

"My partner, Agent Turner, is coming in to question you now," he said. "After that, you'll go into a holding cell. I assume you called your husband."

"Yes." She frowned. "One more thing. Is there any way I could get a pen and paper?"

Nathan looked at her is disbelief. "Are you serious?"

"I'm hoping that's a yes."

Ten minutes later a pencil and a sheet of paper were delivered to her. She madly jotted down the story that was taking shape in her head, remembering all the details she'd put on the tape. Her hand grew tired as she scribbled and imagined the next day's headline. She had quite the story.

After another agonizing thirteen hours went by and when Cameron still hadn't shown up, Olivia began to worry. She sat alone in the darkness reflecting on her day and predicament. Her thoughts tormented her as she paced the jail cell. She realized that, by now, someone else had written her story, and Duncan probably wondered where she was, especially after news like this coming over the wire.

The irony was, she could have cared less what the news reported. She just wanted out of jail. She also spent time trying to figure out where Cameron was, debating whether or not he was okay. It wasn't like him not to respond to her message. She felt so jaded now, different. She had crossed a line she wasn't prepared to cross with her personal life and her career. This job was killing her. Slowly.

Finally, some time after six the next morning, her husband arrived and posted bail. Relief overwhelmed her when she saw him. He was sweating and seemed highly agitated when he saw her standing behind bars.

"Are you okay, Liv?" He tried to catch his breath.

"I am now."

"I'm so sorry it took me so long. My phone battery died yesterday afternoon, and I didn't think much of it until I realized you hadn't come home last night. I was up late in the study. When I came to bed around one-thirty and realized you weren't there, I went crazy with worry. I finally figured out how to check my messages from a land line."

"Cameron, it doesn't matter. Please, just get me out of here."

55

Olivia wanted nothing more than to be wrapped in the safety of her husband's arms.

"Let's go home," he said. "I'm clearing my schedule for the day because I think we should talk about it this. I just need to run into the hospital this morning for about an hour or so, and then I'm free the rest of the day."

"Okay, but I actually need to talk to Duncan first."

Cameron opened the car door for her. "I'm sure he'd love to know you're okay and what happened."

"I hope so." She sat down in the front seat and fixed her hair in the visor mirror." Do you mind dropping me off at my car?"

"Where is it?"

"I parked by the Lincoln Memorial yesterday when I got the call about the dead body."

"Sure, and while we're driving maybe you'd like to tell me why you spent the night in jail?" He pressed his lips together and kept his eyes on the road.

Olivia knew he deserved an explanation. "Cameron, I was arrested for obstruction of justice. I stole evidence from a crime scene."

"What?" He turned his head and stared in disbelief. "You've got to be kidding."

"I got a call from Sandi Starr who found a dead body. Turns out he happens to be the latest victim of The Punisher."

Her husband sat in silence.

She sighed and massaged her temples. "I know what you're thinking."

"Do you?" He gripped the wheel so tight the veins in his forehands protruded and pulsated.

"You're wondering how I could be so careless...and I'm not really sure what to say. I don't expect you to understand."

"You're right. I don't." His face tightened. "You're in over your head. You could've gotten yourself killed, but you can't see it because all you care about is another by-line."

"That's a little unfair, don't you think?" But she wasn't surprised by his lack of support. "Don't you think you're being a bit melodramatic? How was I putting my life in danger?"

He looked at her in disbelief. "Do I really have to tell you?"

"I guess you do." She watched as they made their way into the city.

"You're a reporter. Not a detective."

"Yes, and I have a job to do," she stated. "To report the news on crimes."

"I just hope that in the process you don't become a victim."

"What's that supposed to mean?" She threw her head back and sighed.

"Yes, Olivia, you do have a job, a very important one. One that you've been recognized for because you're extremely good at it. I respect that."

"But?"

"But, you need to realize the limitations of your job and set some healthier boundaries," he said. "You're not trained to be a criminal investigator. You're not trained to defend yourself if this killer was staking out the scene after he or she dumped the body and saw you messing with it and decided to attack you. Did you think of that?"

Olivia didn't respond. He was right.

"Plus, now if you contaminated the scene, you've only made it harder for the detectives or FBI to do their jobs. Not to mention the legal implications." He shook his head and frowned.

"I'm well aware of that. Thank you. I believe that's why I was arrested." She crossed her arms and looked straight ahead. "Tell you what. Just let me off here. My car is around the corner."

"I can drop you closer." Cameron's tone suddenly softened.

"No, this is fine. I could use some fresh air. I'll see you at home." She hopped out of the car and walked away.

56

Olivia made a brief stop at her cubicle before approaching her boss. She dropped her scribbled story and notes on top of her desk and went to face the music. Duncan paced the floor of his office. His rage blistered his cheeks crimson red. Olivia took a chair across from him and fought back tears.

"What were you thinking?" he demanded. He slowed his steps and turned to look at her.

"I guess I wasn't." She stared at the floor.

"You're right. You weren't!" He pounded his meaty fist into his desk. "How could you have messed with a crime scene and stolen a key piece of evidence? And argued with a cop!"

"It's not necessary to rehash the last twenty-four hours of my life. I am well-aware of what just happened, Dunk."

"Well then, explain it to me. No, better yet – I really don't want to hear it because it doesn't matter right now."

He stopped pacing, and she could feel his eyes burning a hole through her skull. She'd never seen Duncan this angry before, not in the eleven years she'd known him. She hated to disappoint people, especially herself. She couldn't swallow the knot in her throat or escape the shame she felt.

"This little fiasco of yours made the front page! With all of the other news out there, you getting arrested made the front page."

She tried to imagine the headline that morning. *Pulitzer Prize Winning Journalist Arrested.* "Think of all the papers it sold," she retaliated, dismayed by her witless delivery.

"Yeah, for the Tribune, not the Post!" Duncan rubbed his head hard with the palm of his hand, messing up the little hair he had left. He plopped down in his chair. "It's not about selling papers any more with you, is it? Not only did the Tribune probably have one of their most satisfying scoops in the history of their paper, they also actually had a news story about the murder of Brendan Campbell, which is more than I can say for us. We had our top investigative reporter on the scene but couldn't even get a decent story out of it because you spent the night in jail."

"Please calm down, Dunk. You would've done the same thing."

"Oh yeah. You think so? Tampering? Trying to trump the local law enforcement. You're wrong. I never would've done that."

"Yes you would…if you found what I found." She stood up, convinced she was right.

Duncan looked at her, wide-eyed. "What did you find?"

"I have a story that no reporter has. The Punisher left another note on the body, but this time he also left a quote. A clue. This murder is somehow different than the others, yet still connected."

"It doesn't matter what you found," he said. "The FBI won't allow you to run with any information you retrieved illegally from the crime scene. We can't print anything you write. Not a word of it."

"What?" she yelled, now almost in a state of delirium. "I have to talk to Special Agent Spencer. Now."

"Olivia. He's the one who directed the gag order."

She couldn't believe what she was hearing. She had to get through to Nathan. Was this his way of getting back at her? Why had he done this?

It was as if Duncan read her mind. "He's just doing his job," he said. "You've really crossed the line this time, Olivia."

She took a deep breath. "I know I did. I'm sorry, and I'll make it up to you."

"That isn't good enough this time. At least for the North Wall."

"What are you saying?" She was afraid to ask and feared the worst.

He sighed. "Effective immediately, you're suspended."

57

Olivia closed her eyes and rested her face in her hands. She couldn't believe she was being suspended. For an entire month. She couldn't control the tears any longer. This wasn't the first time Duncan had seen her cry, but she couldn't remember the last time.

"And what's this about paying off a bum?" he asked. "Seven hundred dollars. Is that true?"

"How did you know about that?" She had really backed herself into a corner.

"She called here looking for you when she didn't receive her payment."

"Don't worry about it," she said. "It's coming out my own pocket."

The last concern on her mind now was that she had not lived up to her word. She was good for it. Sandi would just have to understand. "I just spent the night in jail, and now I could lose my job. Please. Can we talk about this later?"

Just then, Emily Morgan, appeared in the doorway of Duncan's office. Olivia turned, noticing Emily had a look of satisfaction in her eyes.

"Am I interrupting?" She leaned her body into the doorframe.

"As a matter of fact you are," Duncan said. "Is this urgent?"

"No, it can wait," she said. "I just wanted to run a story idea by you, and I thought this might be a good time to move on it." She adjusted the top button on her business suit and smirked at Olivia.

"What is it?" Duncan asked.

189

"Given the incident yesterday with the man in the slug line," Emily began, "I was thinking that I could go out and interview some sluggers at different locations. You know, to get a feel for what it's like, how the public feels about what just happened. Try to put a positive spin on this type of alternative transportation. After all, there's never been a crime reported to date within the slug community."

Olivia turned her back to Emily, but the harshness of her voice penetrated the resounding headache that was pounding in her head.

"Sure, that's a good idea." Duncan dismissed Emily with a flip of his hand.

Olivia could feel the woman's antagonizing smile moving right through her. She wiped the tears from her eyes before turning around to get in the last word, not fooled one minute by Emily's innocence.

"Oh, Emily," she said. "I'm just curious, what will your angle be?"

"I'm not sure yet," Emily said, appearing a little caught off guard by the challenge.

Olivia turned to face the woman, noticing the confidence dwindling in her stance as she slumped against the doorway. "Here's a thought, just an idea...how about, I can't think of story ideas on my own, so I go snooping around my co-worker's desk until I find what I'm looking for and try to pass off her ideas for my own."

"I don't know what you're talking about." Emily spun around and scurried away.

"Wow," Duncan said. "That was a low point, even for you." He sat down on the corner of his desk. "Listen to me. Go home and get some rest. You aren't acting well, and I'm worried about you. Just do the time off, and I promise your job will be waiting for you when you return. I need you here, but not like this."

"Right." Olivia felt her blood start to boil, and there was nothing she could do about the situation. "Emily Morgan's been waiting for an opportunity like this since she started here."

"She is hungry and determined, I'll give her that much," Duncan said.

Olivia didn't like what she was hearing and thought about the text from her MsgPost. "Well, I don't trust her, and I wouldn't put anything past her."

58

Olivia knew her life was about to change. She was grateful that Cameron had canceled his afternoon appointments and come home. She longed for his company and felt relieved that he took the news of her suspension so well.

"Sounds like you've had a rough two days." He pulled his wife into his arms.

"To put it lightly." She buried her face in his chest.

"Liv, everything is going to be okay."

"You think?"

"I know." He kissed her head, and she melted into his warmth.

"Now I want you to do me a favor. Actually, I want *you* to do *you* a favor."

"Oh no, I don't know if I like the sound of this." She pulled away from him.

"I think this suspension is a good thing." He kissed her on the forehead and smiled. "First of all, it's got your attention. Now I want you to really take some time off and focus on the important things in your life."

"I know, I know." She didn't like to admit when he was right.

"That means no writing, no working, and no worrying." He raised his eyebrows. "Do you think you can handle that?"

She closed her eyes and pouted. "Yes"

"Good."

"But I'm not going to lie. It's not going to be easy. I'm angry with Duncan for suspending me."

Cameron grabbed her by the shoulders and looked into her eyes. "What did you expect? You broke the law."

She could count on Cameron to be honest with her. She had always appreciated that about him, but for some reason it was difficult to hear. She rubbed her eyes and yawned. "I think I should take a nap."

"Excellent idea." His eyes lit up brightly. "You get some rest, and when you wake up, I'll be waiting for you."

She closed her eyes again and sighed with relief. "What did I do to deserve you?" She cupped his cheeks between her hands and kissed him.

Olivia wasn't sure how long she'd slept when she finally woke up later. The sounds of Mozart filtered down from above, and she made her way up the stairs that led to the rooftop. When she opened the door, she saw Cameron reclined in a lounge chair in a pair of cargo shorts and no shirt. A nice suntan was forming across his rippled abs. He had a bottle of champagne chilling along with a cheese and fruit plate. He looked gorgeous basking in the sunlight.

"What's the occasion?" She startled him from his slumber.

"Oh, I must have dozed off," he said in a sleepy voice. He smiled, and Olivia recalled never having been so attracted to him as at that very moment. She wanted him.

Straddling his body she began to kiss his ears and neck. He pulled her down on top of him, and they melted into each other. They made love right there in the lounge chair. The warm rays of the sun tickled her bare skin.

An hour later, after they had devoured the fruit and cheeses along with the champagne, they made love again. She didn't care if anyone saw them. These were moments she'd never forget. They were euphoric. She was so grateful to have him there to take her mind off of everything. Maybe this suspension wasn't such a bad thing after all. It felt incredible to reconnect with her husband.

She could have stayed wrapped in his embrace for hours, but her fantasy faded at the buzzing of a phone.

"Is that mine or yours?" She rolled out of his hug.

"It's mine." Frowning, he grabbed the device off the table where the empty bottle of champagne sat.

Olivia watched her husband's eyes move as he read his latest email off his Blackberry. "What is it? A patient?"

"Yes, one that's on suicide watch." Cameron shook his head. "I'm sorry but I've got to go to the hospital. It's an emergency. Can we continue this later?" He kissed her on the cheek.

"Sure, do what you need to do. I'm not going anywhere."

59

The Punisher paced the room. He waited. And waited. Then he began to second-guess his decision to let Sam go to the hospital to finish off the comatose slugger.

"Let me do something," Sam had pleaded earlier that morning.

"Why should I? I'm The Punisher. You're just…Sam."

"You need me."

"Oh." The Punisher rolled his eyes.

"I have good ideas." Sam stomped his feet into the floor.

"Yes, but you don't have the means to carry them out without me." He knew he needed to make Sam feel important, like things were *his* idea. Even if it wasn't the case.

"Would you feel better if perhaps you pulled the plug on the man who jumped from the car the other day?"

Sam beamed ear to ear. "That's exactly what I had in mind."

But The Punisher started having doubts after Sam left. He knew things hadn't gone according to plan with the last murder, but they had ended up working out just fine. He also knew he needed to be more meticulous with his next kill. More disciplined. He sighed with relief when he finally saw Sam walk through the door.

"Is it done?" he asked.

"Of course it is," Sam said. "Now nobody will ever be able to identify you. Although, it wasn't as easy as I thought it would be."

"Why is that?" The Punisher stopped pacing.

"Because we didn't count on the man being a high ranking official in the Department of Defense."

"What!" The Punisher grabbed his chest. "What are you talking about?" How do you know that?"

"Apparently his name is Stanley Baldwin," Sam began. "I overheard some family members talking about him in the waiting room. I think he may have been the Chief of Staff for the Army from the bits and pieces I heard. Plus, there were men guarding his door off and on. But luckily, I was able to slip past them long enough to unplug the life support equipment. Then, I blended right into the scene."

"Well done."

"We're taking too many risks now." Sam shook his head. "When it's made public that The Punisher is linked to this man, there will be huge political ramifications...especially after the Secretary of State's recent death."

The Punisher thought about this and smiled at the ironic twist of events. This could work to the advantage of his reputation.

"Why are you smiling?" Sam asked. "Don't you understand what we've just done?"

He laughed. "Yeah, and when the president finds out, he's going to be devastated. This calls for a celebration." He walked over to his stash of Maker's Mark and poured himself a couple of inches.

"Yeah, I think it's safe to say we've got his attention."

"Well, are you going to thank me now...for allowing you to be a part of my master plan?" His belly warmed as he sipped and let the alcohol soothe him.

Sam's eyes opened wide. "Thank you? You're the one who should be thanking me for cleaning up your mess. You've gotten sloppy."

"You've never been able to see the big picture, Sam."

"The big picture?" Sam walked over to the liquor cabinet and poured himself a tall glass of whiskey. He took a long sip. "This master plan of yours was never supposed to be political, remember? We're supposed to be punishing those who cheat on their spouses and who cheat the

American public. Not murdering innocent politicos who happen to get in the way."

"He's simply a casualty of war."

"He was innocent, and we killed him." Sam downed the rest of his drink. "Do I need to remind you of the rules we established?"

The Punisher watched his friend and allowed him to carry on.

"We don't see race, gender, religion, political affiliation, rich or poor. The only thing we see is high profile infidelity."

The Punisher laughed. "The rules have changed."

60

The next morning Olivia went for a run down to the National Mall, managing to resist the temptation of reading the newspaper that lay at her doorstep. Until she returned. Then, she read every page. Word by word. The first thing she noticed was the front-page story.

As she skimmed through the content about the latest "Punisher" murder, the story sounded very familiar. After further examination she realized that it *was* her story, only with another person's name in the by-line. Emily Morgan's. Details, like the note The Punisher left, had been omitted, but it was still her story. And it had made the front page. The woman really had a lot of nerve.

Olivia suddenly remembered how she'd left the story she'd written in jail on her desk the day before while she was talking to Duncan. Emily must have stolen it. Olivia grabbed the phone and dialed Duncan's cell. He picked up on the fourth ring.

The fury inside her temporarily made her lose sight of sound reasoning. "Wow, Dunk. Emily's certainly making a name for herself, according to this morning's paper."

"Olivia...please..."

"My reputation is ruined, and she's not only trying to take my place, she's resorted to plagiarism!"

She hung up on him. Probably not the best move, but it sure made her feel better. In fact, thinking back on it, she suspected her anger had little to do with Emily. It probably had more to do with her own fear than anything else. The thought occurred to her. Without her work, who was she? The answer saddened her. Her career consumed her.

It was impossible for her to relax, focus on anything but work, especially after three more cups of coffee. Plus, she wondered how many more by-lines by Emily she'd have to endure over the next month. A by-line was a by-line, and it was clear that Emily would stop at nothing to take Olivia's place. When her phone rang she figured Duncan was calling back to fire her, but it was Cameron.

"I was just thinking about you and calling to see how your morning's going," he said. "I figured this first morning might be rough, having no place to be, and I just wanted you to know how much I love you. I'm here to support you through this."

She instantly felt better. "I love you too, and I'm glad you called." She smiled and forgot about Emily for a minute. She didn't want to tell him she was wrapped up in work issues. She was supposed to be relaxing.

"Maybe one day this week we can meet for lunch," he said.

"I'd like that."

"I better run. Call me if you need anything."

She plopped down on the couch, flipped on the television and found the *Today Show*. A rolling tag at the bottom of the screen indicated that the local news team was interrupting for a breaking news update.

The local anchorwoman had come back on and wore a serious expression as she reported. "We learned early this morning that the man who jumped from a moving vehicle on 495 in Virginia Monday died late last night at GW Hospital. He's been identified as Samuel Baldwin and served as the Army's Chief of Staff for the Department of Defense. The police have declined to comment at this time as to whether his death could be linked to the body found at the Lincoln Memorial Monday afternoon. If you'll recall, NBC was the first on the scene to report this murder…"

Olivia caught her breath, realizing the magnitude of the situation. She suspected that The Punisher had returned to finish what he started with Samuel Baldwin, and now the only witness who could have identified the killer was dead. The media didn't know about the note at the Lincoln Memorial yet, or they would have had a field day with this angle.

The wheels in her head suddenly started to turn. She made her way upstairs to her office and grabbed a pen and paper. After she sat down at her desk, the words started to flow and she couldn't get her next story down on paper fast enough. It was time to reveal to the world that there was a serial killer on the loose in Washington. As she'd told Rex, people needed to sit up and listen. She had an obligation to deliver the news; she'd kept the truth to herself long enough. Even if she didn't get the credit for her next story, it was time it was told. She imagined the headline to read:

SERIAL KILLER TARGETS TOP D.C. OFFICIALS.

She had the facts. She had the sources. And, now she finally had the story.

"He calls himself The Punisher," she said out loud and jotted down the first sentence of her story. "D.C. power players with explosive secrets are his targets. His goal: high profile murders in the nation's capitol."

Hours later she put the finishing touches on the article and emailed it to Duncan, unsure how he might respond. She didn't expect him to run it with her by-line since she was suspended, but she did expect him to run with it. And, above the fold. It was the truth. And it meant papers would sell. It also meant that he would succeed despite her failures.

She simply wrote, "Dunk, here are a few ideas to call your own. Run with it however you see fit. This story is long overdue." It was the masterpiece she'd been leading up to all year.

She was totally enthralled in her work when she heard the doorbell ring. She contemplated not answering it at first. When Olivia made her way downstairs, the last person she expected to find at her doorstep was Emily Morgan.

61

Emily stood at Olivia's doorstep and smiled as if she knew something her co-worker didn't.

"What do you want?" Olivia asked.

"I was hoping we could talk." Emily tilted her head to the side as if trying to look sympathetic. "May I come in?"

"No, I don't think so." Olivia blocked the doorway.

"This won't take long."

"You're right, Emily. It won't." Olivia took a deep breath and tried to keep her composure.

Emily put her hands on her hips and looked down at her. She still towered above her, even being a half foot below her.

"I can see that you're angry, and I don't blame you," Emily said.

"I'm not angry, I'm indifferent." Olivia squinted her eyes through her lie.

"Either way, I need your help."

"*My* help." Olivia shook her head, unable to hide the disgust she felt. "What else could I possibly help you with?"

"You're the only reporter who knows the other details at that crime scene. Olivia, I need your notes for a follow up story. I know there was more to this story. What else did you see?"

Now Olivia was furious. "This is a bold move. Even for you."

"I was sure you'd want to tell me," Emily said. "I know you have a theory. You do want to do what's best for the paper, don't you? Of course you'd get an attribution."

"Attribution? Is that what you call your by-line running on the front page of the Post, on top of my story? How do you suppose that happened?"

"You can't prove anything." Her face turned hard and cold.

Emily was right. Olivia had scribbled the story out on a loose piece of paper in jail. "Tell you what. You can have that story because I can always write another one."

"We'll see," Emily said. "You should know that Duncan thinks I have real potential."

"Oh really." This amused Olivia. "I think you underestimate him. You know, people without journalism integrity don't make it long in this field."

"You're entitled to your opinion on integrity, but I think you're the last person to be giving me advice considering you spent the night a jail for breaking the law."

Olivia's blood started to boil. Who did Emily think she was? She wasn't playing fair, but she'd gotten this far. She decided to challenge her.

"I know exactly why you're here," Olivia said.

"I told you, I want-"

"You want my job." She stared up at her, realizing if Emily wanted to she could probably take her out without breaking a sweat. "Good luck with that." Olivia stepped back to shut the door.

Emily leaned into the door to stop it from closing. "With the way things are going, I don't think I'm going to need luck."

Olivia pulled the door back open again, wondering if Emily might be right, but she couldn't resist learning what her true intentions were. "Why did you really come here? You didn't actually think you'd get my notes, did you?"

Emily laughed. It was an evil sound that came deep from within her. Her entire personality seemed to change.

"You don't fool me for a second, Olivia. Somewhere deep down I know you felt proud that your story ran, even if it did have my name on it. I'd be willing to bet you pored over every precious word you wrote. So, I thought you might have something else you'd like to offer to the world. I thought I'd be doing you a favor by giving you the opportunity to continue sharing your ideas and seeing them in print. After all, at the end of the day you're still Olivia Penn...*the* Olivia Penn. People cherish the words you write, especially The Punisher."

62

Olivia tossed and turned all night, but it wasn't the strange encounter with Emily that kept her awake. The nightmares triggered by Stacy's disappearance had returned. She couldn't get them out of her head.

The only highlight of her day was seeing her latest article above the fold. Duncan had run with it. She'd spent the rest of her day screening phone calls from media around the country, wanting to interview her. They all wanted to know more, but she didn't want to be bothered. She hadn't even been able to talk to Terry when he'd called.

Olivia felt completely drained, defeated. Despite the high from her article being published, the only thing she could bring herself to do was sit on the couch. She was relieved when Cameron came home early from work and sat down next to her. She needed to talk. His brown leather brief case slipped to his feet. He looked handsome in his white button-down and khaki slacks.

"Saw your article this morning," he said, a disapproving tone in his voice. "It's all anyone can talk about. And thanks you to, Washington is in a state of pandemonium. I thought you agreed to take this time to rest."

"Please don't start in on me," she said. "Not now."

"Look at you. You're a wreck. You haven't even gotten out of your pajamas today."

She pulled her knees to her chest and wrapped her arms around her shins. "I don't have the energy to argue about this right now."

"I don't want to argue with you either, but I would appreciate some honesty." He sat up straight and looked down at her. "Why didn't you tell me you were working on a story? Especially one this big. Do you know how embarrassing it is to have friends and co-workers come up to me all day, asking me questions, and I have no idea what they're talking about. Until I pick up a copy of the Post. No more secrets, Liv. Sometimes I feel as though I don't know you any more."

"I wasn't intentionally trying to keep anything from you. I knew you'd react this way."

"I'm worried, that's all." He stood up and untucked his shirt. "You're all over the place these days."

"I just started writing the story on impulse and couldn't stop. It's a theory I've been working on for a long time, and I finally had enough pieces of the puzzle to go public with it. People have a right to know. I sent it to Duncan and didn't expect him to run my by-line since I'm suspended."

"Why not?" He paced back and forth in front of the couch. "It's a huge story. Duncan isn't the type to take credit for your work. You knew that when you sent it to him."

"I don't know what else to say. Why are you so angry?"

"I'm not angry."

"Yes, you are," she said. "Can we please talk about something else?"

"Fine, but we're not through talking about this." He pinched the bridge of his nose and squinted.

Olivia stretched her legs out and sat up straight. She let him stew in silence for a minute before she said, "I had another dream about Stacy. More like a nightmare."

"Oh. What was it about?" Cameron sat back down beside her.

She rubbed her temples. "It was awful...so real. It was the kind of dream that makes you never want to close your eyes again."

"Do you want to talk about it?"

"Maybe," she said. "I don't know."

"What do you think triggered it?" He kicked his shoes off and sat down again. "Besides stress."

Olivia's eyebrows furrowed. She couldn't think of what to say.

"I had a flashback of that night I thought I saw her on the street and chased after her." Olivia played with her hair, pulling it down around her ears. "Maybe that had something to do with it."

He leaned forward and began to stroke the back of her head. "It's okay if you don't want to talk about it."

"No. No. I do. I'm just trying to get past this knot in my throat. I was on the street again, waiting for the light to turn so I could cross. There was a crowd of people, and I looked over. That's when I saw her. But this time it really *was* Stacy."

Cameron gave a supportive nod.

"She looked great, and she was talking to other people around her with a huge smile on her face." Olivia paused for a moment. "I walked up to her and called her name several times before she turned to look at me. It was like I wasn't even surprised to see her, but I was, if that makes sense."

"Hmmm…"

"She just stared at me with a blank expression for the longest time."

"She didn't recognize you?" he asked.

Olivia bit her lip. "No, she didn't. She was Stacy, but she wasn't."

"Then what happened?"

"I realized that I finally had her back, yet she was still gone…and I remember that my heart literally felt like it had stopped. Everything stood still for a moment, and I couldn't breathe."

"Oh, Liv. I'm sorry. I know this is hard for you."

She sunk back into the couch. "What do you think it means? Do you think maybe she's still alive and I'm sensing it?"

"You miss her, and you're still grieving for your best friend."

The tears finally came and crawled down her cheeks. Cameron pulled her into his arms and held her in silence. "You have to find a way to let her go."

"But what if she's still out there? What if she's alive?"

"Don't do this," Cameron pleaded. "It's only going to make things worse."

63

Olivia didn't know how to feel about what her husband had just said. How could things possibly get any worse? She pulled away and propped herself up on the opposite side of the couch. "I don't have enough answers. It's not just Stacy. I know she was in love with Senator Price, and he disappeared that same night. What do you think happened to him?"

"We've been over this. He's probably dead. Or maybe he's living it up on some deserted island. Just because they both disappeared at the same time doesn't mean the two are related."

"Maybe, but you have to admit it would make sense if they were," she said. "I just want to know the truth."

"I don't blame you. You're not the only one."

"I know what you're thinking," she said.

"Oh." Cameron played with his lips.

"That I should be over it already."

"You've suffered some huge losses in your life. I'm empathetic."

"But?" Her eyebrow raised.

"But nothing," he said. "I think it's healthy for you to talk about it and feel what you feel."

"Talk but not obsess."

"I didn't say that." He pushed himself toward the edge of the couch and looked into her eyes.

"She just vanished into thin air," Olivia said. "I still have questions."

"That's completely normal."

Her shoulders slumped and her gaze fixed on the floor.

"Do you think when her body is eventually found you'll finally find some closure?" Cameron asked.

"*If* her body is ever found," she said, "but yes – until it is I'll always have some lingering doubts."

Cameron got up and walked toward the kitchen. "Coffee?"

"Sure, why not?" She scratched her head. "Actually, I think what I could really use is a glass of wine."

"Wine it is, then." He smiled and turned away.

Minutes later, Olivia heard the pop of the cork then a sound that she'd grown accustomed to over the last two years of their marriage as a wine glass crashed to the floor. She smiled thinking how many things Cameron had broken in the past. How could one person break so many things?

"Oops," he said. "Don't worry, I'll clean it up."

Her eyes were still fixed on the floor when he returned and handed her a glass of red wine. She took it but didn't look at it.

He cleared his throat. "When you went to Stacy's apartment that morning..."

"The door was ajar, the lights were on, and her purse, keys, and wallet were still on the counter."

"What about her cell phone?"

"I didn't see it. She must have taken it with her."

"You said there was no sign of the clothes she had on when you were at dinner the night before," he said.

"That's right." She palmed the glass. "She must have thought she was coming right back to her apartment – because women don't typically go anywhere without their purses." She had to have known the person she went to meet and thought she was coming right back.

"Or, maybe she set it up to look like she'd been abducted." Cameron took a long sip of his wine. "But why would she do that?"

"If she meant to escape, then she was running from something. Or someone."

"She wouldn't have gotten too far without any money or identification," he said.

Olivia turned to look at her husband. "You and I both know that arrangements can be made. Maybe she had enough cash and another form of ID to get where she needed to go."

"Or perhaps things are exactly as they appear to be," he said.

64

Olivia knew something Cameron didn't, but she'd been afraid to tell him. Now was the time. "Stacy was writing a memoir, and I think she was planning to blackmail Senator Price."

"What?" Cameron stood up and began to pace the floor. "How do you know *that*?"

"I found a CD last week when I went through an old box of her personal things. She hid it in a Miles Davis CD case. After I helped her parents pack up her belongings, they told me to keep anything I wanted, and the CD was in the box."

"So her memoir's on the disk?" he asked.

"Two hundred pages of it."

Cameron stopped pacing. "I wonder why the police didn't find it on her lap top."

"She either didn't save it on her hard drive or they weren't looking for it," she said. "Stacy had never mentioned she'd been writing a memoir, but I think she wanted me to find it."

"Why do you say that?"

"Because she hid it in a CD case I loaned to her. She left a clue."

"What do you mean?"

"The CD had a post-it attached to it in Stacy's handwriting," Olivia said. "It said, 'don't blame me,' which just happens to be the title of a song on that CD."

"What do you think it means?"

"I have no idea, but I intend to find out."

"Imagine finding something this big after all this time," Cameron said. "Obviously the articles you wrote were substantial enough to win you a Pulitzer, but if you had included excerpts from her memoir…"

"Don't you get it?" Olivia's tone shifted. "The Pulitzer doesn't mean anything to me. Never did. It doesn't replace Stacy, and it certainly won't bring her back. Plus, I'd never expose her life like that, even if I'd had this information then. You know I'm ruthless when it comes to getting my stories, but there are some things I would never do. Selling out a friend is one of them."

Cameron stopped cold in his tracks. "I'm sorry," he said. He seemed unsure of what to say next. He stared at the untouched glass of wine in her hand. "Are you going to drink that?" he asked. "Because personally I could use another one after hearing all of this."

"Oh, yeah." She took a sip and puckered at the tannins.

"So what now?" He brought the bottle over from the kitchen and poured himself another. "I'm assuming you've handed it over to the police."

"Yes, I printed off a copy and gave the disk to the FBI."

"I wonder if they'll re-open the case."

"As far as I'm concerned it was never closed."

He sipped his wine and looked up suddenly. "Is there anything you haven't told me?"

She didn't say anything.

"There is something else, isn't there?" he asked. "Liv?"

"Okay. Okay." Olivia couldn't look him in the eye. "I haven't told anyone this because I really didn't want to believe it at first. Stacy was in love with Price…and she wrote about Price's idea of fantasies of having her kill his wife so she could be with him. The title of her memoir – *Holiday*—was symbolic of the place where Stacy was supposed to help him kill his wife by drugging her and pushing her overboard off a cruise ship in Alaska."

"Wow, that's unbelievable." Cameron gulped hard.

Olivia played with her glass. "The only thing I'm certain of is that she was not the person I thought she was. I never really knew her at all."

"I'm sorry." He walked over and put his hand on her shoulder. "You didn't feel you could trust anyone with this information until now? Even me?"

"No, I just haven't been able to process it," she said. "I just found out. And if the FBI does re-open the case, her parents will know who she *really* was. Stacy wouldn't have wanted that."

"Liv, you did a good thing by giving it to the authorities," he said. "Maybe they'll find something in it that could help them solve the case."

"I hope so." They sat in silence for several minutes.

"Do you think anyone else knew about the memoir?" he asked.

She nodded. "Yes. If she's dead, maybe that's why."

"I'd really like to read it," Cameron said. "Do you really think it's possible that Stacy's still alive?"

"I'm beginning to believe it might be true," she said, swirling the wine around in her glass. She sat mesmerized, watching the legs run down the glass.

"Maybe Stacy faked her death and is roaming the streets of D.C. as The Punisher."

"That's crazy, Cameron. I can't believe you'd say something like that." But something deep within her began to entertain the idea. Especially since Terry had suggested the same thing.

She knew she needed to speak with Sarah again, to find out more about the conversation they'd had the night Stacy disappeared.

Before she did that, she planned to comb through Stacy's memoir one more time. If Stacy had left it for Olivia to find, there must be a clue to her disappearance she'd overlooked. She'd find it, no matter how long it took.

65

Sure enough, the next morning Olivia found what she'd overlooked the first time she'd sifted through Stacy's memoir. Cameron had left a note on the kitchen counter she found while making coffee. He'd gone to the hospital for a couple of hours, which meant she had some time to herself.

After re-reading her friend's fantasies of how she'd like to kill Price's wife and details of their sordid three-year love affair, she came to the part where Stacy talked about being raped.

But it wasn't Price's name she mentioned. It was someone called Sam Camp. Stacy described Sam as a childhood friend she'd reconnected with in D.C. by shear coincidence. He'd become obsessed with her after they'd gone out a few times. Then she'd started dating Price, who had swept her off her feet and made her forget about Sam. Stacy's entry about Sam stalking her chilled Olivia to the bone.

Stacy wrote: "I heard a noise while I was in the shower but thought it was my air conditioning crackling again. The next thing I knew my shower curtain had been ripped open and Sam stood there, completely naked. He had an odd look in his eye I'd never seen before. I couldn't move. I think I was in shock and very terrified. He ripped me from the warm comfort of the water and threw me down on the cold bathroom floor. All I remember is the initial pain of him forcing himself inside me. Then I blocked it all out and thought to myself – this isn't happening.

I'm not really here. This is all a dream, and I can wake up any time. I will wake up soon. Wake up. Wake up.

I don't recall him beating me afterward. I didn't feel it until I looked in the mirror and saw the blood all over my face. The last thing I remember was Sam's breath on my face and his threatening tone when he said, "If you don't leave the Senator, you'll be sorry. I'll chop you into tiny little pieces. The police will never be able to identify you, even if they do find what's left of you." Then he left me there. At that moment not only did I want to curl up and die, but I thought I was already dead.

Sam Camp was the kid in Stacy's sixth-grade picture whose face had been rubbed out. The name Sam also appeared on a book of matches found in Stacy's purse that she'd only bought a month before she'd disappeared. What had happened after she'd left Stacy that night?

Olivia suddenly felt sick to her stomach, thinking about what had happened to her friend. Was the rape really true or had Stacy made it all up? The thought of Stacy being chopped up into little pieces made Olivia's stomach rise to her throat. She wanted nothing more than for this to all be a bad dream. And when she woke up, Stacy would be there, Patrick would be there, and life would be the way it was supposed to be.

66

Finally Olivia pulled herself together, and she decided it was time to talk to Sarah and find out more about the conversation she'd had with Stacy that last night. Sarah's answering machine picked up her call, but a minute later she rang back.

"Olivia, I've been thinking about you. There's someone here I'd like for you to meet," Sarah's smile could be heard in her voice. "His birth mother had him about a week early."

"It's a boy?" Olivia's heart dropped.

"Yes, and he's perfect."

Why would Sarah want to rub it in her face that she didn't have a son and Sarah did?

"That's great, Sarah. Congratulations. I'm really happy for you."

"I was hoping maybe you'd be able to drop by some time and say hello."

"Actually, I'm free now." The last thing Olivia wanted to do was to go see Sarah's new baby and be reminded of her own loss, but she desperately needed some answers. "I was hoping we could chat some more about Stacy's phone call to you that night."

Sarah was quiet. "Sure. It's funny you brought that up because after your last visit, I started thinking about it again, and I do remember some other things she said. Not sure if they'd be helpful or not. It haunted me for a long time, but then I sort of put it out of my mind."

"I understand. Whatever you can tell me will be helpful. Can I swing by in the next hour? Around eleven?" Adrenaline swept through Olivia.

"Sure, that's fine."

Forty minutes later Olivia arrived at Sarah's home. She spent the ride over trying to mentally prepare herself for seeing Sarah's new baby and all of Patrick's things again. *This is a good thing*, she told herself. *A family in need, and Patrick's baby things put to good use.* She tried to focus on the reason she was there.

Sarah greeted her at the front door, smiling ear to ear, cradling her baby boy in Patrick's blanket. Olivia had a hard time looking at him, even though he was completely covered up from his head to his tiny toes, but she tried to muster a smile.

The scent of baby powder on his newborn skin teased her nose. When she entered the living room she had an overwhelming sensation that Patrick was alive, and her heart, though it wanted to burst, felt a joy she hadn't felt in a long time.

Sarah stayed quiet and so did her baby as Olivia examined the room. She shut the door and swayed back and forth.

"Would you like to hold him?" Sarah finally asked, even though the silence didn't feel awkward to Olivia.

"Oh, I don't know…"

"Here, you'll be fine." Sarah walked over, reached out and put the baby in Olivia's arms.

Olivia had to catch her breath as she held the precious being against her body. She peeked at his peaceful, sleeping face and thought of her son again. How peaceful he'd looked when she'd held him in her arms the day she'd given birth. Then they'd taken him away, and she'd had to bury him.

"He's beautiful, Sarah. What a gift." Olivia smiled away the tears. "What's his name?"

"We named him Patrick, after your little boy," Sarah said.

Olivia's jaw dropped. How sweet. "I don't know what to say." Olivia could no longer hold back the tears.

"I hope that's okay," Sarah said. "We just really liked the name and felt it was the perfect fit. You did such a wonderful and selfless thing by giving us *your* Patrick's things, and we just didn't think any other name would work."

Olivia thought her heart was going to explode. "Thank you. Thank you. You have no idea how much this means to me, and I know Cameron will be so touched."

She looked down at the baby in her arms and rocked him gently. Patrick. Even though he wasn't hers, he was truly a gift to all of them. She reflected for a moment on how Sarah and Rob's lives had become connected with Cameron and hers, and how odd it was that Sarah had known Stacy long before she had. She was glad her path had crossed Sarah's.

"If you want, I can put him down and we can talk," Sarah said.

"Sure." Olivia handed Patrick back to his mother and followed Sarah into a small dining area off of the living room after she'd laid him in the crib.

"Sorry, the place is such a mess," Sarah began. "We're pretty tight on space right now, but we make do." She had a lovely smile. "Can I get you anything to drink or eat?"

"No, I'm fine, thank you. I appreciate you letting me come by." Olivia squirmed in her seat. She hadn't even noticed the clutter, which normally would have bothered her. "I need to know more about your last conversation with Stacy. You said you remembered something else she said?"

"Yes, I think she called around eleven that night, and she sounded wasted." Sarah looked away. "I was asleep, kind of out of it when she called, but we talked for a few minutes. I really didn't think much of it, Stacy always used to drunk dial me…but now that I think about it, I think she was upset."

"Yeah, she was." Olivia flashed back to when she dropped her off and regretted leaving her that night.

"She said something about getting another note from her stalker, and that was it."

217

"Someone was stalking her?" Fear shot through Olivia's veins. Why hadn't Stacy told her this? Was there any chance it might be the same person who was stalking Olivia?

"I'm not sure, I hadn't talked to her in a while," Sarah said. "I didn't even know she had a boyfriend until she said he'd stood her up. Then, like I told you, she said if anything ever happened to her he wouldn't be responsible for it. That's such a weird thing to say now that I think about it. I should have told the police. Maybe it would've helped."

"Don't worry, I have a feeling it's not too late," Olivia said. "Do you recall her saying anything else?"

"I don't remember. Our conversation got cut short because she told me her boyfriend was beeping in on the other line and she had to go. Then she hung up on me."

So Senator Price *did* end up calling Stacy that night? Maybe Stacy ran away with him after all. Had she blackmailed him with her memoir or had she told Price about her stalker and pleaded for help to get away? The note Stacy received that night at dinner must have been from her stalker. Was it Sam? Olivia shuddered at the thought.

She needed to find this Sam. He was the key. He'd know if Stacy was dead or alive!

67

Olivia's head was still spinning when she got back home. A package rested on her front steps. She picked it up and went inside. She wasn't expecting anything, but maybe Cameron had ordered something.

Her husband got off the couch and greeted her with a hug and kiss when he saw her. "There you are," he said. "I was wondering where you went. Sorry I missed you this morning – I went to the hospital for a little while, and didn't want to wake you. You looked so peaceful."

"It's been a crazy day." She walked over and put the cardboard box down on the kitchen table.

"Dare I ask?" His expression grew somber.

She grabbed his hand and led him back to the couch. "Well, I finished reading Stacy's memoir this morning and learned some very interesting details of her life."

"When do I get to read it?"

"You probably should look at it, so you can put your psychological profile together – of a person I never really knew." Olivia nestled under his shoulder. "This feels nice, just being in your arms." She tilted her head and kissed him on the cheek.

They sat in silence for a moment. "What else did you do today?"

"I went and saw Sarah again," she said.

"You did? Why?"

"Stacy called her the night she disappeared, and I wanted to ask her more about it." Olivia told him what Sarah had said about their last conversation and about Price's late night phone call to Stacy. "After everything I read in the memoir and learned today about her stalker, I actually think she might still be alive."

"Here we go again…"

"Cameron, please. New things are beginning to surface, information that the police didn't have before. Maybe there is still a chance of finding her. And Price."

"It's surfacing because you're digging it all back up again." He stood up, walked into the kitchen and poured a glass of water from the Brita in the fridge. She followed him. He turned to her and sighed. "Okay, Detective Penn…maybe your hunch is right. Maybe Stacy is alive. Who can really say?"

Olivia ran her hand across the dry cardboard surface of the generic-looking package.

"What's in the box?" Cameron took a long sip of water.

"I don't know. Did you order something?"

"Nope."

"Hmmm…that's odd, there's no return address, but it's addressed to me." She wondered what it was. A gift? "Will you hand me that pair of scissors over there by the knives?"

Cameron turned around, retrieved the scissors, and she cut through the clear packing tape around the sides of the box. He stood over her shoulder, and when she opened the two flaps, they both gasped and stepped back, horrified by what they saw.

68

Olivia stood in their kitchen and looked at Cameron. The ghosts of Senator Sterling Price and Stacy haunted her as she stared, wide-eyed at a picture of the two of them holding hands and smiling at each other. The photo was taken from behind, but caught a moment when they had turned and looked at each other. There was no mistaking it was them. Whoever had taken it had been following them. A stalker?

"There's a note, too." When he picked it up a man's wedding band fell out and rolled across the floor. Olivia chased after it and suddenly felt sick to her stomach. Instantly, she knew it belonged to Price and had been sent as a message. As Cameron began to read the note, Olivia walked closer and noticed the writing on the backside. Once again, the same handwriting and stationery that she'd seen at the Lincoln crime scene and on Stacy's note.

Another quote the killer left as a clue? Was The Punisher responsible?

Cameron read out loud. "It says, 'I've been a bad boy, and I deserve to die.'" He hesitated and looked at Olivia.

"What? What else does it say?"

"Liv, I'm so sorry...."

"Tell me. What is it?" But she knew. She already knew what it said.

"It says, 'And Stacy does too.'"

She suddenly felt possessed. "That's it! I've had enough! Who does this freak of nature think he is, and why is he screwing with my life? What does he want from me?"

"I'm calling Nathan at the FBI and Rex," she said, her voice steady. She wasn't ready to give in to the pain she felt at the moment. "I need to see the note. There's a quote on the back, and I want to see if it could be linked to the Punisher, especially since the line about deserving to die already does."

"Liv, are you okay?"

She looked him in the eye. "I will be. As soon as I find out the truth – about everything and how it's linked to me."

Rex arrived a half an hour later, but he stayed out of the way when Nathan and the other federal agents came in to examine the evidence. Olivia knew he was there for her, not the crime. She introduced Cameron to Rex and Nathan, and watched her husband walk away with Nathan to answer the agent's questions.

"Are you all right?" Rex asked when they were alone.

"I think so," she said. She kept her eye on the scene in her living room.

"I can't imagine how shocking this must have been for both of you." He put his hand on her shoulder. "Is there anything I can do?"

Olivia turned and looked at him. "You can help me find The Punisher."

"You know it's out of my hands now. The FBI is handling this."

"But someone is stalking me, just like he did Stacy. And I think she really is dead."

"We don't know that."

"The note in the box indicated she probably was. I'm almost certain it's from The Punisher. And if that's Price's wedding ring, which would make sense given the symbolism and fitting the killer's M.O. on infidelity...then where is his body? I just hope it doesn't end up on my doorstep too." How had she gotten so close to the terror? Was she next?

69

That evening after the madness died down, she and Cameron made sure all the doors and windows were secure. They stood in the kitchen, and she wrapped her arms around his waist and buried her head into his chest.

"You were incredible this afternoon," he said. "You took charge of the situation and made things happen. I'm proud of you. I know how difficult this is for you right now."

"Something just clicked in me."

"You're probably exhausted after everything that's happened today. Why don't I make us some dinner?"

She smiled. "Can we make it a late dinner? I think I just need some time to decompress."

"You're a terrible liar, you know that?" He kissed her on the nose and backed away. "Tell you what…I know all you want to do is retreat to your office and write your next story so you can get it to Duncan before press time. It'll run on the front page of the Sunday Post."

She crinkled her nose. He knew her too well.

"Since I don't have the energy to argue with you right now, I'll give you some space and go read Stacy's memoir. I'm intrigued. Let me know when you decide to come up for air."

"Thanks," she said and turned to walk upstairs. "I'll bring you the copy I printed out."

The only thing Olivia wanted to do was write. She needed to express what had just happened. After leaving Duncan a message about the breaking news, she sat down and got to work. Being in her office instantly put her at ease.

Somehow she was able to remove herself from the emotion of recent hours and days. She didn't want to think about Stacy being dead. It was easier to imagine that she'd run away.

The story was easy to write since she'd lived it. It was difficult to write because she included the contents of the letter and, for the first time, was revealing that her friend was also probably a victim of The Punisher, along with Senator Sterling Price.

70

The next afternoon, Olivia and Cameron sat snuggled on the couch watching an episode of Antique Roadshow when the doorbell rang. Olivia could sense Cameron's annoyance when he opened the front door to find a strange man on the doorstep. She was surprised that Terry hadn't called first, but she was still glad to see him. They had a lot to talk about.

"Is Olivia here?" Terry asked. "I'm a friend of hers – Terry Carson."

"Right, you used to be with the FBI," Cameron said politely.

Olivia walked to the front door when she heard his voice and let him in. "This is my husband Cameron." The two shook hands.

"I see you've seen the Post this morning," she said, noticing the copy of her article in his hand.

"Sure did," Terry said. "I was in the neighborhood. Thought I'd take a chance and stop by. You free?"

Cameron gave her a disapproving look, which Terry respectfully ignored.

"I am, we were just watching television, but I have something I want to show you," she said. "Why don't you come up to my office and we can catch up?" She tilted her head and smiled at Cameron. Her eyes said, thank you for understanding.

He plopped back down on the couch and didn't say another word.

Olivia led Terry up the narrow wooden staircase to her office and invited him to sit down in the leather recliner parallel to her desk. She spent the next hour filling him in on the contents of Stacy's memoir, showing him her sixth-grade photo with Sam and Monica, told him about the book of matches with Sam's name and number on it and the contents of the letter that came with the Senator Price's wedding ring and incriminating photos.

"That was smart of you to write it down before the FBI took it."

"There was another quote on the back of the letter," she said. "I'm convinced it's another clue, but I have no idea what they all mean."

Terry thought for a moment. "This killer is toying with you," he began. "He knows you're looking for him or he wouldn't have sent you something so important."

"I think the key is to find out who Sam Camp is."

"The kid in Stacy's class photo?" He picked up the picture and studied it. "I agree. Do you know where Stacy's from? I want to track down some of her old classmates and see what I can find out about Sam."

Olivia had to think for a minute. "She grew up in Granbury, Texas. It's just so bizarre that she knew Monica Habershamm at one time. If Sam is The Punisher or involved in some way, he's known at least two of his victims since childhood."

71

The next morning Rex paid Olivia a visit. She was still in her pajamas, cup of coffee in hand when she answered the door.

"What are you doing here at this hour?" she asked and bent down to pick up the Post on her doorstep.

"Can I come in?" He looked solemn. "I have something I need to tell you."

"Sure, come on in. You want a cup of coffee or something?"

"No, I'm fine. Can we sit down?"

"You look like you've seen a ghost," she said, worried. They both took a seat at the dining room table.

"I'm not sure how to tell you this…but-"

"Is Cameron okay? Did something happen to him?"

"No, he's fine."

"Okay, what is it?"

"At about five-thirty this morning a man walking his dog came across two bodies in Rock Creek Park."

"Oh no…Stacy?"

"We don't know yet." Rex sighed. "The bodies are badly decomposed."

Olivia tried to relax the tension in her shoulders.

"But I did overhear that one of the bodies is thought to be female."

Olivia held the warm coffee cup in her hands and let the heat soothe her. How had these bodies suddenly turned up after two years…and a day after she'd received that package in the mail?

"How did you know about this if the FBI is working the case?"

"The 911 call came across on the scanner this morning, and when I heard it, I called Nathan and went to check it out. Pretty gruesome scene."

"Do you know anything else?" She was thankful he was there with her and the one who'd delivered the news. He was a good friend, and even if he didn't get emotional, she knew he understood what this news meant to her, and she appreciated that he'd done it in person.

She closed her eyes, attempting to push away the visions of Stacy's body in Rock Creek Park for the past two years.

"I think we have to accept the fact that Stacy might have met her end two years ago and that their deaths were connected." He reached across the table and placed his hand on hers. "You may finally have the real story. I'm sorry."

72

Nathan was looking forward to meeting up with Steve and a couple of friends in Annapolis for the weekend. He couldn't wait to take his boat out and relax, dine on some crabs and indulge in more than a few beers. Nathan almost wished he had a girlfriend he could take along. He wasn't sure why Olivia Penn popped into his mind.

First, he needed to get to the FBI lab and see if there were any new results on the The Punisher's murders. He figured the lab technician, Seth Rider, would be in his usual mid-week dramatics, but this visit couldn't wait any longer. Seth had on a pair of skin-tight black jeans and a muscle t-shirt, minus the muscles. The attire didn't leave much to the imagination. His hair was black with highlights that were in need of maintenance, pushed back by a silver sequined headband that matched his flip-flops.

"Oh, do I have lots to tell you." Seth looked up from filing his nails and delicately put both hands up to his cheeks. "You're going to want to sit down for this Nate."

"I'm ready when you are." Nathan grabbed his pen from behind his ear and opened his notepad.

"You know Seth loves you because I was able to push some of your DNA results through in record time."

"I really appreciate it," Nathan said. "I can see how busy you are."

"Yes, well anything for you…but you should know that I have DNA test results backed up from last year."

"I'm glad you appreciate the urgency and the delicate nature of this case." Nathan smiled.

"Okay, let's begin with the wedding ring."

"Pretty sure it belonged to Senator Price based on his wife's identification and photos. But since we just got the body, it'll take a little more time for the lab results. I'm working all the magic I can, but unfortunately I'm not Houdini."

"Now about the tennis player and the Secretary," Seth said. "Unfortunately no other DNA samples were found except the two women's. I mean this guy was good. Martha Stewart during spring cleaning good."

Nathan scratched his head and frowned.

"The most disturbing part is that both bodies revealed evidence that they *were* sexually abused, more than likely post-mortem. Oooh." Seth made a face.

"Really?" The thought sickened Nathan. He originally thought the killer hadn't gone that far. He remembered how the bodies had been staged. Pretty typical serial killer behavior – sex post mortem. Nathan looked up from his notes and realized that Seth was staring at him. "What else can you tell me?" Nathan asked.

"Well. We found two sets of DNA on Brendan Campbell's clothing, and we were able to rule out his wife and the passenger from the slug line who opted to take his chances dancing in the streets."

"What does that mean?" Nathan swiveled back and forth on the stool.

"What it means is that it's likely this killer has an accomplice."

"Interesting, since serials typically work alone."

"Apparently not this one," Seth said.

"And what was the cause of death on Brendan Campbell?"

"That's the most peculiar part. He was poisoned."

Nathan put his hand on the counter to steady himself. He certainly wanted to make sure this victim suffered, but why? This murder was different. No blood, but complete humiliation. The biggest mystery was how he got the body to a public place like the Lincoln

Memorial. The killer wanted to demonstrate how powerful he was, to show the world he was in control. He certainly was, and Nathan wondered who would be next. Again, Olivia Penn came to mind.

73

Benjamin Funkhouser sat in his bedroom in front of his computer, reflecting on his latest message to Olivia. The sounds of Joni Mitchell's song about "clouds getting in the way," remained on repeat.

Thankfully, the smell of his Subway meatball sandwich disguised the stench from the New Balance tennis shoes he'd just removed. He leaned back in his chair, clasped his hands behind his head and smiled. It was almost time to complete his plan. He'd been very patient.

He knew his diligence would be worth the wait. He had Olivia right where he wanted her, and he felt proud of himself and the self-discipline he'd exhibited all these months. His brilliance would be fully appreciated soon enough. He read his latest message over and over, savoring every word and the satisfaction that was soon to be his.

Dear Ms. Penn,

It's been a while since I wrote. I've been busy. I consider it a compliment that you published my emails weeks ago. Now I'm a published writer like you. I always knew we'd have a lot in common. I understand you're suspended from work, yet you managed a way to still have your voice heard. I admire that about you, always have. The way you follow your heart and don't let anything or anyone get in the way. I wonder what you do now, with so much time on your hands. I wonder if you think of me, while you're home, alone. I think it's time we meet. I'll be in touch. I remain, Your Biggest Fan.

The fact that the FBI was surveying the library didn't faze him. At least anymore. He'd still found a way to reach Olivia, even though it took some creativity and unforeseen risks. But, by the time his latest message got traced, it would be too late.

74

Olivia got up early with Cameron that morning and made coffee while he made omelets. Then they'd gone back to bed and made love. She let herself go and melt into him. The intimate feeling lingered with her long after he kissed her goodbye for the long weekend. He was traveling to Boston for work and would be gone for three days, and even though she was looking forward to the uninterrupted time, she would miss him.

For the next several hours she enjoyed the silence of her office... until Benjamin's email came through. She clutched her stomach as she read it, a wave of nausea hitting her. Immediately she forwarded it to Nathan and debated whether or not to tell Cameron because the last thing she'd want him to do was postpone his business trip and lecture her again.

She was in her bathroom getting ready for the day when the next email came through. It was from Nathan, and it shocked her. It read: We may have a new lead in The Punisher's case. How are things with you? Run across anything I should know about?

The message indicated that he had sent it five hours prior. Strange. For some reason the email had just come through. When the doorbell rang, she wondered if it was Nathan, coming to deliver his news in person. She left her iPhone on the bathroom counter and walked downstairs. She noticed that the afternoon sun had invited itself in and warmed up the living room. Shielding her eyes from the brightness, she smiled. When she opened the door, she was greeted with a gorgeous arrangement of flowers.

"What's this?" She beamed.

"Hello, I have a delivery for you," a voice called from behind the bouquet. A young man with a Washington National's ball cap and clean-cut brown hair peeked around the flowers. He had a very nice grin.

"For me? Do you know who they're from?"

"No, but I think there's a card." He almost fell backward down the concrete steps.

"Oh, watch your step." Olivia reached out a hand to help steady him. She couldn't help but gush. "They must be from my husband. He's so sweet."

"Uh-huh."

"So many beautiful flowers. Roses, daisies, and I love tulips." She reached out and touched a yellow one. The aroma of soil and spring filled her nose. "I'm not sure if I can carry those. They look really heavy."

"They are." He stood there awkwardly until she waved him in.

"Okay, watch your step. You can put them right over there on the dining room table. Thanks."

"No problem," he said, his voice strained.

She watched the young man, who looked like he couldn't have been more than eighteen, waddle carefully over toward the kitchen. She scanned the living area for the spot where she always left her purse. It was lying on the floor, open-mouthed, like a hooked fish.

"I really appreciate your help," she said. "I would have dropped it."

"Yeah, it is a little heavy."

"I'd like to give you something for your efforts." She dug in her purse for some money.

"That won't be necessary." He placed the massive vase down, carefully arranging it in the middle of the dark wooden table. "There, I think it looks good right here."

"Yes it does. Thank you so much." She walked toward him with a five dollar bill pressed into the palm of her hand. "Please, take this. You certainly deserve it."

His eyes lit up. As he reached for the bill in her extended hand, his skin touched hers and felt warm and clammy.

"Thanks a lot." He grinned.

"You're very welcome." He seemed like a nice young man. She imagined he had a beautiful girlfriend and was attending college somewhere in the area, delivering flowers part-time.

"Enjoy your flowers." He made his way to the door. "I'll let myself out."

"Have a good one." Olivia bent over to smell the arrangement and took in the beauty. Suddenly she felt an overwhelming urge to call Cameron and thank him. She was semi-aware of the front door shutting softly behind her.

She found the card buried in the myriad of floral wonder and rescued it from the snares of the rose thorns. Delicately pulling it from the tiny paper envelope, she looked forward to the loving words from Cameron.

Instead, her heart felt like it had just been pierced. The card said, *Enjoy. From, Your Biggest Fan.* She found it impossible to breathe, and then the breathing came too fast. She stood there for what seemed like hours, letting the words sink in. An eerie, unsettling feeling washed over her as she sensed another presence in the room.

Slowly, she turned around. A shiver ran through her body and made her cringe. The sun had retreated behind some clouds and darkness now enveloped the room. That's when she saw him. Still standing there. Watching her.

75

The young man who'd delivered her flowers locked the front door and stood there. His startling presence had turned the safe haven of her home into a place she feared. What did he want? Who was he? Instinctively she experienced remorse for the brief amount of time she'd chosen to let her guard down. Now she was vulnerable. How could she have been so blind?

"What do you want?" she demanded.

He stood still, saying nothing.

"What do you want?" she repeated. "Who are you?"

The young man, who moments before had been so obliging to her every request, had taken her by surprise. Inside she was trying her best not to panic as she watched a cryptic grin creep across his boyish cheeks. She backed herself against the kitchen table.

"Answer my questions." Her voice sounded foreign to her. Not strong like she'd tried to make it be.

"Ms. Penn." The young man paused for a moment, took off his baseball hat and ran his fingers through his short brown hair before continuing. "I told you it was time we meet."

"What?" She shook her head and tried to focus. With his hat off, why did he suddenly look familiar?

"Do you like the flowers?" He tilted his head to the side as he approached her, waiting for her response. "I heard they were your favorites."

"Yes." She stood there, inwardly shaking, trying to think of her next move, not registering what he was saying or what was happening. Breathe, she kept telling herself. She refused to believe it as the realization hit her if the man standing in front of her was...The Punisher. No. No. No. He didn't fit the profile, did he?

He walked closer and calmly placed his hat on the kitchen table by the flowers. "How could you not know who I am after all this time? I'm your biggest fan."

Olivia's heart sank. Was this really happening?

"I know what you're thinking," he said. "You're wondering what's going to happen next."

His words made her tremble, reminding her of the note Stacy had received that night. He no longer sounded like the young man who had come to her door pretending to be a delivery person. Was he the same person who stalked Stacy? Was he Sam? Or could it merely be a coincidence that they both had stalkers?

"Is Benjamin your real name?" she asked. She knew she needed to engage him, keep him talking.

He smiled and fingered the flowers in the vase, taking his time to admire several before answering. "Of course not, but that doesn't matter. I just want to talk to you. I feel like I've known you for a long time, but you've never known me."

She slowly moved her way around the table, and he moved with her. "Tell me about yourself," she said.

"I'm a great writer, just like you. And one day I'll be recognized for it, like you have.

Run, she thought. You've got to run and get away. "You don't understand – I didn't expect or want the fame I have...it just happened because my best friend disappeared."

"But that's the beauty of it, and I know all about Stacy," he said. "I used to read her columns too. I know you'll find out what really happened to her one day because that's just you. You won't give up until you do. And Ms. Penn...I know you'll find her."

"How can you be so sure?" Olivia put her hand on the table to steady herself. Was Benjamin dangerous? Had he come to harm her or just talk? "Did you have anything to do with Stacy's disappearance? Do you know something I don't?"

"No." He looked down at the ground. "It's just that I understand how much you hurt. I lost someone I loved too once. I know your pain. I can see it in the haunting ways you tell your stories. I've always admired your work. You're my idol, my inspiration."

"Thank you." She didn't know what else to say. While she knew she should be thinking of how to get out of the house, she was drawn to what he was saying. Why was such an attractive man so desperate? Why had he fixated on her? She felt afraid to make any sudden moves, not sure if he had a weapon or not.

"I'm sorry I broke into your house." He looked down at the floor again. "I just wanted to know more about you and how you lived." He paused. "I think you're wonderful. Don't you see how much we have in common? We're perfect for each other."

Had he lost his mind? He was too young to be having a mid-life crisis.

Caught up in the moment, he moved toward her in a swift movement, grabbed her cheeks in his two hands and kissed her. His passionate embrace was powerful and took her off guard. When his tongue went inside her mouth she pulled away in disgust.

"What are you doing?" She pushed him away and wiped her mouth off with the back of her hand. "What makes you think you can just steal into my home again and assault me like this? I'm married! You should leave before I call the cops." Instantly she regretted her reaction when she saw the look of shock on his face. He looked like a wounded deer. She hadn't wanted to hurt him. She just wanted him to leave. To get out of her house and her life.

76

enjamin began pacing Olivia's kitchen floor. "All this time, I've waited for you to realize we should be together. Why haven't you listened? Why haven't you noticed me, until now?" He stopped and looked at her. "I know if you'd just give me a chance you'd see how right this is."

She needed to get to her phone and call for help, but she had to distract him. "I'm sorry," she said. "You're right." She could visualize her iPhone on the basin in her upstairs bathroom. How was she going to get to it?

"I just want us to be together," he said, moving toward her again.

She didn't move away and stood her ground. As much as he gave her the creeps, she needed for him to trust her. "Maybe you're right, maybe we would be good together."

His face lit up. "Really?"

"I don't know, how do you think you could make me happy?" she asked. Just keep him talking.

"For starters, we could write something together." He took another step closer to her. "You've always wanted to write a book, right? I could help you...even edit if nothing else." He reached out and gently touched her cheek with the back of his right hand. This time she didn't pull away, just cringed inside. "And I know how much you love children and long to have another one. I'm sorry you lost Patrick. But we could make more. As many as you want."

"Maybe it could work," she said over the knot in her throat when she heard Patrick's name. Benjamin was young and naïve. He had no idea what he was talking about. "You're a handsome, intelligent man, and I do want more children-"

"And I love you, Olivia." He looked longingly into her eyes. "I know if you just spent some time with me, you'll see you can love me too."

He was freaking her out. He wasn't some middle-aged pervert. He was a handsome college student who'd become obsessed. Was he harmless? She still needed to figure out a way to get him out of her house because she couldn't physically remove him herself. He needed help, and she had to make him believe she could help him, until help arrived.

She put a hand up to his warm, flushed cheek. "Why don't you open the bottle of white wine in the fridge while I freshen up. Then we can sit down and talk some more. Get to know one another better." She kissed him on the forehead and took a step back.

"Okay, but why the sudden change of heart?" His eyebrows furrowed.

Think fast, Olivia. "My husband's out of town, so this would be the perfect opportunity for us to talk. Maybe work things out."

He smiled. "I like that idea. I don't know much about white wine though. You'll have to teach me."

"That won't be a problem." She winked, trying to play into his fantasy and made her way toward the stairs.

"Don't be long. I'm keeping an eye on you, and this better not be a joke."

"I'll be back in a minute." She gave him a lingering smile. "The wine opener is in the second drawer on the left and the bottle's in the fridge. You might even find some cheese and crackers in there too if you're hungry."

She tried to make the most of the time she had, calmly making her way upstairs to her bathroom. Locking the door behind her, she grabbed her iPhone. A new email from Nathan had come in, the subject said: False alarm on the lead. The Punisher is still out there. She noted the time. The message had been sent hours before. She fumbled to respond

241

and found that her fingers were numb as she typed: Help! Intruder in my house. Could be him. Come quick.

She hit the send button, yearning for an instant response or a miracle of some kind but saw that it returned to her in red. The message didn't go through. She didn't know what to do. Then she heard Benjamin's voice outside the door.

"Are you coming?" He knocked. "What's taking so long?"

"I'm coming…be right there." She was trembling. What was she going to do now? She had no way of calling for help without him knowing.

"You're making me nervous." He rattled the doorknob. "Unlock the door."

"Please, give me another minute," she said.

"What are you doing in there?"

"Trying to clean up." She kept trying to send the email to Nathan and it continued to fail. "I want to look as good as I can for you."

They exchanged an eerie silence. "I don't believe you," he finally said. "You've been up here for a while. If you don't open the door, I'm coming in."

What could she do? Could he really get through the door? She searched frantically through her make-up bag for a weapon and found a metal nail file that she hid in the side strap of her thong underwear. Hopefully she wouldn't have to use it because if she did, she wasn't sure how she would.

She looked at the phone again. Still no signal. Benjamin started kicking in the door, and it flung open suddenly. He was stronger than he looked. She stood against the far wall of the bathroom with the phone still in her hands. It all happened so fast, but she could tell by the glare in his eyes that he was livid.

"What's this? You tricked me? Who did you call?"

"Police," she managed to say. "They're on their way. They'll be here any minute." She prayed he believed her. It was the only thing she could think to do.

77

enjamin grabbed Olivia's arm and yanked her back down the stairs to the kitchen. "I can't believe you called the police! How could you do that?" He threw her down in the kitchen chair, grabbed a butcher knife from the wooden knife holder on the counter, and waved it in front of her.

Think, Olivia. Think. He's scared too. Stay calm.

"I've been pouring my heart out to you for months, to no avail! Why is that? Why would you ignore me, dismiss me, pretend I don't exist?" She could only imagine what he planned to do next. How could she calm him down?

"I'm sorry." She couldn't take her eyes off of the knife.

"Do I scare you?" Tears welled in his eyes. "I just wanted to come here to talk, so you'd know how much I cared about you. You made me think you understood that for a minute. Now this."

"Is your real name Sam?" she asked, trying to keep him talking. "*Are* you The Punisher?" She felt that he wanted to tell her things, and this subject seemed to pique his interest.

"Maybe." He shrugged the suggestion off, but she sensed it flattered him for her to think he had that kind of power.

"How could you have killed all those people?" she said.

He circled her with the knife, seeming unsure of what to do with it but growing angrier by the minute. "You think you have me all figured out," he said. "Well, you don't. You'll never know. You! Are undeserving of the truth. You! Make mockery of the truth."

"I don't know what you mean," she said. "Please. Put the knife down."

"You know exactly what I mean." He grabbed the back of her hair and pressed the knife to her throat.

"I don't. I really don't. Please tell me. What is it you want me to know?"

"You really don't remember, do you?"

She could smell blood. It tickled as it ran down her neck. "Remember what?"

"How we first met," he said.

She wracked her brain for something. Earlier when he'd taken off his baseball hat, she thought he looked familiar. But why?

"Last year," he began, "you spoke at the journalism conference at American University."

She suddenly remembered the event and searched her brain for a memory with him.

"I thought we shared a moment, a special one." He wiped the sweat from his forehead with the sleeve of his shirt and kept the knife firmly against her neck. "After your speech I came up to you and told you how much I admired you and your work. That you'd been an inspiration to my own dreams of writing for the press someday. You told me, 'we have a lot in common' and I believed you. I've been your biggest fan ever since, even though I'd been following you long before.

She scarcely recalled something like that. "I think I was talking about writers, in general."

"That's obvious to me now." He shook his head back and forth in disgust. "I just thought that if we could meet, then you would see how much I loved you. How many things we have in common and that we should be together."

Did he fit the profile of The Punisher? Why had he fixated on her?

"You seem like a very charming man, but this is the wrong way to go about this." She sighed. "Do you really want to spend the rest of your life in jail?"

"No, I wanted to spend the rest of my life with you. But, you've changed everything. Now that can't happen."

She was desperate. "Who says?"

"Please, don't patronize me. Not after everything that's happened."

She didn't know what to say to him. She didn't know how to get through. He backed away for a moment, and she studied him. Something about his eyes triggered a memory, and when he turned and looked at her, she knew.

"You work at the Post, don't you?"

He rolled his eyes. "Only for the past two months."

"I saw you there once." She gasped. "It was the day I got that threatening email on my Message Post. I knew it had to be someone on the inside." She paused. "Did Emily Morgan put you up to that?"

But before he could answer, she heard the sound of a key fumbling in front door. Thank God. Who was it? Just then, the door opened and Cameron walked through. He removed his key from the door and peered in her direction. He wasn't supposed to be home for another three days.

"What's going on here?" He dropped his bag on the floor when he saw a stranger standing over Olivia.

"He's got knife," she said. "Watch out!"

Cameron lunged toward Benjamin with great speed, tackled him to the floor and began punching him, viciously. She screamed as she watched the scene unfold and couldn't comprehend what was happening. The two men struggled like animals on the floor. She saw the knife, still wedged firmly in Benjamin's hand, until he planted it in Cameron's thigh.

Cameron groaned and removed the knife, blood oozing onto the floor. Everywhere. Then, he struck the young man over and over and over in the face, until he was unrecognizable. He picked up the knife, looking ready to kill when Olivia screamed, "Cameron, don't! He's just a kid. He didn't hurt me."

She'd never seen her husband's violent side, nor did she recognize the vindictive look in his eyes when he turned and said, "What's he doing here?"

Tears ran down her face. "Stalking me."

78

Groaning with pain, Cameron put the knife down and rolled off of Benjamin. "This is who's been stalking you?"

"That's what he said." She still couldn't believe it herself.

"How did he manage to get back in our home?"

Tears filled her eyes. "He brought me flowers…and I thought they were from you."

The savage look that had been in his eyes moments before disappeared. Olivia stared in horror at the bloody scene in her kitchen. It appeared Cameron had nearly killed the young man by beating him to death! She couldn't believe it had come to this.

"Cameron, are you okay?" Suddenly she snapped out of her daze and rushed to his side. She kept an eye on Benjamin to make sure he was still breathing but not a threat to them.

"Yes." He looked down at his leg and winced. "Are you?"

She figured they were both probably in shock. "I'm fine," she said. "I'm just worried about you. We need to get you to the hospital right away. You're losing a lot of blood."

"Liv, I don't think I can stand up." He crept toward the phone, glancing warily at Benjamin. "We need to call the police."

"I'll do it." She rushed toward the phone hanging on the kitchen wall and dialed.

Ten minutes later Olivia watched the medics arrive and go to work on Cameron's leg. There was nothing she could do to help him. He had almost been killed because of her. She knew he was going to be all right, but at that moment she wasn't so sure she was.

Several policemen she didn't recognize rushed into her home and arrested Benjamin Funkhouser. She knew she'd never forget the look he gave her when he regained consciousness and realized what was happening. He looked like a wounded animal, slumped over in pain. Betrayed, and appearing to be hurt more by her rejection than the physical pain Cameron had caused.

As the officers escorted him out of her house, he turned back to look at her with his eyes full of contempt. "This isn't over," he said.

She shuddered.

"Oh yes it is." One of the officers yanked him out the front door.

His words haunted her. Something within her told her he was right, but at the moment she couldn't have said why. Her top priority was making sure her husband was stable. She thought she heard one of the officers ask her if she was hurt, and she shook her head.

She went over to hold Cameron's hand. He was quiet, and she wondered if he was confused due to the pain. She squeezed it and kissed him on the forehead.

"We're taking him to GW Hospital," the medic said. "You can either ride with us or meet us there." He propped up the gurney and started to roll Cameron toward the door.

"I'll be right behind you," she said. "You're going to be okay."

She looked up and saw Nathan standing in the doorway. He approached her with a sympathetic look on his face. The ambulance crew and the rest of the police officers cleared out of her living room, and she and Nathan were the only ones left. She stood there, trying her best to hold herself together and absorb everything that had happened. She realized that standing there with Nathan she felt safe for the first time in months.

"I'm sorry," he said. "I just heard. You okay?"

She thought about this question for a minute. "Yes...no, I'm fine but I have to get to GW." Olivia ran her fingers through her hair and fought back the exhaustion.

"Don't worry, I'll take you." He put his hand gently on her shoulder and guided her to his car.

The night air gave her a chill, and she wrapped her arms across her chest. Nathan put his windbreaker gently around her shoulders and opened the car door for her.

"Thanks," she whispered.

Nathan pulled away into the night, and she couldn't help but notice how life continued as usual around her. Why hadn't it stopped? Why were people still going about things as though nothing had happened?

"We really need to talk," Nathan finally said.

"I know, but I want to make sure my husband's okay."

"I'll wait. I can stay as long as it takes."

"You know, I could really use some coffee." She massaged her temples. "Everything's a little fuzzy right now."

"How about I go get us some food and coffee and be back in an hour. Does that sound good?"

"In all honesty I'm not sure how much help I'm going to actually be to you tonight," she said. "I'm so tired, and I'm still not sure what just happened."

"I understand, Olivia. I know you've been through a lot, but it's important that we talk. Tonight."

She looked over at him as he pulled into the emergency drive to drop her off. "Okay." She knew it must be important for him to be so insistent. And from the way his eyes had lost all their light, she feared the news wasn't good.

79

Olivia floated into the emergency room of GW Hospital in a reflective daze. She found Cameron conscious but groggy on a gurney in the hallway.

"Liv…," he said, although she wasn't sure how he managed to smile. "You're here. Are you sure you're okay? Did he hurt you?"

"I'm fine, and I'm so sorry, Cameron."

"It's not your fault." He closed his eyes and winced in pain.

"Yes, it is…I've been so naïve." She stood over his bed and looked down at the bandages over his leg.

"I'm not sure what would've happened to me if you hadn't shown up." She wiped her palm over his forehead, soothing him.

"It's okay. The only thing that matters to me is that you're okay." His eyes fluttered.

"Why did you come back home? I thought you'd already left for your trip."

"Fortunately I forgot some of my research and the talking points for my speech," he said in a soft voice. "I was on my way to the airport when I realized I didn't have it, so I rescheduled the flight and headed back home."

"I can't believe everything that's happened."

"It's over now." He seemed to be drifting in and out of sleep.

"Is it?" She could tell he needed rest. "I'm going to talk to the FBI while you sleep. I'll be right here if you need me."

Cameron didn't respond. She stood there for a moment and watched him before she made her way back out into the waiting room. She was glad to see that Nathan wasn't there yet because she wanted to try and gather her thoughts before they talked.

She sat down and put her head in her hands and wept silently. She didn't care who else saw her. Once again she'd allowed her career to blind her, and it could have cost her her life. She didn't know how she hadn't seen it coming, but she'd always had a way of letting her passions get the best of her.

Now her stalker was behind bars, but what about The Punisher? Up until now she'd thought they could be the same person. Was it still possible? After Benjamin's obsessive affections, it was hard to believe he'd been capable of violence, until he'd stabbed Cameron.

But maybe it was just self-defense. If she hadn't demanded Cameron stop, he might have killed Benjamin. That was a side of him she'd never seen before. She figured anyone might be capable of anything, given the right circumstances.

If this wasn't a wake up call, she didn't know what was. She was chasing a serial killer and to understand him she'd have to be insane. She suddenly smelled coffee and food and looked up.

"Stop beating yourself up." Nathan sat beside her and put the coffee within her reach.

"Thank you." She took the lid off the coffee cup and took a huge gulp. It instantly perked her up. "I deserve it. I've been an idiot."

"No you haven't," he said. "You couldn't have known."

"I really have been so naïve about everything, thinking I could actually solve this case." She opened the McDonald's bag and surveyed her choices. "Is that a quarter pounder?"

"With cheese." Nathan leaned back against the chair.

"Perfect."

Minutes went by before she spoke again. She devoured the burger while Nathan sat watching her and giving her all the time she needed.

"I should have taken his emails more seriously, Olivia."

She nodded. "We both should have."

"The strange thing is that earlier today we thought we had a new lead on The Punisher, but it turned out to be a crank."

"Yeah, I got your message, but my phone's been acting up so it came in five hours after you sent it."

"Hmm…well, it was a false alarm."

"What makes you so sure?" she asked.

"I'm not completely sure. The guy we brought in for questioning seemed to know things about the Lincoln Memorial crime scene that he couldn't have known without being there." Nathan reached in the bag and retrieved the other burger.

Her clarity seemed to be coming back to her now. "Yes, but isn't it fair to say that I might know more about that crime scene than possibly any other reporter, or police officer – especially the one who arrested me – or even the FBI might know?"

"I hope not, but why do you say that?" He took a long sip of his soda.

"Because I was one of the first on the scene…supposedly." She stopped chewing.

"What are you suggesting?" he said.

"Maybe this guy who you suspect actually did have something to do with this. Maybe The Punisher has an accomplice."

Nathan rubbed the blond stubble on his chin.

"Think about it." She swallowed the last bite of her burger, forgetting to taste it. "And if Benjamin or whatever his name really is, and The Punisher are connected somehow, he couldn't have done all of this on his own, could he?"

"I had the same thought too, at first," he said.

"But?"

"But. Now I'm convinced we have the right man." Nathan put his drink down and looked her square in the eyes. "I feel confident that we finally have this so-called Punisher behind bars now."

How could Nathan believe this? The kid didn't fit The Punisher's profile in her opinion. But, maybe he was an accomplice? Was he telling her this so she'd back off and stop writing stories about serial killers terrorizing Washingtonians? As much as she wanted to believe the words that were coming out of his mouth, she couldn't. Something didn't add up.

80

Nathan drained the last bit of his soda and scanned the ER waiting room. "You know, I have to write up a report," Nathan said.

"I understand that's why you came." She swallowed her last bite of burger.

"One of the perks of my job."

"I know." She wiped her mouth with a paper napkin and sighed. "Look, I'll tell you everything I can."

"What I really want to know is how this guy got into your house?"

"He posed as a flower delivery boy," she said. "Very clever if you ask me."

"We certainly underestimated him." Nathan started to jot down notes.

"What do you mean?" she said.

"We found out that the emails were being sent from computers in the library at American University, and we've been surveying the place and investigating for weeks."

"And?"

"And, nothing." Nathan hesitated. "The FBI has also been watching your house and your movements."

"What?" Olivia said. "You thought I was involved?"

"No, I just wanted to make sure you were safe." She thought she saw Nathan blush as he looked down at the floor. He grabbed his pen and continued making notes. "Trouble is, I called off the watch last week or we would have caught this guy sooner."

"Maybe." She wasn't convinced. She did her best to fill Nathan in on all the details of her time with Benjamin.

"Sounds like you were very brave," he said.

"I wasn't brave." She frowned. "In fact, I've been a complete coward throughout this whole thing. If Cameron hadn't shown up, I might not be sitting her right now."

"Give yourself some credit." He smiled politely.

"I'm sorry." She looked away to catch the tears gathering in her eyes before he saw them. They sat there in silence for several minutes as she reflected on the root of her problems.

"What are you thinking?" Nathan asked.

She couldn't explain where her thoughts were coming from or why they were consuming her. It was at that moment she figured out what had been bothering her this whole time.

"Do you remember much about the Stacy Greenburg case?" she asked.

"Of course, and how you tried to help the FBI find out what happened to her," he said.

"At the end of the day, I didn't find out anything you didn't already know."

"You still won you a Pulitzer."

"That never mattered to me," she said. "All I've ever wanted was to get Stacy back, or at least to find out what happened to her."

"I don't think you should worry about that right now." Nathan put his hand gently on top of hers. "You're under a lot of stress, and I'm sure this whole experience has been very traumatic for you."

She wasn't really listening to what he was saying. She sat there and stared into space. And then she vocalized everything she'd been feeling since the whole ordeal began.

"You want to know why finding The Punisher has been so important to me?"

"I have a guess," Nathan said.

"You do?"

"Well, if it was me, and I'd won a Pulitzer, I might feel that after that there was no place to go but down, so you have to stay on top of your game. Nothing wrong with that."

Olivia considered what he was saying for a moment. She sat back in amazement that he'd actually given this some thought before. "Stacy and I were friends, you know?"

"Oh."

"We were actually very good friends. And I was with her the night she disappeared. I think I've always felt that if I could find out what really happened to her, I would be able to keep living."

Nathan started to put away the trash around them.

"I don't think I've really ever been able to forgive myself for her disappearance," she said. "Or put it behind me."

"I can't imagine." He looked sympathetic.

She wondered why he kept listening and how far beyond his duties this went. She tried to remind herself that he wasn't her therapist. "Maybe I thought by finding The Punisher I could finally lay Stacy's spirit to rest."

"That's interesting."

"It's ridiculous now that I think about it, but I've really struggled with it over the last two years." She massaged her temples.

"Now that he's finally behind bars, do you feel a little more at peace?"

"You know…I don't think I'll ever be completely at peace about Stacy's death until her body is found and I find out what really happened to her. Besides, I'm not convinced The Punisher *is* behind bars. I think he's still out there."

81

Olivia wasn't sure Nathan knew how to respond to her last statement about believing The Punisher was still out there, so she figured that's why he didn't say anything at all. The waiting room was unusually quiet.

Nathan studied her for a long moment. When he finally spoke, his usual warmth was missing. "Are you keeping anything from me, Olivia?"

She was taken off guard by his question. "I don't think so. In fact, after all that's happened today, I think it's time I let the FBI do their job."

"Probably a good idea." He relaxed a little and smiled.

"This has all gotten way out of my control." She pulled her hair down over her ears. "I'm scared…"

"About?"

"I don't – " She looked up and saw Rex hurrying through the door. He rushed over to the front desk, looking frantic. "Rex, over here."

"Are you okay?" He ran over and gave her a hug. "I came as soon as I heard. "I can't believe this happened. How's Cameron?"

"He's going to be fine," she said. "The doctors just wanted to keep him a while longer to monitor him, but he should be released first thing in the morning."

Rex shook his head.

"Spare me the lecture." She motioned for him to sit down. Olivia rubbed her eyes while he and Nathan exchanged hellos.

"I'm just glad you're okay," Rex said.

"You and me both," she said. "Kind of gives me a new perspective on life."

"Me too." Rex leaned over and rested his elbows on his knees.

"I told Nathan I'm through playing rookie detective," she said.

"I'll believe that when I see it." Rex winked at her.

"I'm serious," she said, not believing the words that were actually coming out of her mouth. "But I would love to know what progress Nathan's made in this case. Just because Benjamin's in jail doesn't mean we have our killer. I'm not convinced he's The Punisher."

"You know I can't discuss those details," Nathan said.

"I just thought I could help you." Her energy had returned.

Rex seemed deep in thought as he changed the subject. "You know, I hate to say it but that last victim, Brendan Campbell, deserved everything he got."

She noticed a strange look wash over Nathan's face. "Did you know him?"

"That's a terrible thing to say." She'd never heard Rex talk that way before, and it surprised her.

"Yeah, I met him once," Rex said. "Brendan had quite a reputation. The night I met him, we were at a Christmas party, and he hit on my wife."

"Wow, really?" she said. "That's interesting."

"Oh you don't forget a scene like that." Rex said.

"I guess not." Nathan stood up to leave. "I'm going to take off. I'll be in touch."

"Okay," she said. "Just tell me one thing before you go. Did you ever figure out what the quote meant on the last letter The Punisher left? It was hand-written, and it sounded familiar."

"Wasn't that hard." Nathan smiled. "I read a lot of Ralph Waldo Emerson in college."

She made a mental note. "Any idea what it meant?" At least now she knew who had written the quotes.

"Not sure," he said.

Just then the emergency room came alive as several medics burst through the door with an injured victim. All she could see was blood, and she experienced a flashback to earlier that evening.

"We've got a live one," one of the medics shouted, "but not for long."

A doctor came out of nowhere and rushed to the victim's side. Olivia watched in awe as the scene unfolded.

"What happened?" the doctor asked.

"He said someone tried to kill him," another medic said. "He's unconscious now, but from the looks of things, his killer may have succeeded.

"Let's get him back. Now." The doctor led the way.

Olivia caught Rex staring at her as Nathan moved closer to the exit. "Looks like you have a heads up on your next story," Rex said.

She shook her head. "No thanks. Let the Emily Morgan's of the world have this one. I'm through writing stories for a while, at least until my suspension is over. Besides, aren't you the one who told me there will always be another story to chase tomorrow?"

"That's right." Rex smiled, reached over and patted her on the back.

82

Olivia spent the next week at her home, resting. She took care of Cameron, even though he'd bounced back quicker than she would have imagined. He seemed content as long as she wasn't working on stories about The Punisher. Did he enjoy seeing her so low, without a purpose?

She couldn't shake the unsettling feeling that something terrible was about to happen…that the nightmare wasn't over yet. She hadn't read the paper or watched TV in a week, which helped to clear her head. She also hadn't checked her email in days.

She was doing the best she could to deal with the trauma she'd experienced with her stalker. She'd kept busy doing spring cleaning, attempting to free herself of his presence in her house.

Olivia finally decided she couldn't put off checking her emails any longer and made herself comfortable in her office. Her bathrobe had become her second skin. She scrolled through about fifty emails she didn't need to read right away, but one caught her eye. The subject line read: From Your Biggest Fan.

Chills ran down her spine.

Was this some sort of sick joke or was Benjamin contacting her from prison? She noticed it had been sent two hours earlier. At first afraid to open it she at last let curiosity get the best of her. The email read:

My dear Olivia, You didn't think this was really over, did you? It's just begun...and do I ever have a story for you. This could be what you need to jump start your career again. Trust me. At 2860 28th Street, NW, there is a messenger waiting for you. The house is open. He will give you what you need to know. I remain, Your Biggest Fan.

The email was all she needed to spring her into action. Olivia quickly forwarded the message to Nathan, grabbed her phone and ran up the stairs to throw on some clothes. Then, she frantically dialed Nathan's number and waited. No answer.

"Nathan, it's Olivia." She left a message. "I just forwarded you an alarming email I received. Says it's from my stalker, and he has a message for me. Could be nothing more than some copy cat, but I'm going to check it out. Please call me back. It's urgent. I'll meet you there. I think the address is somewhere in the Woodley Park area."

The next thing she knew she was in her Mini Cooper traveling north on Connecticut Avenue toward Adams Morgan. It was less the two miles away.

Olivia contemplated calling Rex but didn't know if that would complicate things, so she decided against it. The address seemed familiar for some reason, and her car steered its way there easily. She stopped in front of the charming three-story brownstone with the address from the email. It had been a few years since she'd been inside, but she remembered who lived there. It was Rex's home.

She drove around the block until she could secure a parking place on the street. None of this made any sense. Why had the email directed her here, and who had sent it? As she was getting out of her car, Nathan called.

"Where are you?" she asked.

"I'm in Baltimore." His voice cut in and out. "I took the day off, now that things have died down. I got your messages. Stay put. Do *not* go into that home alone. Do you hear me?"

"Why not? I'm here right now." She reached for the paper with the directions to double check the address. "The home belongs to Rex."

"Are you sure about that?"

"Positive. I was here a couple years ago."

"Olivia, this sounds like a trap. I'm sending some men over now. Please, just wait."

She looked at her watch. "Okay, but hurry." The connection suddenly died.

She decided to listen to Nathan, and got back in her car and waited another fifteen minutes. She also tried calling Rex on his cell and at home and left a message. When nobody showed up and neither he nor Rex called her back, she decided she had every right to go in. After all, the message had come to her.

The tall concrete steps up to the front porch zapped all the energy out of her heavy legs. The house looked dark inside. She rang the doorbell and waited. No response. She rang it again and stood there, anxiously. Still no response. The email had said the house would be open, so she let herself in. She flipped the light on next to the door. Nothing could have prepared her for what she saw next.

Olivia fell to her knees and cried out in horror. Rex sat slumped in a reclining chair, his body butchered. Gaping holes stared at her from where his chest had been sliced open and ripped apart. It looked like some of his organs had spilled out onto the floor along with so much blood. The blood looked fresh. Rex's face held a blank, lifeless expression. He'd been tortured.

She couldn't stop her stomach from creeping up her throat and threw up all over the hard wood floors. She tried to stand far enough back not to get any blood on her. When she backed up against the far wall, that's when she saw the message.

The killer had written the words in blood across the wall behind Rex's body. The words made her gasp for air.

You're next Olivia.

She stumbled out of the house and fell into the arms of a man with a gun and an FBI hat on coming up the steps. "He's dead," she screamed. "Rex is dead!"

"Stay here, ma'am," the agent said. "Don't go anywhere." He turned to go in the house, gun drawn. "Turner, stay with her."

She felt someone grab her shoulders and lead her down to the sidewalk.

"Call the paramedics," he said. "Looks like she's going into shock."

83

Nathan sat beside Olivia in the interview room at FBI headquarters. A paramedic had arrived at the scene earlier and treated her. She was still so numb she couldn't feel a thing. Her head was pounding, and she was seeing double. She sensed the onset of a mental breakdown. Nathan was dressed in khaki shorts, a Hawaiian-printed button down shirt and flip-flops. His hair looked windblown, a nice reddish tan settling in.

"Was it The Punisher?" She was almost afraid to ask.

Nathan looked as broken as she felt. "Appears so."

"But the signature was completely different, nothing like the other murders." She massaged her temples, willing away the tension headache building.

"We found another note like the others," he said.

"But Rex's murder had nothing to do with infidelity." She sighed. "Is it possible this time it was about revenge? And it's personally reflected on me?"

"Yeah, and I'd like to know why." Nathan stood up and paced the floor. She knew he was probably angry at her for going in the house when he'd told her not to but at least he wasn't yelling at her...yet.

She had no more tears to cry. How could someone kill Rex? She couldn't believe he was dead. She didn't even want to think about what he must have gone through in those last hours. "I'm responsible for his death."

"No, you're not," he said.

"How can you say that after what's happened and my involvement?" Rex had been one of her most trusted friends.

"Olivia, I'm going to level with you, only because you're so closely involved with this case…and at this point I think you may be the key to solving it." Nathan sat in a chair next to her.

"You think the killer is someone I know, don't you?" She looked deep into his eyes.

"I think it's very possible." He played with his ear lobe. "That's why I'm going to put a surveillance team back on your home. For your protection." He paused. "Look, this murder couldn't possibly be a copycat because we've kept certain details a secret. Even after reading your stories, the general public wouldn't have known about them."

"Like what?" She scooted to the edge of her seat.

"That's all I can tell you for now."

"You mean Benjamin Funkhouser was just a crazy fan? Just like I thought. Which means, The Punisher is still out there."

"That or he does have an accomplice." Nathan made a pained face.

"What else are you not telling me? Come on, if you want me to help, give me something," she said.

"Portions of each note found at the supposed 'suicide' murder scenes were held back by the police and FBI and never shared with the media."

"So the note I found on Brendan Campbell's body wasn't unique, The others had Ralph Waldo Emerson quotes scribbled on the back too?" He certainly had her attention now.

"That's right." He handed her a sheet of paper with a list of quotes. "There's been a different quote on the back of each letter."

She scanned the paper and searched for anything familiar in the quotes. "Can I take this with me?"

He hesitated. "Yes, but this information better not end up on the front page of the Post."

"Okay. Understood."

"I'm showing you because maybe you might see a connection to someone you know."

She scratched her head. "Why didn't I see a quote on the letter Monica Habershamm mailed to Jordan Schelbert."

"That's because it turned up at the crime scene, but it took some detective work. I didn't see it at first."

"I'm not sure I understand why you didn't share the quotes with the public since he didn't write the message himself." She stood up and started pacing the room, her brain alive with questions.

"It's been The Punisher's way of communicating with us over the last year," he said. "We've known this was a serial case for some time, but we didn't want the public to know because it would have caused absolute pandemonium."

"I can't believe this – all this time I was right." She rubbed her face with her hands as if she could somehow make the reality of this nightmare go away. "And, how do you think Rex was involved?"

Nathan pulled at his ear. "The Punisher had been contacting Rex directly after he started investigating the case."

"Rex never mentioned that to me." She thought he had trusted her more than that. There had to be a reason he'd withheld that information, especially after he knew she was going to run with the first serial killer story.

Nathan hesitated. "I also have another theory, but I'm not sure you'll want to hear it."

"Nothing would surprise me at this point." She motioned with her hand for him to continue.

"Well, I now believe Benjamin was just a crazy fan. Maybe he wanted the attention and notoriety of The Punisher's deeds and got them by default. But, he's made it clear he is dangerous and guilty of a crime against you. I hope he spends a good amount of time in prison thinking about what he did before he gets released, and I'll do all in my power to ensure that."

"And?"

"And, I think there's another possibility we need to consider here… which is that Rex was somehow involved in these murders."

"What? I can't believe that." she said.

"I know, but think about it – "

"I've known Rex for years, and he could never do something like that."

"That doesn't mean he isn't guilty," Nathan said. "Killers live next door to people all the time without being detected. That is until they want to be. Besides he had the motivation – you heard him talking about how he thought Brendan deserved to die just because he had hit on his wife at a party once…"

"I think he was just blowing off some steam. It was late, and we were all tired." The idea that Rex could be involved disturbed her.

"What if he started this and he pissed off his partner, and that's why he was killed?" Nathan proposed. "If that's true, we may have an even bigger psychopath on our hands."

Olivia just sat there, thinking how maddening this all was. It was starting to make her crazy. The Punisher was still out there. Watching *her* now.

"I knew this nightmare wasn't over yet," she mumbled. "It's just beginning, isn't it?"

84

As soon as Cameron got the news, he rushed to be at Olivia's side. He seemed to be at a complete loss for words as he embraced her. Nathan left the two of them alone and went back to work.

"Are you okay, Liv?" He stroked her hair. "I mean, really okay?"

"I'm not sure right now."

"Let's go home." He put his arm around her shoulders and led her outside to the car. On the drive home he said, "I'm sorry to hear about Rex. It's horrific, and I can only imagine the pain you're feeling right now. I just can't believe everything that's happened!"

Olivia stared blankly out the window and didn't say anything.

"I'm not really sure what else to say...but I'm here if you need me."

"Thanks." She turned and put her hand on his thigh. "I know you are."

"What would you like to do tonight?" he asked. "I can go rent a movie. That might be a good escape from everything..."

All she wanted to do was close her eyes and wake up to a different reality. After thinking for a minute, the perfect solution hit her.

"I want to work on the baby's room together." Chills ran over her body.

"You do?" He asked.

Olivia had never seen him smile so big. "Yes, let's go shopping," she said with renewed energy. "The first thing we need to buy is a baby blanket."

He took his eyes off the road and looked at her. "I love you. Nothing would make me happier."

"I love *you*." Olivia needed a distraction, and if this didn't do it, nothing else would. "You've already bought a new crib and rocking chair, so let's go see what else we can find to make the room more complete." She leaned back in her seat and closed her eyes. "I think I'm ready."

"This is a terrific idea, Liv."

"Thanks, I thought you'd like it." She leaned over and kissed him on the cheek.

The next several hours, while strolling through Baby's R Us, she tried to forget about seeing Rex's mutilated body earlier that day...and focused on shopping with her husband for toys and necessities for a baby.

When they got home that evening, Cameron ordered a pizza and they shared a bottle of Chianti while decorating the baby's room with the new treasures they'd found. Olivia felt like she was on autopilot. She was just going through the motions while shopping with Cameron. She wanted to be strong, and this was the only way she knew how to be. She tried to keep her mind on the possibility of a new baby and how happy that would make her. And for a moment, she felt hopeful. Until she had another black out.

85

Although the black out hadn't lasted long, it still frightened her. What had caused it? She remembered Cameron saying something about it being a big day and helping her upstairs…just like the night she'd come in from dinner with Stacy and had too much to drink.

She suddenly recalled flashes of walking in the door that night two years before and Cameron greeting her with a kiss and carrying her to bed. She should have never had that last glass of Merlot with Stacy. Why was she remembering this now? Cameron's kiss on the forehead, the way he felt snuggling beside her as he crawled into bed with her. Just like now. She drifted off to sleep in his arms.

The next day, she showed up at Mimi's for another emergency session.

"I recently recalled the dream I had the night I came back after leaving Stacy," Olivia said.

"After the first black out?" Mimi asked. She wore a bright red suit with black pumps, but her hair looked in need of attention.

"Yes." Olivia pulled her hair down around her ears. "I remember dreaming about water and getting up to go to the kitchen for a glass. But before I got all the way downstairs I saw Cameron with another woman, and she had her arm draped around his neck."

"Did you know the woman in this dream?" Mimi asked.

"No, I don't think so. She was blond and didn't look familiar, but I couldn't really see her face because she was hunched over. But I do remember deciding against getting the water, so I went back to bed...in my dream."

"What was the woman wearing?"

Olivia thought for a minute. "She looked liked she'd been running. She wore a white sleeveless top and black shorts with running shoes."

"These are all interesting details," Mimi said. "Are you certain this was a dream?"

"Yes," Olivia said. "I wonder why I would dream something so strange. Probably just insecurity, right?"

"Maybe, but you've also mentioned having several blackouts, which alarms me."

"What do you think is causing them?"

"Blackouts can happen for numerous reasons," Mimi began, "including anything from dehydration or emotional stress to seeing something that frightens you. And, almost fifty percent of the time there is no explanation for what really causes loss of consciousness."

"But there were no warning signs," Olivia said. "And why am I just now beginning to remember when and why I've had them? Why am I having flashbacks of things?"

"Are you on any medications?" Mimi asked. "Maybe you forgot and accidentally took too many."

"No, I don't take medication." Her eyes darted back and forth. "So that's not possible."

"Then, is it possible you were drugged? Remember, each time you had been drinking."

Olivia had never thought about that possibility before. "No, no." But was she sure?

"Go home and get some rest." Mimi uncrossed her legs. "Then go back to work."

"What do you mean?" Olivia raised an eyebrow at the suggestion.

"Find out what happened to Stacy." Mimi smiled. "I believe you know where she is deep down. Keep searching. She's trying to reach you. You'll

find her. Just keep listening. Last time I told you to live in the present…
but sometimes in order to live in the present, you have to relive the past."

Olivia was being given permission to pursue what her gut had been
telling her to do all this time. She hadn't seen this advice coming, but it
excited her, and she felt a sense of relief.

"And one more thing," Mimi said. "When you find out where The
Punisher is, I think you'll find out what happened to Stacy too."

Olivia sat back in her chair in awe.

"What? You think I don't read the papers…or keep up with my cli-
ents?" Mimi smiled. "Go and do what you were born to do. Just be careful. And always, trust what that inner voice of yours is saying."

86

That afternoon, Olivia went back to work. Maybe Mimi was right. Everything that was happening in her life was connected to Stacy. She made herself a pot of coffee and got comfortable in her office.

Now that Nathan had told her about the significance of the Ralph Waldo Emerson quotes on each of The Punisher's letters and given her a copy of them, she decided to Google them and see if she could find any cross references.

She scanned the first pages of references and spotted the one that was at Brendan's scene, "what lies behind us and what lies before us are tiny matters compared to what lies within us."

That was a scary thought when viewed through a serial killer's mind. She was curious about Mr. Emerson's original intent and wondered whether The Punisher had bastardized his quotes. How were his words being used or misused in modern day? Then, she saw another quote left at the crime scene.

"As soon as there is life, there is danger," she read out loud and kept scrolling down, searching for the next one on the list. It said, "None of us will ever accomplish anything excellent or commanding except when he listens to this whisper which is heard by him alone."

Another one was, "Trust your instinct to the end though you can render no reason." She kept going, reading, reading until she came across, "Truth is beautiful, without doubt; but so are lies." She re-read the list but couldn't find any real significance. She wasn't sure where she was going with any of this or if this was just a colossal waste of time.

Then, she thought about the note she'd found that day at the Lincoln Memorial. There was something about it that was more significant than the message or the quote itself. The letter was written in the killer's handwriting. Or was it? And, if it was, did that really matter? It wasn't as if they had a DNA database for penmanship. Of course there were graphologists who studied penmanship characteristics to derive conclusions about the author's personality. But, from what she'd heard, consulting a graphologist was like going to get your palm read.

She had taken a class several years back on handwriting examination and remembered being fascinated by the theory that, without even realizing it, people left imprints of their individuality in their writing. But, at this point she wasn't sure how useful digging into this was. This killer was steps ahead of her, and time was not a luxury she could afford. The Punisher made it clear from the message he left at Rex's – he was coming after her. It was just a matter of time.

87

Olivia knew she was overlooking something. The stationery at the Lincoln Memorial had looked familiar to her. She knew she'd seen it before, but where? After going through ten more pages of links, she'd almost decided that getting her palm read might not be such a bad idea. Her palm. *Body* parts.

She began to read back through the quotes again and something strange occurred to her. All the ones she had jotted down could have related to respective parts of the body. The first one, "as soon as there is life…" could refer to the body part responsible for creating life. The second, "he listens…" with an ear. The third "trust your instinct…" with your heart. And, "truth" and "lies" were spoken with a mouth.

But why Ralph Waldo Emerson? Did all his quotes relate to the human body? If so, maybe The Punisher was a doctor. What if The Punisher hid a clue in the body part of each victim that the different quotes referenced? Or, what if there was some significance in the victim and body part referenced? How were the quotes connected to the murders? They referenced parts of the body that contributed to infidelity.

This killer seemed to have some qualities of a magician. She still hadn't figured out how he managed to get Brendan's body onto the steps of the Lincoln Memorial without being seen. He certainly knew how to blend in. An expert in the art of distraction.

It wasn't until she was on the very last web page of references to Emerson that she found a link to a magazine article entitled, "Mind

Full Ways: The Healing Powers of Ralph Waldo Emerson." The article was written by a mental patient. Sam Camp! Unfortunately a photo of the man did not accompany the byline. Journal entries were woven into the story. The entries described Sam's childhood abuse from his father, his trauma after his father killed himself and the mess he left behind.

His mother's words had always haunted him. She'd told Sam that his father got what he deserved. His father's suicide note was included, which explained all his sins against his family, including sexually abusing his son and his infidelities against his wife.

Her thoughts were interrupted by a loud banging on her front door below.

Moments later when she saw Terry Carson standing in her doorway, her spirits lifted. She invited him in and couldn't wait to share what she'd found. She suggested they get some air on the rooftop, and he seemed to like that idea and followed her up there. They got comfortable in the lounge chairs, the spring air feeling warm but brisk.

"Olivia, I can't imagine what you've been through in the past few weeks. I'm sorry about Rex and for your loss." He put a hand on her shoulder. That was as far as his sentiments went, but she suspected that was hard enough for him to say.

"Thanks." She half smiled.

"I wanted to talk about The Punisher and Sam," he said.

"Great. I've got something to show you, but first...any luck on finding Sam's classmates?"

"Yes and no." Terry squirmed in his seat, looking as though he was still trying to process what he'd discovered. "I got in touch with three of Sam's classmates, and they all said the same thing. Cute kid, but weird. He was shy and withdrawn and didn't have many friends."

"That's interesting." She pouted her lips and looked up at the sky.

"When I mentioned Stacy and Monica, they'd all heard about it on the news and remembered going to school together, but hadn't kept in touch over the years. None of them remember Sam after the sixth grade, which is strange since Granbury used to be a small town."

"That's odd," she said. "I wonder if he moved away."

"Don't know, but one of them was nice enough to go through old scrapbooks and sent me the sixth-grade photo." Terry pulled out the eight-by-ten photo and handed it to her. "*This* is what Sam Camp looked like as a kid."

Olivia stared at the photo of the face Stacy had rubbed out. Sam looked familiar, but she wasn't sure why. He was young, had blond hair, and a difficult smile. "Can I keep this for now?"

"Sure, see what you can come up with," he said.

"I will, just need to think on it for a bit." She put it aside. "Thanks."

He reached for a piece of paper in his back pocket, unfolded it and handed it to her. "I've been looking at my crime timeline every which way I could, and I think I've come up with something. Tell me what you see."

She took the paper and studied it for several minutes. "All the murders happen on no particular day of the week."

"Look closer…"

She did some math in her head and calculated the number of days between each murder. She thought about it for a minute. "Do you see a pattern?" "I think these numbers may be a clue." His eyes frowned.

"Symbolic of something?"

"Maybe so," he said.

"Couldn't something be random and make no sense for once?" She laid the paper down in her lap, her brain overloaded. She glanced at the dates on the page again and noticed something but was afraid to vocalize it.

All the dates were significant in Olivia's life. One was her birthday, another the day Patrick died. A murder fell on the date she'd won her Pulitzer, her wedding anniversary, the number of years she'd worked at the Post, her lucky number, and her age. For the time being, she pushed the thought away. It was more than inconceivable. It was disturbing. It seemed that something in her life was connected to each of the victims and their killer.

88

Olivia was lost in her thoughts while she and Terry sat on her roof-top lounge. A warm afternoon breeze blew through her hair. She closed her eyes and tilted her head toward the sun, soaking in the warmth that crawled over her.

"What are you thinking?" Terry finally asked.

"These numbers *could* mean something." A knot formed in her throat.

"What do you think it is?"

She chose her next words carefully. "For some reason, all of these murders have something to do with me, but I can't explain why."

He leaned forward, his eyes bright, intent on her words. "Tell me. Don't hold back."

"It may mean nothing and is probably just a coincidence." She put her face in her hands and rocked back and forth. "All of the numbers stand out to me because they're significant dates or anniversaries in my life."

"Are you serious?" Terry massaged the stubble under his chin.

"It's as if he has intimate knowledge of my life. Knows things about me only my closest friends and family know," she said.

"Or he's taken the time to learn about you through those who know you well. A psychopath like this often becomes obsessed with a person. And I've always wondered why this case keeps coming back to you. Do you own a gun?" he asked out of the blue.

"No, but Cameron does. It's hidden in the basement."

Terry reached behind the crest of his jeans and pulled out his weapon. "Here, I want you to take mine. Don't worry, it's just a loan."

"I can't take your gun." She fell back in her seat.

"It's not loaded. Yet."

"Then what's the point?"

"Trust me on this one," Terry said. "I want you to keep this on you at all times. But use extreme caution."

"Are you going to leave me with some bullets?" She reluctantly picked up the gun and held it in her hands. It was heavy and felt awkward.

"I'll load it before I go."

"I've never even seen a gun before, much less tried to shoot one."

"And I hope you don't ever have to use it," he said.

"I still don't understand how I'm supposed to protect myself if I have no idea how to use it."

"It's just a precaution, but you're right…guns aren't easy to shoot, but they are easy to miss your target if you aren't experienced. So don't use it unless you have to."

She shook her head in confusion, sure he had his reasons. "Let me show you something," she said. "Actually two things. I'll be right back, I just have to run down to my office and get my notes. Can I get you anything while I'm up?"

"Whiskey…if you have any." A sly smile crept across his cheeks.

"I'll see what I can do." Cameron had a liquor cabinet in his study, and she was sure he wouldn't mind.

His office was dark and messy. She tripped over a pile of newspapers on the floor and wanted nothing more than to clean up the chaos that surrounded her. The glow from his computer screen lit the way as she searched. Minutes later she returned to the rooftop with a tumbler full of Maker's Mark, her notes and the article she'd found.

"That's more like it." Terry looked pleasantly surprised as he took a generous sip.

She explained the research she'd been doing on the quotes and her "body part" theory to Terry while he enjoyed his libation.

"That idea's not far fetched at all." He winked at her and took another swig of his drink. "You realize the FBI or whoever did the autopsies would have found anything unusual?"

"IF, they were looking for it, but maybe they weren't," she said. "I know...it's a crazy idea."

Terry studied the amber liquid in his glass as if it contained all the answers. "You have the mind of a killer, you know that? But I happen to like crazy ideas, Olivia. And I like the way you think."

"I forgot to mention that I also think The Punisher may be a doctor," she said. "He's clearly into anatomy."

"A doctor, huh? Not bad, detective. Or, maybe he was a vet."

"I just thought of something," she said. "He could even be an artist. I know its way out there, but think about it."

"So considering this body part theory of yours, what could The Punisher have possibly hidden in each of the victims' bodies that would be significant?"

It suddenly came to her. "Maybe evidence of their sin."

"Like what?" he asked.

"A token of affection – something that belonged to their lovers."

"Still, what would that prove? I think you've given The Punisher too much credit. Plus, like I said, the pathologist would have discovered these items."

"But why the quotes then?"

Terry thought about it for a moment. "Who knows? Maybe he did it to throw the police off." He drained his glass. "It's certainly proved to be a good distraction."

89

Olivia handed Terry an extra copy of the online article she'd print-ed: Mind Full Ways: The Healing Powers of Ralph Waldo Emerson. "What's this?" he asked.

"Right before you came I found this article. It sure is an interesting twist."

She read it again while he had a chance to review it. The heat from the afternoon sun beat down on her back, and she welcomed the breeze.

"Well. Well. Well." Terry rested the article in his lap and looked over at her. "When was this written?"

"Looks like about ten years ago." She stared at the article and twirled her blondish hair around her fingers.

"What's so ironic about the article is that he claims the works of Ralph Waldo Emerson got him through some difficult times." Terry scratched his head.

"Do you think Sam or his accomplice is The Punisher?" she asked. "Stacy mentioned him in her memoir, and Sam's connected to both Stacy and Monica."

"Could be," he said. "I'm just trying to figure out how he disappeared."

"My guess is that he goes by a different name now," she concluded.

Her finger skimmed back through the article as she spoke. "The motivation is all there. The infidelity, the traumatic childhood, the ref-erences to Emerson." She rolled the paper into a tube in her hands.

"Looks like Sam was an out-patient case study, one who should have been studied longer."

"I still don't understand the link to Emerson." He shook his head.

"Maybe he found some truth in the poems, some interpretation of a faith that became his religion and way of justifying his actions."

"We have to find this man." Terry got up and paced the rooftop. A blustery breeze tossed the papers from his hands, and he scrambled to chase them as they fled in every direction.

She didn't move to help him, remaining focused. "It's too coincidental," she said. "What are the chances that I'd find this article? We don't know if this is even the same Sam Camp that's in Stacy's sixth-grade photo."

"I think it is, and if we can find him, we'll at least have a link to The Punisher."

"But this was years ago, and there's no telling where this guy might be." Olivia looked around, noticed a red bird perched on the railing of the roof deck. It pecked around for a moment and flew off. She suddenly longed to be a carefree bird that could simply fly away. She felt Terry's eyes on her.

"I think he's right here in Washington," Terry said. "You said Stacy mentioned him in her memoir and that they'd reconnected in D.C. There's no telling how long these murders have been taking place. I just wish we knew why and where it all started. Olivia. Do me a favor. Keep researching while I try and locate Sam. We've got enough to go on now; I should be able to call in a few favors from my old pals at the bureau."

"Maybe I should give this information to Special Agent Spencer?" she said. "He's the one who's been the lead agent on this investigation."

"Please don't do that just yet." Terry looked her straight in the eye as if he was asking her for a huge favor. "Trust me, I've got a plan. Just give me a couple of days to sort this out."

She thought about it for a moment and agreed. "Okay, but please hurry. This all seems to be closing in on me, and I'm scared."

90

Two days later Olivia found herself pacing the kitchen floor, her chest growing tighter by the minute. Realizing she had absolutely no control over anything in her life at this point, she felt like climbing the walls with all the unknowns. She now questioned whether she'd done the right thing by not telling Nathan about the article with Sam Camp and her theory on the Ralph Waldo Emerson quotes, especially if they were linked to The Punisher.

Her thoughts turned to Rex. She missed him and still couldn't believe that the week before he'd been alive, and now he was gone. His funeral the day before had left her numb and shell shocked. She had managed to keep a low profile and pay her respects to her good friend. She still refused to believe he had anything to do with The Punisher's murders.

Feeling helpless, she decided to do some more research to work through her pain. It was late afternoon, and she poured herself a steaming cup of coffee before heading up to Cameron's office. She was sure he wouldn't mind if she used his computer since the Post had decided to confiscate her laptop for the remainder of her suspension. Duncan had apologized the day before when he'd come by to get it.

"It's out of my control," he'd said, "but don't worry, you'll get it back soon. It's just a technicality I think…when someone down in inventory realized you were on suspension and it was unaccounted for. Ridiculous if you ask me."

Olivia was insulted by the gesture, given her tenure, but she tried to blow it off. The thing that upset her most is that she didn't own a personal computer since she did all her work on her work laptop. It was time to buy one. She refused to let the Post have that much control over her life and take away the tool to her happiness.

She held her coffee mug in her hands, letting it warm her insides as she got comfortable in his chair and waited for the machine to come to life. She realized she'd forgotten her notepad in her office and went rummaging through Cameron's desk drawers for some blank paper.

She opened the first drawer and found what she was looking for under a nice box of stationery. She fingered a few of the sheets that stuck out of the box, noting the nice color and texture. Then she grabbed the notepad and pulled up the Google homepage to start a few searches. First, she did a random search and typed in the word "criminal clues."

Suddenly a list of the last several searches Cameron had made appeared on the drop down menu. The subject: cyanide poisoning jumped right off the page. Strange. Why would Cameron have searched on that topic? She completed her search and when thousands of sites instantly appeared in reference to criminals, she realized she needed to be more specific. She typed in the words, "body parts," not exactly sure where she was going with her search. Again a list of the most recent searches dropped down, revealing the subject of bullet wounds.

Olivia's thoughts ran wild. She typed in a few other words to test her theory, and what she ended up with was a search for every major key word linked to The Punisher case. Suddenly it occurred to her that maybe Cameron had been researching these same subjects for his portion of the book he was writing for work. If so, she was curious why he hadn't mentioned it since she could have been a valuable source for him.

Then it dawned on her as she searched through almost every letter of the alphabet of his last searches, that he'd been researching criminal subjects *very* intently. The words, "decomposition," "vital organs," "Secretary of State," "Monica Habershamm," "forensic evidence," and "serial killers," led her to believe that this had gone beyond general research. She made a mental note to ask him about it. It wasn't like him to keep secrets.

91

Nathan had never been able to make sense of the locket he'd found on Monica's body or the photos of the two young women. One, he was certain was Monica. But who was the other young woman, and how were they connected?

However, after going back through Monica Habershamm's journal again and reviewing each page carefully, he'd found something significant. After looking closely he'd seen that one page had been ripped near the inside of the binding. At the time, he was tempted to grab a lead pencil and rub the blank sheet to expose the impression from the sheet underneath it. But he knew that would have destroyed evidence, so he decided it would pay off to be patient.

Evidence was crucial at this point and he could not afford to lose any. Nathan flipped through the journal once more as he waited on lab results from forensics. A business card fell out and floated to the floor. It must have been hidden in the journal's leather covering before. The card landed blank side up as Luke Simpson, one of the FBI's forensic document examiners, walked up to Nathan's desk.

"I'm sorry to say that I'm not sure I have any news that'll help you." Luke cleared his throat. "The only thing the blank page revealed was some sort of random quote."

"What does it say?" Nathan reached for the series of photographs in Luke's hands.

"See for yourself. We shined an oblique light at the grooves of the indented writing on the blank page. The photos reveal shadowed depressions of the writing from the torn-out page above it. That's how you see what you're looking at." Luke smiled in satisfaction at the results of his magic.

"As soon as there is life, there is danger," Nathan read out loud. He stared at it for a moment, not believing what he was looking at. It was the same quote that had been left at the crime scene at Monica's condo.

"What does it mean, just out of curiosity?" Luke said.

"I'm not sure..." Nathan stared at the quote, brainstorming all the other possibilities of the meaning.

"Well, I'll leave you to it," Luke excused himself.

"Thanks."

When Luke lifted his shoe, the business card that had fallen to the floor flipped over like a pancake, revealing a piece of the puzzle that took a minute to put together, but once it did revealed a horrifying realization. The card appeared to be from a doctor. More than likely *Monica's doctor* since the card was in her journal. Nathan stopped and thought for a minute. Was that the common thread to all the victims? The victims' doctor? How else would The Punisher have had so much personal information about each victim? And why was the business card hidden in the journal along with that quote? All of a sudden, it made sense. He just couldn't believe that he hadn't seen it before.

Nathan sprinted down the long corridor, past security and out of the building. He jumped in his car and peeled out of his parking place and around the corner. He would call for back up on his way. He floored the accelerator and tore up E Street. His car was flying, past pedestrians, tourists at the hotdog stand, the Gallery Place Metro stop...

Nothing could have prepared him for what happened next. A toddler stumbled out into the street and right into his path. Nathan swerved to miss the little girl and did a U turn into the on-coming lane. He didn't see the black suburban that crashed into the side of his car, but he certainly felt it. The impact knocked the wind out of him and flipped the vehicle upside down.

His last thought before losing consciousness was Olivia Penn. He had failed her. He had been so close to saving her, but now she would surely die.

92

He waited patiently in his '75 Mustang convertible and watched Olivia's home from the street below. Sheets of rain rushed down his windshield, and thunder grumbled in the distance. O Street was quiet this time of the morning, except for the homeless man across the street, who seemed to be deciding whether or not to call it a night.

He watched the man swagger back and forth before eventually stumbling to his knees and passing out. Soaking wet. He turned his attention back to the windows of Olivia's house. He could not afford to be distracted. Not now. Not when he was *this* close. It was becoming increasingly difficult to find the courage to do what needed to be done. He wanted so badly to see Olivia. Right then.

When he saw a light come on in the top story of her home around 4:20 am, Terry Carson decided it was time to make his move. He grabbed his gun, got out of his car, gently shut the door, and made his way to the back entrance of Olivia's home. The rain gave him the chills. When he'd been there several days before, he'd made sure to leave one of the bottom floor windows unlocked so it would be easy to come and go from her place whenever he needed to.

***

Olivia woke up with a start early that morning. She wasn't sure if it was the flash of lightning that lit up the room or the crashing thunder that had woken her. She couldn't breathe, and at first she thought she'd had another nightmare. Only this time, if it had been a nightmare, she would have welcomed it because then it would mean it wasn't true.

She lay very still, paralyzed with fear. Her heart raced as she held her breath. Earlier the thought had escaped her, but for some reason it just hit her. The stationery in Cameron's drawer. She knew where she'd seen it before. It looked like the same stationery as the note left at the crime scene at the Lincoln Memorial and the note Stacy had received that night. Then something else dawned on her…and she realized why Sam Camp's childhood face looked so familiar.

The idea was inconceivable, and she just wanted the realization to go away. No, it couldn't be, she thought. She turned to look at her husband, who appeared to be fast asleep by the slow rising and falling of his chest. She looked down and gasped as a bolt of lightning lit up his face.

Could it be possible that the man she thought she'd known and was in love with had something to do with the awful murders plaguing the city? *Had she been sleeping with a serial killer all this time?* Thunder rattled the walls of the room.

She needed to convince herself this couldn't possibly be true. If she looked once more at his stationery maybe she'd see that it was different from those left by the killer. Maybe she was imagining all of these strange connections. She hadn't had a chance to ask him about his research the night before or what topics he was writing about for his book. Deep down, she knew she'd been avoiding the subject.

She actually couldn't recall what they'd discussed at dinner. She thought back on the events of the evening. Cameron had cooked spaghetti and poured her a glass of Merlot. She did remember that she'd only had two glasses and fell asleep on the couch after dinner while he must have cleaned the kitchen. But, how did she get to bed? He couldn't have carried her up the narrow flight of stairs.

She must have had another black out. What was happening to her? Then, she thought about what Mimi had asked. Maybe Cameron was drugging her. But why? What didn't he want her to remember? It suddenly dawned on her...if she was out of commission, he could get away with murder and she'd never know it. Was it true? She needed proof.

She exhaled softly and tried to slow the quick breaths that threatened to erupt into panicky gasps. She had to make sure she didn't wake Cameron.

Slowly, she peeled the covers off her body. The floor kissed her bare feet and sent tingles up her body as she tiptoed out of the room. When she got to the door she looked back at Cameron. He still appeared to be sleeping soundly. She just needed a few minutes. She prayed that the stationery was some sort of weird coincidence.

Olivia thought about grabbing Terry's gun she'd hidden in her desk drawer, but she was in too much of a hurry. She figured she wouldn't need it for now. She took the stairs to Cameron's office two at a time and flipped on a small green desk lamp. Adrenaline shot through her body and sent her heart racing even more.

Frantically she looked around the room for some confirmation that his research was justified. She opened the drawer where she'd found the stationery the day before, but it was gone.

She glanced across the room at the liquor cabinet, where she'd gotten into Cameron's Marker's Mark whiskey for Terry. The cabinet door was slightly ajar. Slowly she walked over to it, opened it and picked up the bottle. It was completely empty. She thought she remembered it being at least half way full the day before.

Nothing made sense as she looked around his office. She also remembered it had been cluttered with piles of papers. Now it was neat and clean. She turned around to scan the room one more time, and her hip bumped into the liquor cabinet. She had never realized it was on wheels until it shifted slightly from her weight.

She didn't think anything of it until she started to walk across the room and her foot kicked a crumbled sheet of paper that had come into view when the cabinet moved. Olivia bent down to pick it up and slowly freed the paper. What she saw was a list of names. The first few she didn't recognize. "Anne Cavenaugh and Candice Barreto," she whispered aloud.

Then she began to see the same names from her crime timeline. The four after that, along with Monica and Sandra's, were all too familiar to her. She knew the list by heart. These were all the victims of The Punisher. The last name on the list sent chills up her spine. It was her own.

93

Terror overcame Olivia when she realized what she'd been looking for had been right in front of her the whole time. The man she was married to, the man she loved…was The Punisher. She tried to comprehend the reality of the situation. This whole time she'd shared her life and her bed with a serial killer.

For a minute she thought she was going to throw up. She felt hot and could hear her heart thumping loudly. This couldn't be happening. This couldn't be true. She didn't want to believe it.

Olivia relived days and conversations that slowly began to add up. Somehow the shock kept the tears and the hysteria at bay for the moment. She had to figure out what to do next. She crumbled up the list of victims in her hand and put it back under the cabinet. Out of sight. She couldn't let him know she'd found it.

The sound of someone coming up the stairs suddenly threw her concentration. Cameron. He must have woken up. Did he know? There was no time to call anyone for help. She turned her back to the door and switched on the computer. Suddenly she felt a presence in the room with her. Just like before, with Benjamin…and the flowers. She couldn't breathe. She had never been this petrified in her entire life.

Olivia knew before she even turned around that Cameron was behind her. She had to somehow make him believe that she didn't know he was The Punisher so she could get out of the house. She wasn't convinced she could pull it off as frightened as she was, but she had to try. It was her only chance.

"Oh Cam, you scared me."

"What are you doing in here?" He stood wide-eyed in the doorframe.

She forced herself to relax so that he wouldn't read the tension in her body. "I couldn't sleep and thought I'd get caught up on some emails I've been avoiding the last couple of days," she said. "Since the Post confiscated my computer, which is annoying, I didn't figure you'd mind if I used yours." She could hear the nervousness in her own voice.

"Oh?" he said.

She longed to know what was going through his head. "I hope I didn't wake you," she said. "Or could you not sleep either? This storm is pretty loud."

He didn't say anything. Even though they'd only been married two years, she knew that her husband, the psychiatrist, could read her like a book. He must have sensed something was wrong.

"You know, I'm actually getting kind of sleepy now," she said, thinking as quickly as she could. "Maybe I'll try to go back to bed."

Everything had changed. She could hear the storm outside his office window growling with fury. Olivia felt her body fall back against Cameron's desk as her hands grasped for some sturdiness. The sudden blank expression in his eyes terrified her. He made a move in her direction and suddenly pulled out a gun.

"You're not going anywhere, Olivia," he said. "You should've listened to me." His words were devoid of emotion. "I really never wanted it to come to this, but I should have known that you wouldn't stop until you got your story."

"What are you doing?" she asked, playing dumb. "Why do you have a gun?" The only thing she knew to do was to try and talk to him.

"How long have you known, Olivia?"

"What are you talking about?" She managed to say. "Stop pointing that thing at me."

"Don't patronize me." He moved closer, the gun pointing at her chest. "Not now."

She tried her best to keep looking him in the eye. She no longer recognized the person staring back at her. He was not the husband she'd known.

"Cameron, it's me...your wife," she pleaded. "Don't do this!"

"You really made a mess of things now, didn't you?" He asked, his expression void of humanity.

"Please tell me it's not true," she said. "I can't believe it. How could you have done these terrible things?"

"They deserved it." His voice was cold. "And it's my purpose." Cameron looked to his left suddenly and appeared to be listening to the silence. It was an eerie moment.

"You're the only one with the power to stop these murders." Empower him. Disarm him. She guided herself back, circling along the walls of the room, attempting to get closer to the door. It was working. Cameron was moving with her. Now if she could just get downstairs to her office for Terry's gun. But when she took a second look at the gun in her husband's hand, she realized the gun he was holding *was* the one Terry had given her.

"Please, talk to me. I'm your wife. I love you." The words sounded sincere because up until five minutes before they had felt real.

He didn't answer.

"Why are you doing this? What made you do these things?" She continued to inch her way toward the doorframe. She desperately needed to keep him talking.

"You want to know? You really want to know!" Until now Cameron had remained calm and in control, but now his anger took over. He swiped his arm across the desk and knocked the lamp onto the floor. The light bulb shattered, and darkness took over the room.

She felt him move toward her and grab her by the throat. The next thing she knew he had shoved the barrel of the gun in her face. Then he threw her down against the floor where she landed on her tailbone and hit her head against the doorframe.

"I never wanted to hurt you, but you've ruined everything," she heard him say. "Now I have no choice."

94

Olivia struggled to regain her vision, blurred from the pain and the darkness. Occasional flashes of lightning illuminated her husband's shadow. "You really are a monster, aren't you?"

"I'm not a monster. I punished those who deserved to be punished. Don't you see? It's my destiny. It's what I'm meant to do."

She scooted back against the wall and sat with her knees curled up to her chin. She had to figure a way out of this while Cameron kept talking.

"What about me?" She cried. "Did you punish me too – by drugging me?"

"How did you know about – "

"The blackouts I've had – they've never made sense until now." Then something occurred to her that brought tears to her eyes. "Maybe that's why Patrick died. Because you drugged me."

"Don't you dare say something like that!" Fury erupted in his eyes. "He was my child too. I lost him just like you did."

"Why Cameron? Why have you done all this and killed so many innocent people?"

"They weren't innocent, and they deserved to die."

She looked up at him and brushed away the tears in her eyes. "I don't understand."

"They all came to me," he said. "I was their psychiatrist, and they trusted me with their sordid little affairs…their nasty little secrets. The timing of it all couldn't have been better. It just fell into place. I couldn't just sit there and let them go about their lives, portraying one false face to the public and another to me. People trusted them, believed in them….and their families and the public didn't deserve all the lies. They deserved to die." His voice trailed off. He seemed to have stopped talking to listen to something again.

"Why is my name on the list?" Olivia asked. "I've never been unfaithful to you."

He didn't answer.

"Did you kill Stacy too?" she asked. "At least tell me that!"

"Sam was right. He said you were getting too close. Even after I pleaded with you to focus on other things besides work, you still couldn't let it go." His voice was calm and steady again.

"What happened to Stacy?" Olivia demanded. "Where is she?"

Cameron got a strange look in his eye. "I don't know…I didn't kill her. I had planned to. She got away. I have no idea where she is, but I'll find her."

"I don't believe you. Why won't you tell me the truth?"

"I am."

"Fine! Then, who is Sam?" She looked around. "Have I met him before?"

"Of course you have," Cameron said. He sounded perplexed. "Sam's standing right over there."

She looked around the room, confused. What was Cameron trying to do? Make her think she was crazy? Or did he honestly believe there was another person in the room with them?

"I don't see anyone." She glanced around, and it finally registered. *Sam was merely a figment of Cameron's imagination.* Sam *was* Cameron.

"There's no one here."

"Nice try, but you can't fool me." He motioned to the empty space in front of the door. "It's time to get on with this."

She tried her best to think. At this point, she knew he had every intention of killing her. She could only guess how. She suddenly heard footsteps on the stairs. The sound was subtle at first but someone was definitely in her home.

"Who's there?" she asked.

"Sam," he said.

"What?" It couldn't be. But she knew she wasn't imagining this. Someone was definitely there. Maybe Sam *did* exist.

Olivia shot up from her position on the floor and clung to the inside wall right next to the door. Silence followed. The footsteps had stopped. Whoever it was seemed to have vanished…or he was hiding somewhere in the house. Olivia felt the still silence in the room. Cameron didn't appear to be breathing either, but she could only get a glimpse of him in the darkness when the lightening flashed. The calm before the storm.

Then she heard a floorboard creak softly, right outside the door. Someone was on the other side of the wall she was leaning against. She froze in fear. What should she do? She could feel the intensity of Cameron's gun still pointed in her direction. Thunder crashed and shook the glass in the window above Cameron's desk. Lightening followed. She waited for Sam to step into the room. He never came. But Terry Carson did.

"You're Sam?"

Terry didn't answer her. "Put your gun down Cameron. It's over."

Cameron reacted quickly and fired. Olivia screamed and watched Terry fall to the floor. She wasn't sure what came over her, but she flung her body into Cameron's, aiming for the area on his leg that was still recovering from the stab wound. Cameron grunted in pain and buckled as she made contact. His gun flew out of his hands and spun across the floor.

Olivia grabbed the butt of the broken desk lamp, raised it above her head, and heard the crack as she smashed it into her husband's skull twice as hard as she could. It made a thud, one of the most disturbing sounds she'd ever heard. She released the lamp and stumbled back as his body collapsed. At that moment she wasn't sure if he was unconscious…or dead.

"I thought I told you to keep my gun on you at all times." Terry pulled himself up and leaned up against the doorframe and clutched his wounded arm.

"Are you okay?" She moved toward him.

"I'm fine." He grunted in pain. "Thankfully he doesn't have the best aim. Now do me a favor and call 911."

95

The Punisher sat in his jail cell. He was having a hard time understanding that he'd been caught...by his own wife. This wasn't part of his master plan. But at least Sam was there with him.

"What would I do without you, Sam?" he asked. His voice echoed off the concrete floor of the empty space.

The voice inside Cameron Penn's aka The Punisher's head said, "You know I'll always be there for you. You need me, right? I have good ideas."

It had been Sam's idea to leave California all those years ago, especially after the movie star. It had been Sam's idea to move to Washington. And, it had been Sam's idea to target high-profile people in the city who were up to no good. The Punisher reflected for a minute. He wondered how Stacy was doing and where she was. He reveled in the way he'd tried to set her up. But in the end, Stacy had decided to do her own thing and had foiled his plan, even though he still intended to kill her. Unrequited love.

It had been so easy to corner Senator Price that night. He'd relieved Price's driver and picked him up from a black tie dinner.

The Senator had glanced anxiously at his watch in the back seat. "I just need to make one quick stop," Price said and gave him the address to Stacy's place in Dupont Circle. When they'd arrived, Price called Stacy from his cell phone and said he was downstairs.

Minutes later Stacy stumbled down the stairs of her apartment building. Cameron could tell she'd been drinking, and that annoyed him.

She climbed into the back seat, and he heard words exchanged. They were fighting. When he rolled the window down that separated the front seat from the back and saw Stacy, she gasped.

"Hello Stacy." Cameron smiled.

"What are you doing here?" Terror filled her eyes.

"You know the driver?" Senator Price furrowed his eyebrows and sat back.

Cameron kept an eye on the road while he slipped a gun out of the glove compartment.

"He's an old friend…" she said.

Cameron recalled firing three shots at the Senator, hoping none had hit Stacy. He wasn't through with her yet.

Stacy started crying hysterically and cursing. "Let me out. Let me out of here! What have you done?"

He looked in his rear view mirror and realized he'd hit his mark. The Senator was dead. He pulled over, against his better judgment on Rock Creek Parkway. All he wanted to do was talk to Stacy. But, he also needed to figure out what to do about the body. He put the car in park, turned off the lights…but he never expected Stacy to run off in the woods. He started to chase after her, but then he knew she'd be back. She wouldn't last long out there. He was wrong.

That was the last time he'd ever seen her. She'd simply vanished, just like his wife Anne had. He'd loved Stacy since sixth grade, and they'd shared a strange relationship over the years. He would never let her go. Never. Looking back, he should have chased after her but didn't want the police to find the car with the body in the back seat. It was late.

He acted impulsively, turned off the car and went in search of an area to bury the body. This time of year, the greenery was in full bloom. The body would be easy to hide. After an hour of searching for the perfect place, he'd found one, grabbed a shovel out of the trunk and dug into the dirt as much as he could to bury him. Then he went back to the car.

He threw Price's body over his shoulders and moved quickly. He threw him down, hidden beneath a thick bush and covered him with as much soil as he could. It would be a while before anyone found him. He needed to get home. It was late, and Olivia would be wondering where he was.

Then he'd heard a voice behind him.

"What are you doing?" a woman said.

Had Stacy come back? He turned around to discover a very young, very pretty woman, out for a late night run. He thought fast.

"I lost my dog," he'd said. "Thought he ran over here in the bushes and was hiding from me. He likes to play games sometimes." He walked closer to her, knowing he'd have to kill her. "Isn't it a little late for a run?"

She smiled, relaxing for a moment. "Not for me. What's your dog's name? Maybe I can help you find him."

"Simpson, his name is Simpson."

She was a pretty little thing. He'd played along with her for the next fifteen minutes. Then, when he was sure they were still alone in the park, he snapped her neck and made love to her body beneath a cushion of leaves. But nothing would compare to what Stacy would feel like when he killed her. After he'd had his fun, he dug another hole and buried the young woman next to Price.

96

Olivia stayed by the side of the two most important men in her life. Nathan Spencer. And Terry Carson. Nathan had been lucky enough to walk away from a potentially devastating car crash with three broken ribs and a bad concussion. Terry rested comfortably at GW Hospital, recovering from a bullet wound to his trigger arm that was far from fatal.

Most importantly, The Punisher was finally behind bars. The *real* Punisher. All Olivia wanted to know at this point was how Terry had found out that Cameron had been involved. She'd decided to visit Terry in his hospital room before she faced her husband in jail. She needed some answers.

"The FBI wouldn't listen to me when I told them who I was and that I had a lead on The Punisher," Terry explained. "When I finally tracked down a photo of the author of the article you found online, I discovered that your husband had a lot of explaining to do. Then, when I couldn't get a hold of you, I decided to get back as fast as I could and watch your house. I still wasn't completely sure."

"I wondered what had happened to you," she said.

"I tried to tip off the FBI, but they didn't appear to give what I said much credit at first, so I decided I needed to take matters into my own hands."

"So what's next?" she asked. "After all this."

An amused look washed over his face. "For starters, I have my old job back at the FBI. Any time I want it."

"Terry, that's wonderful!"

"That's not all. The FBI has offered me a full pardon and an official apology regarding the Jackson Myers case."

"It's about time," she said.

Terry reached up from his hospital bed and pulled Olivia's hand close to him. "Olivia, you're the reason the FBI wants me back. I owe all of this to you. Don't think I don't know that."

She thought she understood what he meant. He'd finally gotten his victory. His retribution. She just nodded in agreement.

"There was only one stipulation in my agreement to return to the FBI," he said. "And it had nothing to do with a long over-due apology or money."

"What's that?" She leaned in toward him.

"You. You gave me my life back. Now I want to give you yours."

She was pretty sure she knew exactly what he was talking about, and for the first time in a very long time, she felt relieved. It was so incredible to be understood.

He looked her straight in the eyes and said, "Someday soon, I want to help you find out what really happened to Stacy Greenburg that night."

97

Olivia drove to the high-security prison outside of the city where the FBI was holding her husband. She had mixed emotions about seeing Cameron, but knew she wouldn't ever be able to find closure without some answers. And, without seeing him one last time.

She hardly recognized him as he sat across from her through the glass barrier with a shaved head. She winced at the wound she was responsible for. And she grew impatient as he watched her for several minutes before finally picking up the phone to communicate. She held the phone to her ear and waited.

"I'm not even really sure what to say at this point," she began. "I guess all I want to know is *why?*"

He didn't say anything. It was all she could do to fight back tears. The devastation of losing him to this madness had not even registered yet. *How could she have been in love with such a monster? What was wrong with her? How could she not have known?* His cold eyes bore through her and made her shiver. She longed to reach his thoughts. To understand what was going through his mind. To understand something!

"You think that you've actually *punished* these people you've killed?" she finally asked.

He seemed to mull over her words for a moment before he answered. "Yes. I do."

"You're wrong. In fact, the only person you've punished in all of this is yourself."

"What are you talking about?" He seemed irritated and uneasy.

"You have to stop punishing yourself for what your father did to your mother. He cheated on her and did unspeakable things to you. But none of that was your fault." Olivia didn't recognize the psychobabble coming out of her mouth and wasn't sure where it was coming from. She was like a woman possessed, numb from unspeakable pain.

"Don't pretend you know me," he said. "You don't understand me at all. You think you do. You write about me, but the person you're writing about doesn't come close to demonstrating how much power I have."

She did her best to follow. "You're right, Cameron. What is it you really want to tell me?"

When he didn't say anything she finally asked, "Your real name is Sam Camp, isn't it? And you grew up in Texas…"

More silence, but he smiled.

"Well, can you at least tell me if you were working with the man who took me hostage in our home? Or with Rex?"

Cameron raised an eyebrow. "The only person I've been working with is Sam."

"So Benjamin really was just a crazy fan?" She asked. "You mean he had nothing to do with The Punisher murders?"

"He was just a dumb kid. A wanna-be."

"But you sent the last email and made it look like it was from my biggest fan…oh…because you knew I would take it seriously…"

"Yep."

"Then why Rex? Why did he have to die too?" Tears came to her eyes. "He was a good man. He was my friend!"

"He failed me." Cameron rolled his neck back and forth, appearing bored by their conversation. "He stopped playing by my rules and turned the case over to the Feds. That's when I had no more use for him. Plus, I know how close you two were…and I knew if I got to him, I'd get to you. Then, maybe you'd stop trying to find me."

She could tell he was enjoying taking all the sick credit for his actions. When Olivia looked into Cameron's eyes, she no longer saw the man she'd married. He was different. He was dangerous, and he was crazy. At that moment she realized there wasn't much point in trying to have a sane conversation with an insane man. He just stared at her, and she shifted uncomfortably in her seat.

"I came to say goodbye," she said.

"Did you get the answers you were looking for?" He smiled again.

She got up to leave. "Funny how in the end, the bad guy never really wins. He usually gets what *he* deserves." She smirked at him, but deep down her heart was breaking.

Olivia had loved him with all of her soul, and he'd betrayed her. It was time to walk away from this chapter of her life. It was finally over. As she hung up the phone, Olivia could have sworn she heard him say, "I'll be seeing you," and his words sent chills up her spine.

98

A month later over dinner with Nathan, Olivia reflected on her life. She enjoyed the connection she felt with him, though it was hard to explain. It was just there. But the dinner wasn't a date, even though he had taken her to one of his favorite places, 1789 in Georgetown. Olivia stared off reflectively across the room.

"You're doing it again," Nathan said, sipping his bourbon.

"What?" She perked up and smiled at him.

"You're zoning out. You're not really here with me."

"I am too," she said but knew he was right.

"You're thinking about someone else, aren't you?"

She looked down and adjusted the napkin in her lap. "I can't help but think sometimes how different my life would be if I hadn't met Stacy Greenburg. If only…"

"- you'd stayed out with her longer that night she disappeared?"

"Maybe things would be different and she'd still be here."

"Do you really think so?" He continued picking at the last few bites of duck on his plate. "You know it's true that everything happens for a reason, Olivia."

"Yeah, I know, but do you really believe that?" She took the last bite of her fish.

"Yes, I do," he said. "Just think about it."

"Well, I think it all boils down to timing." She dabbed her napkin over her lips and retired her fork and knife for the evening. "But at least we finally know what happened to Senator Price."

"And that the woman's body found beside his was not Stacy's, which means she very well may still be alive."

Olivia beamed. "I think she is, and now maybe with The Punisher behind bars, she might come out of hiding."

"You want to know what I think?" Nathan asked.

"What?" She raised her eyebrows and smiled.

"I think getting out of D.C. for a while will be good for you after all."

"I think so too. Terry has a cabin up in Maine that he's offered to let me stay in for a while. He said it's secluded and safe. It'll be good to get away and clear my head."

Ever since Cameron had been arrested for The Punisher murders, she had become restless and worn down from the media circus that had instantly become her life. Every television station, newspaper and magazine in the country wanted an exclusive interview. She couldn't take any more.

In an interview on the *Today Show*, she had mentioned that she planned to write a book about The Punisher and what it was like to live with a serial killer, and several major publishers had immediately contacted her with offers. Duncan had also told her that the Post would hold her job for her as long as she wanted.

"Hopefully this time away will provide the closure I need to put this all behind me." Suddenly she had butterflies as she paused and looked Nathan straight in the eye. "*So*, do you see a trip to Maine anywhere in the near future?"

"I wish." He re-folded the napkin in his lap. "You wouldn't believe the case I just got assigned."

"Wow, the FBI doesn't waste any time, do they?" She did her best to hide her disappointment.

"No, I leave for California tomorrow night and probably won't be back for several months."

She thought about her upcoming journey and smiled. "Well, I guess timing really is everything, *isn't it?*

Epilogue

Six months had passed since she'd left Washington, D.C., and Olivia's life seemed so different now in York, Maine. But she knew it was only temporary. She would have to return to Washington soon enough for Cameron's trial, which she dreaded.

Her family had encouraged her to stay away as long as she needed, to write through the pain once again. To try and heal. She was almost through writing the first draft of her book, *Sleeping With A Serial Killer*. The words had just flowed from her emotions, needing to be released. Before she left, she had cleaned out Cameron's office, along with the FBI and had found two journals he'd written.

The FBI had taken the originals as evidence and allowed her to make copies. Cameron's words had given her more insight into the monster he really was. It was painful to read. The journals described his vicious murders.

Questions were what haunted her the most now. *How could she have lived with such a psychopath all that time and never known the truth?* The guilt she felt for her ignorance sometimes got the best of her, and she wondered if deep down she had somehow known that Cameron was The Punisher. *No, that simply wasn't possible,* she decided. She tried to shift her thoughts to something else, anything but Cameron.

Olivia lit a candle in the quaint, shadowy living area of Terry's old cabin and curled up in a rocking chair with a blanket and a hot cup of tea. She rocked gently and let her mind drift as she stared at the dwindling fire she'd made earlier. The crackling of the wood soothed her.

She caressed her growing belly and reflected on the baby growing inside her. Cameron's baby. The Punisher's baby. Though a little bitter sweet, she was thrilled knowing she'd have a child several months later, even though the fear of miscarrying again wore on her at times. In the back of her mind, she knew she'd always wonder whether her child would inherit a version of its father's terrible illness and become a serial killer too.

A knock at the cabin door interrupted her thoughts. Olivia sat there for a minute until the knock came again. Who could it be? The only two people who knew where she was besides her family were Terry and Nathan. Alarm set in, and she wasn't sure if she should answer it.

She got up slowly, took Terry's gun out of the drawer of the table beside her chair and approached the door. Taking a deep breath, she unlocked the safety latch and opened the door. She couldn't believe her eyes.

"Hello Olivia." Stacy Greenburg stood there and smiled at her friend.

Olivia's knees gave in, and Stacy reached out to steady her. "Stacy, you're alive."

"And you're pregnant!" Stacy smiled and reached for Olivia's belly.

"Seems we both have a lot of explaining to do." Olivia's heart soared at the sight of her missing friend who she thought she'd never see again.

"Terry found me and brought me here," Stacy said. "But, for your own safety I can't tell you what happened or where I've been...at least not yet. He said I'd be safe here with you."

Terry had done what he'd promised and given Olivia her life back. It didn't matter where Stacy had been. All Olivia cared about was that Stacy was alive, and she had a new life to share with her friend and her baby now. Surely they both could handle whatever happened next.

About Melissa Wren

After gaining her B.A. in broadcast journalism from Texas Tech University in 1998, Melissa Wren moved abroad to London, England and began her career in advertising, which eventually took her to Dallas, Texas and then to Monterey, California. After over four years on the West Coast, she relocated to Washington, D.C. to work in communications and with the press for a government agency for four more years.

Wren recognized her God-given passion for creating stories at an early age, finishing her first novel when she was 12 years old. During her time in the nation's capital, she wrote the psychological thriller *Serial Vengeance,* joining such organizations as Mystery Writers of America, Sisters in Crime, Washington Independent Writers and Thriller Fest.

She currently lives in her hometown of Granbury, Texas, and works as a freelance writer/editor for hire, penning anything from professional business copy, human-interest stories, magazine articles, poetry, creative fiction to non-fiction. She's currently a member of the National Association of Professional Women (NAPW).

Wren also compiled *Cancer Chronicles: One Man's Journey to Glorify God Through Illness.*

www.melissawrenbooks.com

13022683R00181